OF SPOOLS
AND BILLOWS

Dear Sarah,
Hope you enjoy
getting to know
these characters a
little more, like I did.

Also By Camilla Tracy

Of Threads and Oceans

Of Flowers and Cyclones

Of Blood and Tides

Soxkendi: A Family of Dragons

Of Spools and Billows

Of Gates and Typhoons

Join my animal loving community and learn about my newest book releases by clicking below or scanning the QR code:

https://geni.us/CamillaTracynewsletter

CAMILLA TRACY

OF
SPOOLS
AND
BILLOWS

THREADS OF MAGIC
BOOK 4

Camilla Tracy

Published by Pudel Threads Publishing

First Printing 2024

Tracy, Camilla, author

Of Spools and Billows / Threads of Magic: Book Four

ISBN (paperback) 978-1-7381915-4-3

eISBN978-1-7381915-3-6

B&N ISNBN 978-1-7381915-6-7

Under a Federal Liberal government, Library and Archives Canada no longer provides Cataloguing in Publication (CIP) data for independently published books.

Technical Credits:

Cover Image: MiblArt

Editor: Bobbi Beatty of Silver Scroll Services, Calgary, Alberta

Proofreader: Lorna Stuber - Editor, Proofreader, Writer, Okotoks, Alberta

Created with Atticus

To Dean and Troy

Prologue

Elric,
I've gone to Alexius's world with Rommy to train, to
master my magic. Alexius will keep the wards up to
protect the palace. Please take care of Indi and Ana and
Bardo, and please understand. I need to concentrate on
this. I need to strengthen my magic so I can help you and
the kingdom. I'll be back in a few weeks.

Love always,
Thali

CHAPTER ONE
Thali

T HALI STOOD ON THE enormous, unenclosed balcony of pale gray marble, her hands clutching the solid rail as she leaned into the wind, her long, dark-brown hair whipping behind her. She leaned onto the rail, pretending the wind was strong enough to lift her into the air so she could fly.

A strong hand fell on her shoulder and Thali jumped, startled. Her shoulders relaxed, though, when she turned and saw her brother's smiling face. Even in the windstorm, he still managed to smile. He stood immovable, unflappable, the wind flying around him as if he was a ship dividing the sea. Thali turned to look back out over the balcony. It jutted out of the palace, and she loved how it felt like she could fly when she leaned over the railing in a windstorm like this. She turned her face up toward the sun and the light-pink sky, struggling to take another breath as the wind stung her face.

Her brother's hand waited patiently on her shoulder, weighing her down, warm, firm, solid. She finally turned around and let her brother guide her indoors. He had to tuck her into his side to keep her from being pushed sideways as they walked. Thali thought about how well her brother looked now. He had regained his health from the last time she'd seen him. He was finally the brother she remembered, slender, but still solid muscle. Once through the doors, Thali felt the calm in the juxtaposing stillness.

"One day, I think you might sprout wings and fly away." Rommy poked her shoulder blade teasingly.

Thali smiled. "Maybe I will." She arched one eyebrow in challenge.

"Just what is Xerus teaching you?" Rommy tilted his head and mirrored her own arched eyebrow.

Thali shrugged, knowing she'd caught his attention. She skipped down the hall to where she normally met Xerus for her lessons. Romulus smiled when she looked back over her shoulder at him. She knew he was trying not to be baited, but his stride quickened and lengthened, giving him away.

Thali reached for the magic around her, formed her familiar threads, and attached them to the majestic doors. She had only been here a couple of days, but she already felt stronger and more at ease. Magic flowed more easily in Etciel. Alexius was always a good teacher, but here, surrounded by magic, practicing her magic felt like sailing on a wind current instead of struggling in dead air.

Thali stopped in front of the white stone doors, shiny and intricately carved with dragons of all kinds. She turned to grin at her brother before turning back to the doors that opened inwardly as she stiffened her magical threads and pushed.

"Now you're just showing off," Rommy said as he caught up to her.

CHAPTER TWO
Stefan

S TEFAN TIPTOED INTO THE royal chambers, where he took hold of Elric's foot and shook it. Normally, he would have chosen the prince's shoulder, but a tiger was draped over Elric's torso, and the tiger's head was dangerously close to said shoulder. Stefan's heart clenched as Elric started to wake, his hand reaching absentmindedly across the bed for his wife. He patted the cool, empty spot until his hand found the great curly-haired dog instead. Elric started to sit up, the tiger's tail twitching in annoyance as she moved to cuddle the dog instead.

"Your Highness, I'm sorry to wake you. But it's urgent," Stefan said.

Elric finally sat upright, running his hands through his golden curls and rubbing his eyes with the heels of his palms. "I assume if it's you waking me, Stefan, it's an emergency." He yawned. "I'll be out in a minute," he said with a groan. "What kind of emergency justifies waking me so early? It better not be a foreign guest demanding to see me about a pillow allergy."

Stefan swallowed as he gently shook his head and began to turn to the door.

Elric looked around quizzically and asked, "Stefan, where's my wife? Don't tell me she's training in the weapons room again because I think I'll have to move our bed in there to spend any time with her."

Stefan froze.

Elric

When the captain of his guard didn't respond, Elric looked up at him, eyes wide and suddenly very awake. Stefan wasn't good at keeping bad news.

"Stefan. Where is Routhalia?" Elric struggled to pause the panic that started to rise in his chest and waited for his friend to answer.

Stefan swallowed, not looking the prince in the eye. "She's missing, Your Highness. She left this note." He handed Elric the note he'd held onto for the last half hour. "Guards are searching the palace. We haven't disturbed any of the guests yet, but we are searching every square inch of the grounds now."

Elric leaped out of bed and grabbed the note. He read it over and over. "Who went with her? Just her brother?" Elric's mind was racing. *Why hadn't she woken me? Why hadn't she asked me to go with her?* His heart cracked as he remembered the empty feeling he'd had when she'd been stuck in her own mind for weeks, unable to move or communicate, thanks to an ancient dragon's control.

"Everyone else is accounted for," Stefan said.

"Her guards, Stefan, who did she take with her?" Elric asked.

"No one, that we know of."

"What of Prince Tariq? Wake him. And Lady Ambrene. They may know more."

"Yes, Your Highness." Stefan strode to the door, stuck his head out into the common room, and spoke quietly.

Elric noticed the animals on the bed start to stir, and he tiptoed into the common room with Stefan, leaving the animals in peace in their bedroom.

"Wait. Alexius. Where's Alexius?" Elric suddenly remembered that Alexius was bound to Thali. The dragon could tell him where she was.

CHAPTER THREE
Alexius

THE POUNDING ON HIS door finally woke Alexius. The small guard's barracks was only a low building of wood containing rows of spartan rooms, so he thought at first someone was pounding on his neighbor's door for the walls were very thin. But it didn't stop, so he got up and stumbled toward the door, rubbing his head. He threw open the door, nearly getting a fist to the face as Stefan was mid-knock.

"Alexius, get dressed. You are to report to His Highness's chambers immediately," Stefan ordered, his face bearing a grim expression.

Alexius threw on his uniform and wondered why his head pounded as it did.

"I see you were out having fun last night?" Stefan growled.

Dragons did not drink. It didn't do anything for them. But right now, Alexius certainly felt like how many of the guards looked the morning of their day off.

Stefan marched Alexius like a prisoner all the way to Thali and Elric's rooms. Nasir nodded at Alexius and opened the door. All of Thali's personal guards filled the room, and Elric, in his nightshirt, was pacing barefoot back and forth, reading and rereading a note he held.

Alexius looked out the windows and realized it was still dark out. He narrowed his eyes, trying to mentally put together pieces that floated just out of reach. A quick glance around the room surprised him. He didn't see Thali anywhere. He dove into his mind and looked in the room he held specifically for her. He tossed a thought into the abyss of that room. *Where are you?*

Where he normally saw a gentle purple flame, he saw only a ghost of it. And no reply came. Something had happened to his connection with Thali. It wasn't where it should be. Shaking his head, he sent feelers out into the whole castle, combing through every living creature on the grounds to find that not only was Thali gone, but so were her brother and Aexie. To his surprise, he also found he held the strings to the protective shield over the palace. He checked them mentally, making sure they were solid, before coming back to the physical world.

Elric paused his pacing and looked up. When his gaze landed on Alexius, he rushed over and handed Alexius the note. "Can you explain this?" Elric was trembling as he held the note out for Alexius to read.

Alexius read it once and felt his heart plummet to his feet. She'd left this world without him, without even reaching out to him. How was he supposed to guide her if she wasn't here? As his head pounded, he realized he wasn't well. Slowly, it came to him. His head was pounding very much as it would from the aftereffects of a sleeping potion made specifically for dragons. Only his siblings and Romulus would know about that. His eyes widened as he realized he'd had dinner with Aexie last night and then had gone to bed feeling very tired. Even if Thali had tried to contact him, he would have been asleep and unresponsive.

"Well?" Elric's eyes reflected the fire in the hearth as he glared at Alexius.

Before he replied, Alexius checked on the protective wards again, giving them a boost as he reread the letter. Then he looked up at the prince. As he opened his mouth, another voice interrupted.

"What do you mean she's not here?!" Tariq yelled, badgering Nasir, the Bulstani guard outside the door, who had been sent to protect Thali. The door burst open again then, revealing Prince Tariq and Lady Ambrene. The Bulstani prince and his intended were finely dressed, as always, but Tariq's eyes were panicked as he looked around. "Where is Lili?" Tariq demanded.

Alexius was surprised to smell such strong fear from the usually bold prince.

"Alexius was just about to explain." Elric crossed his arms.

Both princes stared daggers at Alexius.

"I know nothing of her disappearance," he replied. He winced as the pounding in his head increased.

"How is it that my new wife, the princess of this kingdom, disappeared without even one of her royal guards noticing?!" Elric resumed pacing, staring angrily at each of the guards lined up in his common room.

"At least we know she went to Etciel," Alexius said reassuringly as he took a third look at the note.

"And how do we get her back?" Tariq was now pacing beside Elric.

Alexius gulped. "I ... I don't know. I can't do it. I've been denied access to that world." He looked down, wishing he'd had a chance to talk to Thali before she'd left. He was disappointed in himself that he hadn't known she'd left and embarrassed to have to hear from someone else that his blood-oathed princess was missing. And there had been no opportunity yet to explain what he knew about her brother, about his own siblings. He hadn't even had a chance yet to reveal all the things he'd wanted to before but couldn't. Now that everything had changed because he'd performed the blood oath, he was free to tell her almost all of it, but she'd left too soon.

"Sit down, Tariq." Ambrene, still cradling her injured arm, rubbed her temple as she sat on the couch behind the guards. Everyone turned to the exquisitely dressed lady. "Let's put together what we know. Romulus and Routhalia are both missing. We can be assured that of anyone, Romulus loves his sister and would not harm her. Being that they both avoided detection by the many skilled guards here, we can presume they left of their own will and did not want to be followed."

Both princes had stopped their pacing as the lady had spoken. She took the note from Alexius and read it before turning back to everyone. "She will return. I'm sure of it. She wants to learn to protect her people. If there is anything Tariq and I can attest to, it is that Routhalia likes to immerse herself when she learns. She will eat, breathe, and sleep all that she wants to learn until she has mastered it. Then, she will return to us. Just because you cannot surround her with your own guards does not mean she is not safe." Ambrene took a long moment to stare down both princes.

"How can you be so sure?" Elric squeaked.

"Because I know Thali. Tariq knows Thali. You, Your Highness, know Thali. She hated going to that school at first, yet she begged to finish. She was mastering her skills, and at the same time, learning about her people. She knew that in marrying you, the people of this kingdom would be her responsibility. And we all know Thali does not do things partway. With her new skills and the current circumstances, she will want to be her people's protector."

Elric finally sat down on the couch opposite Lady Ambrene. Tariq stood behind her, his white knuckles gripping the back of the sofa.

"Of all the women I know, no, of all the *people* I know, Routhalia is among the most capable. As a team, she and her brother could take over the world, so as worried as we are, we must have confidence that our friends will return to us. Above anyone, Romulus loves Routhalia most. He will keep her safe." Lady Ambrene raised her chin a little higher.

"What am I going to do until then?" Elric paled as he slumped, looking lost.

"You will do what you always do. You cannot let anyone outside this room know," Lady Ambrene continued.

Alexius glanced at Tilton and Daylor. They stood at the back, soaking it all in. They caught his eye, and it occurred to him that there was one more person that they would have to tell of Thali's disappearance. All of Thali and Elric's personal guards, Elric, Tariq, Ambrene, Daylor, and Tilton were here, and Alexius knew Mia was in her sewing closet listening to every word. But there was one more person who loved Thali deeply and had helped them before. He would do what he could to help again.

Ambrene stood and smoothed her skirts. "You will say that the princess has taken to redecorating your apartments. She will be making no more public appearances until she feels settled in her new home."

Tariq looked at Tilton and Daylor. They exchanged a nod.

Elric nodded too, albeit sadly. "And I will continue attending my meetings as usual and hope that my wife will return soon." He glanced at his guards, who nodded their understanding of their unspoken orders.

Alexius took a moment to catch Tilton's and Daylor's eyes again; they had identical furrows in their brows.

CHAPTER FOUR
Tilton

T HALI'S CLOSEST FRIENDS AFTER Tariq and Ambrene—Tilton, Daylor, Alexius, and Mia—were gathered in Thali's cavernous closet. They stood there, huddled and still stunned, not wanting to disturb any of Thali's things.

"I don't understand how she could have gone without saying anything to any of us," Tilton bemoaned, guessing that Alexius was angry at himself. And given Alexius's wince at that, Tilton knew he was right.

But before either could say anything, Mia interjected. "She doesn't mean any harm by it, Alexius," Mia put a hand on his arm. "She doesn't realize there are people who love her and would help her do anything. She always assumes all the responsibility." Mia smiled at the dragon, who still looked sad.

"We need his help, but I can't go and ask him," Alexius said. "I can't leave the palace. Half the guards think it's my fault, and they're all watching my every move."

Tilton knew that Alexius was a dragon and of his special relationship to Thali. Tilton had heard rumors about Alexius and Thali's closeness, but Tilton knew better. They were not, and never had been, romantically connected. They were close on a different level, and the dragon had protected her many times. Their bond went beyond romance, even beyond familial love. Those who knew about Alexius, about Thali's abilities, and about their bond, knew Alexius was not to blame for her disappearance, but everyone else thought he was.

Daylor stood a little taller. "We will go. Just tell us how."

The thought of contacting that particular man made Tilton queasy, but he'd helped them before, for Thali's sake. Besides, Tilton and Daylor had long ago agreed to do whatever needed to be done to help Thali, their best friend.

That night, Tilton and Daylor dressed in their plainest clothes and darkest cloaks and headed to the city's most notorious tavern. The evening was in full swing, and most of the men were drunk with women atop their laps. The two friends entered, their hoods up, and headed straight to the bar, where they each paid for an ale. They looked around, searching for the man that fit the description Mia had given. Tilton refused to look into the darker alcoves of the tavern for fear of what he'd see. There was obviously a man holding court in the tavern, but he had red hair and laughed too freely, too jovially. He pulled everyone's attention toward him. They were looking for a thoughtful, watchful man in a cloak, concealed but in plain sight so attention would slide off him.

One dark corner caught Tilton's attention. There was no bois-terousness, no lasciviousness, just a man with his hood up, his tablemates laughing and slapping him on the shoulder as he sat motionless but for his eyes. While the whole tavern was raucous with laughter and bawdy jokes and talk, the table in the corner seemed to be the only one that didn't draw attention. Tilton swal-lowed as he thought about how they could approach him.

"Hello, boys." A voice behind them made Tilton and Daylor jump.

Tilton quickly readjusted his hood, as did Daylor. Tilton felt strong hands on his shoulder. He swallowed as panic rose in his throat. He turned only to see Prince Tariq standing next to them, dressed plainly. Even though his clothes were plain, his posture gave him away. "Your H—what are you doing here?"

"I couldn't let you have all the fun. Plus, I've wanted to meet this particular gentleman for quite a while now." He flashed them a smile.

"How did you even know we were here?" Daylor asked. The three leaned in close to speak quietly, but they looked out into the tavern as they spoke.

"You forget I'm Lili's friend, too. Not only did I remember that she had another ally, but it was clear you wouldn't have let Mia go into this tavern alone, and Alexius is being watched like a hawk so he couldn't come. You obviously thought that left only you two, but you forgot about me, so I followed you."

Tilton looked worriedly at Daylor, then wiped his palms on his pants, a different anxiety rearing its head.

But Daylor shrugged and licked his lips. "We don't know how to approach him."

"Leave it to me." Tariq turned to the man behind the bar and slid him a gold coin. "Your best room." He looked the man straight in the eye. The barkeep's gaze shifted momentarily to the table with the hooded man before his other hand moved to a set of keys under the counter.

Tilton knew Garen had already seen them. He and Daylor stuck out like thumbs here, and he knew Tariq must have been noticed the moment he stepped through the door.

Tariq whispered, "I've been looking for an opportunity to meet the man Lili has spoken so highly of, though I was hoping it'd be on fairer ground than this tavern. Every single person in this tavern is a thief or worse."

"First room on the right at the top of the stairs," the barkeep said as he plunked a key on the table. He turned away to serve two jovial customers.

The three slowly made their way to the room upstairs. When they opened the door, Tilton and Daylor scrunched their noses as a smell reached them. Tariq looked around the room, checked the windows, then leaned against the wall, crossing his arms and watching the door.

Tilton sat down on the edge of the bed, and Daylor chose a chair between Tilton and the door. They waited, staring at the door.

"Gentlemen." The hooded man suddenly stepped soundlessly out of the closet door. He was tall, thickly built, and quiet as a cat. His steps didn't make a single sound as he lowered his hood and walked further into the room. They had all been startled, but Tariq was the quickest to recover. Tilton was surprised to see such a handsome face. Dark-brown hair reached the man's ears, and his eyes were as blue as sapphires. But what caught Tilton's attention the most was the man's stillness, as if every movement was calculated and necessary. Otherwise, he was still as a shadow.

"You're him," Tilton whispered. "I thought you'd be in Lanchor."

"I moved," he said.

Tilton saw just the tips of his ears turn pink.

"Your Highness, it's a pleasure to finally meet you," Tariq nodded.

Garen smirked. "The pleasure is all mine, Your Highness." He bowed.

"Garen, right?" Daylor stood slowly, approaching the man and extending his hand. Tilton just stared at him, surprised. Daylor was being bold.

Garen looked surprised at the offered hand, but as his eyes narrowed, he took Daylor's hand.

Tilton quickly followed suit, offering his hand to Garen. He couldn't help but blurt out, "She would say your name, in her sleep, when she was sick ..." Tilton bowed his head, ashamed that he didn't have better control over his words.

Garen's Adam's apple bobbed as he nodded. Then, he backed up and leaned against the wall, matching Tariq's posture as he melted into the shadows. "What's happened?"

"How do you know something's happened?" Tariq crossed his arms, and Tilton caught the brief glint of metal. At least two daggers hung from Tariq's belt, and if he was at all like Thali, Tilton knew he would have at least three more hidden away.

"Because you're all here, in the most notorious tavern in the city, wanting to speak to me." Garen pushed off the wall, struck a match, and lit a candle nearby. Tilton glimpsed a pair of dagger-shaped lumps beneath Garen's cloak as he leaned over to light the candle. He suspected Garen had leaned over specifically to show off the daggers. Tilton had no doubt the man had more hidden away, too. As he stood watching Tariq and Garen posturing like peacocks, his only hope was that he wouldn't get caught in the crossfire.

Chapter Five
Tariq

Tariq swallowed, and Garen's eyebrow raised a millimeter at the twitch of Tariq's fingers. He had never met Garen. The prince of thieves seemed a little underwhelming if Tariq was being honest. Confident, powerful, a skilled fighter sure, but Garen didn't seem very ... flashy? His appearance and mannerisms certainly didn't scream "prince." However, his musculature supported Thali's stories of his many battles and confrontations. Tariq wondered if Garen would move to attack him here since he had the upper hand in his own tavern.

As Garen lit the candles around the room, he slapped his hand twice on the room's door, startling everyone. It opened immediately, admitting two boys, who brought in a table and three more chairs, plus the barmaid, who brought in four ales. The barmaid eyed Tariq, Daylor, and Tilton before leaving the room with the two young boys.

"Please. Any friend of Thali's is a friend of mine." Garen motioned to the chairs and table. As he sat to straddle his chair backward, he studied the friends.

Tariq wondered what exactly Thali's relationship was with these people. Did they know he was aware of her trip to that meeting with all the princes of thieves over a year ago? Not that Thali had told him many details. But if she was of any import to them, the political implications could be huge. Had she thought of any of that back then?

He focused on the here and now, moving deliberately and sitting in the opposite chair, not bothering with the ale on the table. Tilton and

Daylor took this as a signal to take a seat, but Daylor, never one to refuse ale, happily grabbed the mug and downed a gulp.

"You must be Daylor." Garen nodded at him.

Tilton slumped in his chair, his gaze moving between Tariq and Garen as they stared at each other.

"And Tilton, I presume." Garen didn't take his eyes off Tariq as he nodded at the ale in front of Tilton.

"She's gone to Etciel, a magical world, with her brother. Disappeared," Tilton squeaked in response.

"When?" Garen's eyes narrowed a millimeter.

"Yesterday, in the middle of the night," Tariq replied coolly.

"She left a note?" Garen, perhaps realizing who the talkative one was, turned his attention to Tilton.

Tariq's eyebrows raised. *He knew she'd left a note?*

"Yes, here." Tilton took a folded paper from his inside pocket and showed it to Garen. Tariq was impressed that Tilton had managed to pry it from Elric's hands.

Garen scanned the contents a few times, then nodded, folding it and returning it to Tilton.

"What's Elric doing about it?" Garen turned his attention back to Tariq.

"He's sent out pairs of disguised guards in different directions to search for her in case she's misdirecting us, but otherwise, he has no access to the other world," Tariq said.

"He'll keep it quiet, then." Garen didn't break eye contact with Tariq as he nodded ever so slightly. "And Alexius?"

"Distraught, but unable to move between the worlds," Tariq replied.

Daylor tossed back Tariq's untouched ale, then added, "His blood oath ties him to her but prevents him from contacting her while she's in the other world. And his own access to that world was severed when he took the oath."

Garen nodded but Tariq's eyes grew wide. "The blood oath supersedes his ability to go home?"

"It was the only way they could get her out, before the wedding, when she was ... you know ... stuck up here." Daylor tapped his temple with his finger as he took another glug of ale.

Tariq's eyes glazed over, and his head pounded as he chewed on that piece of information. As he swallowed, his shoulders sank a millimeter. "I guess I don't know that much about blood oaths. I mean, I knew he must be watching over her or something, but ..."

Garen pressed his lips together. Tilton and Daylor eyed Tariq carefully, allowing him a moment to process.

Once Tariq turned his attention back to the others, Garen rose. "Why did she leave now? And did Elric do anything to push her away?" His voice was strained and low.

"No," Tariq said. "Besides learning to better control her abilities, I think she didn't want to lose her brother again, so she went with him when he had to go."

"And she wanted to be able to protect the people she loves," Garen said, somehow getting directly to the crux of the matter while glaring accusingly at Tariq.

Tariq nodded, feeling the blood leave his extremities as he thought of how he'd blamed Thali after Bree had been hurt. He gulped down his guilt.

"I'll do what I can. Let me know if you need anything." Garen nodded and took three strides to the door, but just as he reached for the doorknob, he paused. "Is Romulus to be trusted?" He asked quietly, still facing the door.

"I... I don't know anymore," Tariq said. Garen's hand was on the door-knob when Tariq whispered, "You didn't truly want to leave her, did you?"

Garen's back tensed as he let go of the doorknob. Then, his shoulders relaxed a little as he visibly tried to compose himself. He took hold of the doorknob again. "Whatever she needs, let me know." He threw the door open and stepped out, closing it quickly but quietly behind him.

"He still loves her," Tilton whispered.

"So why did he leave her?" Daylor asked.

Daylor and Tilton stared at the door Garen had disappeared through.

"Those were dark days when Thali had been inconsolable," Daylor said.

"She tried to bounce back, but the shadow of sadness never really left her," Tilton whispered.

Tariq nodded. He hadn't been here, but he'd also felt the air of sadness about her after the breakup. Seeing the helplessness and confusion on Thali's two loyal friends faces now, Tariq wished he could tell them about the prophecy, to help them understand that Garen had loved her so much he'd had to let her go for the sake of the kingdom. Shaking the desire off, he chided himself for feeling a moment of empathy for the prince of thieves.

Daylor finished two more mugs of ale before they finally decided to leave. They descended the stairs and found the tavern eerily quiet. Gone was the raucous noise and laughter and the games and drinking. The room was now only occupied by a handful of people, and they all turned to watch the three men as they strode across the floor, flicked up their hoods, and stepped out into the night.

On their walk back to the palace, Tariq could have sworn he saw the shadows stir more than usual in the flickering light of the lanterns they passed.

CHAPTER SIX
Garen

I T HAD TAKEN EVERYTHING he had to walk away from Tariq. He had
also wanted to call out the arrogant foreign prince for accusing
Thali when that horrific lizard-bird creature had attacked him and
Lady Ambrene. Garen had only heard about what had happened
and still knew Thali wouldn't have been at fault. Tariq should have
known better than to blame her. She would have taken it to heart
and done something reckless because she felt responsible. Tariq
had pushed Thali away. Tariq was the reason she had suddenly
left.

Garen walked out of that room thinking of her. He hung his head.
Thali wouldn't have wanted him to blame Tariq. And it was easy
to see how guilty Tariq felt. Despite the arrogance, he knew Tariq
already felt it was his fault that Thali had left the way she did.

Garen reached the bottom of the stairs to find everyone in the
room quiet and looking to him. They knew. They knew their
Princess of Thieves and the Kingdom of Adanek was missing.

Motionless, he stood and looked into each pair of eyes staring back
at him. Even when he had moved their base from Lanchor to the
capital city to be better able to help her when the time came, they had
already packed their things before he'd said anything. Their princess
represented all that was good and their hope for a better future. As he
looked at certain individuals now, he nodded to specific ones in turn,
and they melted away. Garen didn't need words to command his court.
They knew what was expected and would do their work and report
back through the chain of command. He gave a final nod and the entire
room cleared out except for the tavern owners. They all knew what

they had to do. Garen turned and strode under the stairs to a second room he kept as his own meeting place.

Fletch sat on a nightstand, legs crossed on the flat surface, as he polished his favorite dagger. Ilya, Garen's third in command and the muscle he often sent on specific missions, sat on a chair. His massive bulk dwarfed the chair. Despite his size, Ilya easily transformed into different characters and had several aliases all over the kingdom and the continent. Beside him sat Sesda, his red hair a shock of color atop his slender body. He often took Garen's position, a stand-in but also a spy. Finally, there was Ella, Garen's best informant. These were his captains.

"Fletch, I want you to learn more about Etciel. See if you can find anything about any other portals and how someone can get there and come back."

Fletch nodded, unfolded himself, and disappeared through the window as quietly as the wind.

"Ilya, I want you to go to Densria. Find out what you can about her brother. I want you to learn his whole life story and every decision he's ever made."

Ilya narrowed his eyes, clearly uncomfortable with spying on his princess's home and family. Garen stared back, so Ilya slowly nodded.

"Ella, keep your ear to the ground. I want to hear any news related to the palace: who knows what, who does what, and what they think. And keep tabs on any magical creatures you hear about from visitors."

Ella nodded and melted out of the room.

"Sesda, you will stay here and be me. I'm going to visit family."

Sesda nodded and went to stretch out on the bed. Garen strode out of the room and through the back door to his own quarters. He packed a bag, armed himself for travel, and hurried to the docks to board a ship.

CHAPTER SEVEN
Thali

THALI WALKED INTO THE Jade Room and clamped down on the gasp that always wanted to escape her lips. The dragons' training room was unearthly beautiful. The entire center of the floor was a single, circular piece of jade. The flaws in the stone—lighter sections and shadowed sections—formed a double dragon, claws together as if holding each other up. Around the jade circle was pristine white stone that stretched to every edge of the room. The walls were a pure jade green, smooth and perfect along all sides of the cavernous room. The green stone melded into the high ceiling, which was itself a miracle. The entire ceiling was green jade with a perfectly white center, the mirror opposite of the floor. The white center, however, was blurred along its circumference by white clouds that licked at its borders. Thali never stared at the white stone clouds for too long because she had the distinct feeling that one day they might swallow her whole.

Quietly, she sat on the floor across from Xerus. She hadn't revealed much about herself and was glad Alexius had made her practice her mental wall to shield her mind from others. While she trusted her brother, Alexius had hinted that Xerus was much more powerful than he looked, and she suspected he had played a larger role in all the magical attacks than he let on. Her mental walls barely took a toll on her at home, so here, where the magic was like a constant stream of water quenching her thirst, holding the mental protections was second nature.

After an hour's meditation, clothes swishing made Thali's eyes flutter open. Jaxon came in carrying a cage the size of a cart. Thali shook her head in disbelief. She knew dragons were strong, but it was still hard to digest seeing a single person, even one as wide and tall as Jaxon, carrying the awkward cage with just two fingers.

"Where do you want it, Xer?" Jaxon asked.

Xerus motioned to the floor's center, to the jade dragons.

When Jaxon put it down, Thali saw the creature inside was much smaller in comparison to the cage. Inside a cage six times its size, a green toad the size of a large dog sat staring at Thali. She chased away the pang of guilt for having left her own dog, Ana; her tiger, Indi; and even Bardo, her snake, behind.

This toad had giant, light-blue feathered wings folded on its back. As Thali approached, she saw that it had feet like a toad but sharp talons like a bird.

"This is a hornsnoad," Xerus said from beside her. "They are the most difficult creature to infiltrate, mentally. Their teeth will inject venom if they manage to bite you, but their strong mental walls make them very difficult to influence."

Thali knew better than to get too close, and she resisted skipping ahead and attempting to delve into its mind. Instead, she stared at it, barely seeing a hazy, dirt-brown sparkle on its skin.

"Now, use the technique we worked on yesterday to infiltrate his mind." Xerus stepped closer to the cage, folding his hands behind his back under his coattails. This was the normal Xerus stance.

Thali took a deep breath in and released it, closing her eyes to recall the feelings she'd learned the day before. Learning magic, unlike other lessons, was more like stumbling to achieve something blindfolded only to have to remember how you stumbled there again later. Every magic user saw or directed magic in their own way. Xerus had told her that his entire family saw magic as light. Tariq had said he felt magic like flowing water or air. She saw it as threads, but the difficulty came in learning how those threads could be directed. She had to learn how to use her threads as Xerus used light.

Xerus cleared his throat and Thali whipped her eyes open. The first thing Xerus had said was never to close your eyes when trying to concentrate. It left your body vulnerable and prevented you from being subtle with your magic use.

The hornsnoad now sat before her at the edge of its cage, glancing between her and Xerus. It opened its wings, showing off the beauty of its feathers. Now Thali understood the spacious containment. The hornsnoad's outstretched wings just brushed the bars of each side of the cage with light-blue feathers that faded to white at the tips. The creature let out a wet croak, and a putrid brown cloud left its mouth. The cloud stayed within the cage walls somehow, making her suspect a magical shield that protected them from the gaseous deadliness. Then, strangely, the creature absorbed the gas as it folded its wings back in again.

"Its gases will attack the lungs, suffocating you where you stand," Xerus explained.

Thali focused on the creature's mental outer perimeter, focusing the thread in her mind like a sharpened needle to pierce the magical creature's wall. Just as various birds evolved to have sharper beaks to pierce the carapace of insects, magical creatures evolved to have naturally strong mental walls. She poked and prodded at the invisible wall, whittling away at her magical thread's tip to make it sharper and smaller each time, testing it against the hornsnoad's wall. As soon as her needle pierced through, she pushed threads through it like a straw, splaying them out within the hornsnoad's mind.

Each creature's mind was different, and it always took her a moment to orient herself within each new creature she encountered.

Before she had come to train in Etciel, she shoved images bluntly into animals' minds like a broad net being thrown into an ocean. She was now learning to insert a thought so small and delicate that the creature didn't even know she was infiltrating its mind. She hadn't practiced on the truly intelligent creatures yet, but Xerus had promised with time she'd be able to infiltrate anything without blinking an eye.

"What do you want me to do?" she whispered. Thali was in the hornsnoad's mind, figuring out what pathways led to what.

"Dance." Xerus's voice came to her as a whisper, quiet, commanding.

Thali dug through her own memories for a jig that sailors often did when they spotted land after a long time at sea.

She moved the creature's legs now, not by shoving the memory roughly into its mind, but by tickling its fine motor control and taking over its leg muscles. The hornsnoad danced a flawless jig.

"Now, the gas," Xerus said.

She reached with a tendril to that part of the creature that controlled its gas release. As she let it go, she noted its lessened potency, realizing she now knew it took time for the gas to develop and become potent in the special sac below the creature's throat.

As she explored its mind further, she noticed other dark-brown sparkly threads stretching from him.

"You have others like him nearby," Thali said.

"Good. How many?" Xerus asked.

"Eight others. On the other side of the wall there."

"And how many can you control?"

Thali paused, sending out threads along the dark-brown sparkly threads that had caught her attention. Remembering the exact thinness of the sharpened point she'd been able to infiltrate the hornsnoad with, she pierced the others' minds quickly.

Not long ago, she would run out of thread; she'd felt limited by the spool she'd seemed to carry within herself. Now, she never felt like she was going to run out. Surrounded as she was by magic in this world, she felt limitless.

"All of them," Thali finally responded. In her mind, she saw the creatures in their cages, all unaware of her presence and sitting calmly as if they were waiting to be let out.

Xerus's command was quiet and terse. "Gas. All of them."

Thali squeezed every sac. The one before her barely emitted a puff.

"Good. Now leave them."

Thali wound the threads back into their spools, noticing Jaxon at the far end of the other room through the hornsnoads' eyes, standing guard like he often did: feet apart, arms behind his back over the other eight creatures.

"How do you feel?" Rommy was beside her now, concern showing in the crease of his forehead and the purse of his lips.

Thali took a deep breath, assessing her body as Xerus had taught her; it was important to be aware of your own limits, to know you could survive your decisions. "I feel good. Energized even."

Rommy looked to Xerus and nodded.

Jaxon strode into the room then. He stopped at a cabinet in the wall, pulled out two staffs, and continued toward them.

Thali couldn't help the excited flutter that her heart now did. Magic was unfamiliar and new and foreign. But physical combat was like home. And Jaxon was even better than her mother, which spoke volumes. Her mother was the best warrior in the kingdom, but Jaxon was otherworldly good. He knew so many different styles and methods, it was fun to see what he'd try next, what she could learn next.

Jaxon nodded to her and handed her a staff. They took up their positions. As they started the familiar *clack, clack, clack* to slowly warm up, Thali felt Xerus's mind creep up along the wall of her own mind. *So it will be one of these practices,* she thought.

As she and Jaxon squared off and the intensity of their hits and speed of their movements became quicker, so did Xerus's attempt to infiltrate her mind.

Xerus sliding into her mind wasn't like when Alexius did it. Alexius had a direct connection to her, so even if he did get in, it was like snapping an elastic back into its place to get him out. Xerus, Jaxon, and Aexie—on the rare occasion Thali did see her—never asked to create a link between them like Alexius had. They'd never tried to create a foothold in her mind. If they ever got through her wall, they'd back off, retreat into their own minds.

Xerus's physical voice came from the other side of the room. "If I get in this time, I want you to push me out. Consider a way to imagine the threads of your magic are like a net to catch and force me out."

It was like he'd been reading her thoughts. Jaxon smiled just then. He was about to try something new on her. Xerus would probably attack her at the same time.

Suddenly, Jaxon spun around, forcing her staff high into the air. He moved to come down hard, and Thali used her magic to pull her staff back to her hands faster than gravity would have allowed. She braced her hands on the staff closer together than normal, preparing to take the hard blow of all of Jaxon's body weight.

CLACK! CLACK! CLACK!

Thali's gritted teeth vibrated in her head as each blow landed impossibly fast, inhumanly fast. At the same time, Xerus was needling his magic into her mind. She felt his magic like a light trying to pierce the pitch black of her wall. She wove a tight net of threads in her mind, spreading it along the wall to catch any light that threatened to seep through.

She was bracing so hard physically from the onslaught Jaxon was dealing that she inadvertently pushed the net of magic through her mental wall, wrapping it around the light beyond it. The stream of light snuffed out and Xerus took a sharp breath. Jaxon stopped immediately, dropping his staff and running over to Xerus.

Thali was so physically exhausted, she dropped to the floor. Reeling in all her magic threads was habit now, like putting weapons away after practice. She turned her head while she lay on the floor to look at Xerus. Jaxon was holding his brother's shoulders as Xerus sat on the floor.

Thali's forehead crinkled. That was odd. Xerus pushed Jaxon aside and stood, brushing off his coattails. Jaxon immediately smothered his concern with his usual mask of indifference.

"How did you do that?" Xerus swayed as he walked toward her. As he neared, he dropped to his knees beside Thali's splayed form.

Thali explained what she'd done, how she'd accidentally pushed the net out of her to wrap around the light, like a thick hide might snuff out a candle.

"For that moment, you disconnected me from my magic. It was momentary, but I felt it separated from me, like I was being plunged into a dark well," he said. He flopped onto the floor. Thali moved away to give his long limbs space. It was very unlike Xerus to be laying on the ground.

Thali turned, raising herself to her elbows, eyes wide. "I'm so sorry. I didn't mean to ..."

She remembered just a few months ago when she had been locked inside a room in her own head, separated from her own body. She reached out to touch Xerus's arm. "I'm sorry." The coolness of his skin always unnerved her. It was like touching scales.

As Xerus shook his head slowly, his voice floated into her mind. *Routhalia, I don't think you realize how powerful you are.* Xerus turned his head to look at her, his brows furrowed. Out loud he said, "There have only ever been four magical beings capable of separating a creature's essence from their soul. Five now." He looked at Rommy.

Rommy's smile was a proud one, but Thali didn't miss the flash of horror that crossed Jaxon's face as color drained from it.

Xerus finally sat up, then stood. Straightening his clothes, he said, "Tonight and tomorrow, rest. We will resume the day after that."

"Is that—" Rommy started to say.

"She will need it," Xerus explained. "And I will need the time to change our training plan."

Thali wondered if that was because of what she'd done today or if perhaps she wasn't making the progress he'd hoped she'd make.

CHAPTER EIGHT
Alexius

ALEXIUS PACED IN HIS small room, trying to calm himself enough to maintain his human form. He would have a difficult time fitting into the tiny room in his dragon form. He was angry at himself for not taking the time to tell Thali the truth. She had been so caught up in the wedding, he had assumed he had time. Time. Time moved so differently in this world. In his own, these past months would barely have been a blink of an eye. Here, time seemed to move so slowly that he always felt like he had more of it to do what he needed to, and then somehow, it was always too late.

If he wanted to go after Thali, he would have to go through a portal and attempt to break through Etciel's gates. And if he got that far, he'd probably have to fight all three of his siblings before he gained access to Thali. They would have wards around the palace, too. And if, against all odds he did sneak past the wards and get to Thali, would she even believe him? Would she believe that her brother wasn't the hero she thought he was?

There was another problem. If Alexius left Adanek, the palace would surely be attacked. Magical creatures were drawn here given Thali's magic and his and Aexie's magical imprint all over the place. The moment he left, they'd come flocking, and he'd return to ruins. Alexius let himself roar in a pitch not audible to humans or other creatures. That wouldn't help his efforts to avoid attracting magical creatures, but it made him feel better. Not having Thali here, not having that comforting purple flame in his mind, was like an itch he couldn't scratch, uncomfortable and irritating. He'd played her guard for so long. When she finally did return, he would demand to be with her at all hours, to have a room adjacent to the rooms she shared with Elric.

He'd tied himself to her, committed his life to her and did not enjoy having that bond strained.

The blood oath was the strongest bond a dragon could make, but maybe through his familial bond, he could contact Aexie. Even from this other world, he could feel her trying to find a way out of their forced servitude. She didn't have the same confidence in Thali's power as Alexius did, so his sister didn't worry about Thali or how she could be manipulated into doing another's bidding. He knew how powerful Thali was though, even if Thali herself didn't realize it, so he worried that Romulus would trick her into joining his cause, or worse, into servitude like his siblings.

A knock on his door brought Alexius back to reality. He opened it to discover Elric standing there, his hair in disarray. Elric wasn't hiding the fact that his wife was missing very well.

"Alexius, may I?" Elric asked.

"Of course, Your Highness." Alexius sucked in to let Elric pass, then closed the door and swallowed down his nerves. He shoved his emotions in a box and locked it. He would be in an even worse predicament if he were to burst into his dragon form and squish the prince in this minuscule room. Elric started to pace three steps one way and then the other, so Alexius sat on the bed, crossing his legs.

"Alexius, I don't know what to do." Elric ran his hands through his hair. "I can't keep sitting in meetings every day and pretending Thali is fine. I need to know. Are you sure she's safe there? Why didn't she tell me? I would have gone with her."

Alexius watched the golden prince carefully before deciding what to say. It appeared they were both spiraling, so he pushed his own thoughts away to help Elric. "If I may, Your Highness, that's exactly why she didn't tell you. She saw all the work you had to catch up on after her ... illness. I think she was feeling helpless and needed to be of use. These magical attacks, we don't have a way to fend them off, and I know it bothered her that she couldn't prevent Lady Ambrene from being injured."

"What do we do? Wait? I can't. I need her here. I need her safe. I need her with me. We were supposed to do this together." Elric sank his head into his hands.

"What would you like me to do?" Alexius sensed there was a specific reason Elric had come to him.

Elric stood and started to pace again. "I want you to go find her. I can't go. I can't abandon my people and set the kingdom into chaos. Nor can I tell them we just lost our princess, and oh, by the way, there's this magical world that no one knows about, and magical creatures are attacking us, and we don't know why." Elric laughed. "I can't even imagine such an announcement from the palace." He paced a few more steps. "This kingdom hasn't seen magic in so long it's just a fairytale now, like ghosts and unicorns. I mean, you're a dragon! This is *not* what my reign was supposed to be like." Elric finally sank into a chair.

"Your Highness, I cannot leave. My magic is holding the barrier keeping other magical animals from flooding into the city," Alexius said between clenched teeth.

Elric sighed deeply and buried his head in his hands. "We are both prisoners in the palace then."

Alexious nodded sadly.

Chapter Nine
Tilton

T ILTON STEPPED BACK FROM the table and considered the array of paperwork now covering it. All Thali's requests and invitations required sorting, and the enormous stack hadn't fit on the tiny desk in his room, so he had taken the whole mess to the library nearest the royal rooms, hoping for more space and peace and quiet. He had taken his time spreading out all the papers as he'd tried to figure out how to cover Thali's absence.

Sighing, he went over and shuffled some of the papers to different stacks, trying to prioritize which needed responses or action right away. Avery, Elric's secretary, could handle those. After that came the ones he could reply to himself and delay any response from Thali. There was, however, a growing stack that Thali should attend to herself and that he was considering asking Mia to help with. Mia had said she might be able to imitate Thali's handwriting. Shaking his head, he took a stray paper—a letter from the Far North—and wondered whether he should open it, get Mia to read it, or give it to Avery for Elric to deal with when a cough made him jump.

"There's a bigger table in the back if you need it," Elric said.

"Oh, Your Highness, my apologies. I didn't think anyone would be here. I'll get out of your way right away," Tilton said, moving to collect all his papers.

Elric put a hand on a stack. "Tilton, don't worry about it. I don't need the table space. It's usually just me in here, anyway. Please. Stay. I wouldn't mind the company," he said.

"All right," Tilton said. He felt uncomfortable. Elric was the crown prince. Tilton had never spent more than a few minutes with him, and never alone. Tilton took a deep breath and continued to shuffle the papers around, still trying to decide what papers could go where. His gaze darted to his periphery as Elric took a spot at the table behind him, where numerous books were spread out. Elric went to the shelves to pick a few more and returned to the table with them, where he sat and started to flip through pages.

Starting to feel like perhaps he wasn't a bother, Tilton moved to the other side of the table to face Elric, so it didn't seem like he was being rude.

"What do you think of all this, Tilton?" Elric asked, looking up from his book. He closed it, rubbing his temples and running his fingers through his hair. He stood up and leaned against the table, turning his full attention to Tilton.

"Sorry, Your Highness?" Tilton said. He was surprised to be addressed in such a friendly manner.

"You're one of Thali's closest friends. If she trusts you, I do too." Elric's brow crinkled as he spoke. "I've been doing so much research, my eyeballs might fall out, but I've still only run into a couple mentions of a place that could be Etciel."

"I think Etciel must be very old," Tilton said carefully. He wasn't sure what Elric was hoping to get out of this conversation.

"I've been looking, searching through old, old books. But I haven't been able to find much that's old enough," Elric said. He ran his hands through his hair again. This time though, he held his head in his hands. "I miss her so much, Tilton. I really do. I feel like I'm wandering around the halls aimlessly. I don't even know what happened in my last meeting."

"We all miss her, Your Highness," Tilton said. He put his papers down as he focused on Elric.

"You can call me Elric, Tilton. Especially if it's just us. I don't need to be distanced from my friends."

"All right, Elric," Tilton said. He was surprised Elric considered him a friend. Turning to the tea he'd brought with him, Tilton poured an extra cup, then went and pressed it into Elric's hands.

Motioning to the couch, Tilton asked, "Would you like to talk about it?" It occurred to him that perhaps Elric didn't have anyone to talk to. Avery was busy, and besides, Tilton didn't trust Avery's advice. She seemed to be by his side more than any palace staff should be.

Elric went and sat on the couch, taking a few careful sips of the hot tea. "I feel like every single time I'm close to setting us up perfectly, something pulls her away. First there was the incident on that mysterious island, then there was that mind trap thing, and now she's gone to Etciel. I've been preparing my whole life to rule Adanek. I finally found my queen. My father started to hand me more and more responsibility. It was all falling into place. But now ..."

"Magical creatures weren't part of the deal?" Tilton offered.

Elric nodded. "What do I do? I'm helpless. Thali can control them, and I understand it's a good thing that she went to learn about magic and the magical creatures, but what do I do now without her?" Elric said.

"Well, there might be magical creatures everywhere now, but the kingdom is still full of non-magical needs, too," Tilton suggested.

"You're right. I can't neglect my people. I just don't know how to lead them into a future that's so unknown." Elric glanced out the window that overlooked the village below.

Tilton let the quiet settle as Elric became lost in thought. He wondered if Elric had enough silent time to think or if he had too much time to think in silence. After a few sips of his tea, he said, "I've only known Thali for three years, Elric. But I can tell you there isn't a more capable person. She's more resourceful than she realizes, the best warrior I've ever seen, and her brother loves her. I'm confident she'll be safe with him."

"But when will she be back? And will she even be the same person when she does come back? What if the magic land changes something in her? What if her brother changes something in her?" Elric said.

Tilton swallowed. He knew she wanted to learn and come back with more magical knowledge, but he'd not thought of how that might change her. Now, he realized why Elric was so worried. "Love is a funny thing, Elric. I don't think it's easily swayed or changed. I think it stands firm and grows as it takes root," Tilton said.

Elric smiled. "Love is not love which alters when it alteration finds or bends with the remover to remove. Oh, no! It is an ever-fixed mark that looks on tempests and is never shaken," he recited.

"That's beautiful. Who wrote it?"

"Some man named Shakespeare. My mother gave me the book when I first told her about Thali," Elric said.

"Thali might come back changed in some ways, but none bad I don't think. I think she went to Etciel because of you. She wants to help you protect her kingdom and her people."

"I hope you're right, Tilton," Elric said. A knock on the library door made them both turn, and Tilton jumped up, ready to attend.

Avery poked her head into the library. "Your next meeting is in two minutes, Your Highness."

"Thank you, Avery."

Tilton went to busy himself with the tea set.

Elric rose, leaving the teacup on the larger table. "Thank you for your time, Tilton. I'm sorry to have taken you away from your duties, but I appreciate your conversation." Elric offered Tilton a warm smile, and Tilton was glad to have helped the prince feel a little better.

"Elric," Tilton said before he could stop himself.

"Yes, Tilton?" Elric said, his hand reaching for the doorknob.

Tilton swallowed, but the words tumbled out anyway. "If your mother and father hadn't approved of Thali, would you still have married her?"

Elric grinned. "Thankfully, I never had to cross that bridge." He opened the door and walked out without looking back.

Tilton's brow crinkled. For the first time, he wondered if Elric really understood what love was.

CHAPTER TEN
Thali

X ERUS HADN'T BEEN KIDDING. Thali couldn't get out of bed the next day. Her whole body was sore. She felt a good deal better the second day and wondered if it was magic that had helped her body heal. Thali decided that for her second day of recovery, rest could mean walking. She continued to explore the great white marble palace every spare moment she could, and as she walked along the pristine halls, she was glad to have worn the soft leather boots her brother had given her so she wouldn't make a sound on the floor as she walked by alcoves filled with intricate carvings of mythical creatures. Every mythical creature she'd ever heard of or imagined, from unicorns and alcetaurs to many she hadn't known of like this strange flying pillow thing before her now, were represented in the carvings. The carvings looked like part of the wall, and the lighting above each one highlighted their exquisite complexity.

She'd found many unoccupied bedrooms along her floor and then on the floor below her own room, a cavernous ballroom, the Jade Room where she had her lessons with Xerus, and a smaller dining room half the size of the ballroom. Down the hall from the dining room, she had found the smaller study where she'd met her brother on her first few visits to the palace. Today, she explored the door on the other side of that study. Before, it had opened to her own world, but now she pushed it open to reveal a plush carpet with a mountain of pillows in the middle surrounded by chairs and couches of all kinds.

One of the many seating options was a chair and desk, and a stack of blank parchment sat on another table opposite the chair and desk. The back wall was made entirely of glass and looked out onto the lands beyond. Thali rushed over to the window and discovered a red meadow with tiny yellow and purple flowers that dotted its softly rolling hills and valleys. A green sky the color of Elric's eyes and big fluffy yellow clouds stretched into the distance as if they were all lined up to go somewhere. The ever-changing colors of Etciel ever ceased to amaze her. A pang went through Thali as she thought of her husband. She wondered what he was doing and whether he was angry with her.

The sound of a book crashing onto a hard surface made her jump, and Thali spun around to see a small bookshelf. It was only three rows tall and backless. She wondered how she had missed it earlier given it stood right in the middle of the ring of pillows. Like everything else in the palace, the bookshelf was white, and as she approached it, she saw seven books on a shelf and another on top as if it had been tossed there.

"Rou! There you are!" Rommy's voice made her jump yet again, and Thali looked over at her brother in disbelief.

"Rommy, what is this room?"

Her brother grinned at her. "I was hoping to show it to you myself, but I'm not surprised you found it on your own. This is the library."

"But there's only eight books. And isn't that other room the library?" Thali pointed toward the door.

"Oh no, no, no, no. This is the true library, and these are the eight books that you want to read right now."

"What do you mean?" Thali stepped closer to her brother.

"This world is magic, remember?" Rommy looked sideways at his sister, who nodded. "This bookshelf will only bring forth the books that you want to read at this moment. And usually, the one you want to read the most is on the top."

"But where are all the other books? And how does it know what I want to read?"

"It just knows. I can't explain how it knows, but the books are stored magically."

"Eight though? Really?"

"You should feel honored. Jaxon only ever gets three to come out, and there's usually one that isn't appropriate for everyone's eyes." Rommy coughed. "Take a look." He gestured to the books but didn't move closer.

Thali bent down and looked at the bottom seven titles. Sure enough, three she'd started back home and the other four were indeed ones she would want to read. "Will they disappear?" Thali asked.

"No. Once you take them, they won't disappear until you put them back on this shelf."

Thali stood up and looked at the book on the top of the small bookshelf. It was the exact book about an arranged marriage she had wanted to finish reading that she'd hoped to find in the library.

"Amazing," Thali said as she quickly grabbed the top book.

"Would you like to see the rest of the palace grounds?" Rommy stepped aside to let her pass as he gestured toward the door.

Another book appeared on the top of the shelf, but before Thali had a chance to read the title, Rommy put a hand on her shoulder blade and guided her out of the magical library.

CHAPTER ELEVEN
Tariq

"**B**REAKING THE SHIP WON'T get us there any faster." Bree came up next to Tariq, where he stood gripping the rails at the bow. His knuckles were white as he leaned forward in hopes of getting home faster. Bree wrapped her good arm around a nearby rope to hold herself steady.

Tariq let go of the rail and flexed his hands, exhaled, then turned his attention to Bree. He gently took her hand, and gentle as could be, wrapped his hand around the elbow in a sling. "How are you, my darling?"

"Filled with guilt that Thali left because of me. Filled with guilt that I've caused you so much anguish. Sad that Thali didn't confide in me. Sad to be the cause of the anger between two of my favorite people." Bree turned back to the ocean. Tariq glimpsed the tears filling her eyes as she turned away from him.

"I'm sorry to be the cause of so many negative feelings, my darling." Tariq closed his eyes and focused on his breathing. He never wanted to cause so much trouble for his dear betrothed. "I'm sorry I let my temper get away with me. Lili knows we love her. I wish I could have gone with her."

"I'm not as helpless as you both seem to think, you know." Bree jerked her injured arm out of Tariq's hand.

"I know. But you are my whole world. Life doesn't exist without you in it. Not for me, at least."

Bree placed her injured hand on his cheek. "And my world is nothing without you in it. But I've learned that I cannot stifle your brazenness or sense of adventure, nor Thali's, no matter how much you two terrify me. But you can't keep me in a locked box, no matter how pretty it may be. I want to be there with you. She's my friend, too," Bree said gently.

Tariq took a deep breath. "All right, I'll try to harder to reign in my anger and protectiveness." He folded her into his arms. "Have my intentions always been so easily read?"

"To me, yes," Bree replied.

"Then you know I want to go through the gate to Etciel and face whatever dangers lie ahead, face beings with more magic in one toe than we have in our whole being. Yet you still want to stand with me?" Tariq whispered.

"Yes. Out of everyone who wants to go find Thali in Etciel, we're the only ones with a feasible path," Bree said.

"And you're not upset that we didn't make it known? Didn't invite Elric or Alexius to come through the portal with us?" Tariq said.

"No. Elric's kingdom has yet to know of magic's existence. And Alexius needs to hold the barrier. Neither could come without Adanek falling apart. Better they don't know there's a way."

"And the others?" Tariq wiggled an eyebrow and Bree felt it by her ear as he nuzzled her neck.

"We cannot trust anyone else with this," Bree said.

Tariq nodded into her shoulder. They turned and stood staring at the horizon, willing it to come faster so they might get home sooner. He called on his magic to twirl a playful breeze around them, making Bree smile up at him. He would do anything to earn that smile.

CHAPTER TWELVE
Thali

"**C**OME, I WANT TO show you some special sights." Rommy held a hand out to his sister.

As Thali took it, they rounded a corner to see a horseless carriage. "Umm ... are the horses invisible?" she asked.

Rommy grinned. "No. There are none. It's a magical carriage. Come on, I've been dying to show you so much." He leapt ahead into the carriage and motioned for her to join him.

Thali hesitated, still wondering how the carriage would move. It looked like any normal closed carriage, though a bit fancier perhaps.

"What, can't do it without help now, princess?" Rommy smirked.

"I am still recovering, thank you very much, but no." Thali heaved herself into the carriage. She rolled her eyes and fell into the bench seat opposite him as the carriage started rolling forward. She gripped the sides as it toddled along.

"Xerus enchants it," Rommy said as Thali stuck her head out the window and looked ahead of and behind them.

"He can do that?" Thali made a mental note to ask Xerus how he did it as she thought of the many applications magic like that could have.

"It takes a special boost from this land, a special crystal. Actually, let's go look." Rommy kicked open the door while the carriage still moved, and with little effort, flipped onto the roof as he gripped the top of the doorframe. Then he thumped twice on the ceiling and shouted, "You coming, Rou?!"

Thali climbed out the swinging door and used the window's ledge to boost herself up to the roof. She almost missed her mark as her body complained, but Rommy grabbed her ankle. As she sat on the flat roof, her eyes bugged out at the landscape around them. The sight was incredible. The most beautiful rolling hills and mountains she could have imagined stretched out around her. But even more outstanding were the colors. The skies were purple, the mountains yellow, the rolling hills blue and orange.

Rommy sat cross-legged next to her. "It's a sight, isn't it?"

"It's like nothing I could have imagined," she said.

Rommy tapped the roof, and she watched a small door slide open to reveal a white crystal embedded in a box. "This holds magic. Someone powerful enough can siphon magic into it and then the magic can be used for anything. Anyone can use it once it's full. It's a complex method, but Xerus prefers we all travel this way. It's quicker and safer."

"Does he need to put specific magic in it? Or is it more of an all-purpose magic?" Thali asked, examining the steadily glowing crystal.

"I think in this one, he's added safety and cloaking magic so we don't attract too much attention when we're out, plus motion magic," Rommy said. "Oh wait! Look! Watch the horizon, Rou."

Thali looked out and saw a huge flock of winged horses soaring over a hill. "Are those ...?" Thali's eyes widened as she tried as hard as she could to see them clearly.

"Pegasi." Rommy grinned.

They stayed on the carriage roof as it rolled along the countryside of Etciel for so long she didn't even notice she was cold until she shivered, and her brother draped his cloak over her. He never shivered once. She glanced at his arms and thought of how he'd flipped himself onto the carriage roof. He was healthier, stronger, and more energetic than she'd seen him in all the time he'd been here.

Suddenly, he jumped up and pointed to their right. A giant purple mushroom-shaped rock balanced precariously on the orange grass. It rose as high as the palace. Thali shivered again. The colors and objects were so strange here, but she thought it fitting for a magical land.

Finally, the carriage slowed, then stopped at a path of bright-orange rocks nestled among grassy blue hills. Rommy leapt off the roof, landing lightly on his feet. He turned to her and outstretched both arms. Thali smiled as she remembered the dozens of times he'd done this as they'd grown up, then leaped down at him. She was surprised at how strong his grip was as he caught her and lowered her to the ground.

"Oof, you're heavier than I remember," he said.

"And you'd do well to never say that again, thank you," she said as she pulled at her clothes to straighten them.

He just rolled his eyes at her. "More sensitive, too, I see." He grabbed a blanket from just inside the door and dashed off, racing up the path. Near the top, he waited for her to catch up, then stopped her before they crested the hill. "Close your eyes," he said. When she did, he took both her hands and led her up.

Thali felt the path under her feet slowly become less steep before it flattened briefly, then descended before leveling again.

"All right, open your eyes." He let go of her hands and moved out of the way.

Thali opened her eyes and gasped. Before her was a vast lake of pure milky, pearlescent-white liquid. The blue hills made the lake a bowl, and as the hills sloped toward the water, the blue darkened to a deep navy that met the pearly white of the lake with a rim of silver. A forest of red trees graced the opposite bank, the tree branches bushy and full of fluffy yellow needles. The red reminded her not of blood but of a ruby. The sky changed from a luscious purple to a soft lilac, and at that very moment, a flock of glowing golden birds flew across the sky. The whole sight was breathtaking. "It's beautiful," she said.

"I thought you'd like it. Not like anything else you've seen, right?" Rommy raised an eyebrow and headed for the water. She followed him as they stepped off the cobalt-blue path onto the navy shore.

"Want to go swimming?" Rommy asked, already starting to strip.

"Isn't it sacred? It must be. It's so quiet."

"As if that's stopped you before." Rommy ran and jumped into the lake, and Thali watched in awe as the lake's glassy, pearly surface rippled. She had a hard time wrapping her mind around its opaqueness. But she stripped off what she could and approached the edge of the water. Dipping her feet into the silver edge, she felt nothing but the softest sand under her feet as if she was walking on pillows. As she entered the lake, she was strangely aware that there were no other creatures around; not a single mental thread could she detect. Instead, she felt a revered silence enveloping the area.

When she was waist high in the lake, it struck her that she felt like she was swimming in milk. "What is this place, Rommy? There are no creatures nearby." She glanced at Rommy, who had been practicing different strokes back and forth.

He dove into the water and when he re-emerged, the water beading on his face looked like pearls on his hair and eyelashes.

"This is the Lake of Reflection. Legend has it—no, wait. Let me *show* you," he said, swimming closer to her. "Come. It will take some concentration." They swam to a spot where they were standing on the soft sand floor and the water was chest high on Thali. "Remember the drawing you made me when I broke my leg? Of that strange creature you made up in your mind with the big red lips, purple legs, and a fluffy blue body?"

"Yes. I was trying to cheer you up. We'd just been to see those panels with all those strange animals, and Uncle had just given me those new inks. I made it as colorful as I could because you were such a sulky invalid." Thali grinned at how miserable her brother had been when he'd broken his leg jumping from a tree. He hadn't checked the ground first and landed awkwardly on a rock.

"Yes, I admit, I was a miserable patient. But think of that picture now. Think about each body part."

Thali did. She thought back to the creature she'd once imagined, then made the colors as bright as she could. All at once, a squawk broke her concentration, and the flash of a silver thread in her mind made her eyes fly open to see the creature she'd just imagined fly out of the milky water and across the lake. "What?!" She turned to Rommy.

Rommy grinned. "The Lake of Reflection is the birthplace of many of Etciel's creatures."

The bird-creature landed in the water. Before Thali could say anything else, a second squawk pierced the air and a second creature appeared from the lake. Both bird creatures took off, flying towards the red forest. "Where are they going?" she asked.

"To find a home, I imagine," he said.

"So, any creature I can imagine can come to life here," she said.

"Absolutely," he said, eyes wide with wonder as he watched the pair of birds fly away.

Thali spun around and marched out of the lake, though she started to shiver from the wet and cold.

Rommy left the water behind her. "What's the matter?"

"Rommy, that lake is sacred. And dangerous. Creating life, creating a creature is sacred. How many have you created?"

"Only one or two. It was by accident, I promise."

"No more. Don't do it anymore. Promise me, Rommy."

Rommy wrapped her in his cloak before grabbing the blanket from the carriage to wrap himself in. "All right, Rou. Calm down. I won't do it again. I promise," Rommy looked away from her like a sullen little boy.

"It's about life, Rommy. You can't know the effect it will have on all the other creatures around here. In this whole world. And what if they get into our world?"

"And what if they are wonderful and beautiful and fit right in?" he retorted.

Thali didn't have a response for that.

"You worry too much, little sister. Come, let's get in the carriage and get back so we don't catch a cold." He led her back to the carriage, and they sat silently for a long time as it rumbled along the path.

"I thought you'd like the surprise," Rommy said, pouting.

"I do. It's a beautiful place, Rommy. Thank you for showing it to me. And I can't describe the overwhelming sensation of seeing what was in my head appear in real life. But you have to look at the big picture, Rommy. Think about the consequences."

"Most of the creatures find a home in the red forest. It's been peaceful there for centuries." Rommy looked hurt that he'd been chastised.

"How do you know that?"

"Xerus told me. He brought me here and told me some magical creatures don't reproduce like most others do. They reproduce by visiting the Lake of Reflection."

Thali's mouth formed a surprised "oh." Then, she grabbed her brother's hands. "I'm sorry. I should have let you explain."

"That's all right. You always were hotheaded. I should have known better and told you first."

"Forgive me?" Thali asked.

"Always." Rommy moved to sit next to his sister, rubbing her arms to get warmth back into them.

CHAPTER THIRTEEN
Elric

E LRIC TAPPED THE END of the quill on the table absentmindedly. He stared at a spot on the table as he thought of where Thali had gone. Why hadn't she reached out to him since? Was she was all right? He knew Rommy loved her dearly, but Elric had never quite trusted Thali's brother.

A persistent cough broke into his thoughts, and he finally looked up and realized the room was empty except for his assistant, Avery, who raised her eyebrows when he looked at her.

"You seem distracted, Your Highness," Avery said.

"When did the meeting end?" Elric looked around again, seeing not a soul.

"About five minutes ago."

Elric stood. "Where to next?"

"You have a few minutes to get changed and meet Master Quinto in the inner courtyard," Avery said.

Elric nodded and led the way out of the office. He strode down the hall, smiling and nodding to the few lords who lingered conversing in the hall. At his chambers, a guard opened the door for him as Avery waited for him in the hall.

Elric's smile faded the moment he walked into the room. He felt the emptiness. Indi was curled up on the couch again in what Elric assumed was depression. The tiger was asleep every time he walked in. Ana also lay on a couch, but she perked up a little when he came in. She hopped off and padded over to Elric for some ear scratches before returning to her post, chin resting on the armrest as she stared at the wall beside the door. They both faced the wall, staring blankly at it. Bardo had barely moved from the tray of decorative rocks on the table. The animals looked how he felt, and he didn't know how to help them.

He changed in his cavernous closet, then popped into the bedroom he shared with Thali to grab a coat he'd left there, but he paused when he heard the soft sobs of someone in Thali's closet. He walked in to find Mia sewing, streams of tears running down her cheeks, her brown hair a mop over her face.

"Mia? Are you all right?" Elric asked.

Mia jumped, stabbing her finger. "Ouch!" She put her index finger in her mouth and sucked on it before looking up at Elric. "I'm sorry, Your Highness. I'm just upset that Thali hasn't come back yet. I miss her terribly. I thought she'd only be gone a few days, but it's been more than a week now."

"She'll be back," Elric said, putting a hand on her shoulder.

"How are you doing?" She turned her face to him and wiped away her own tears.

"I miss her. I wish I could contact her, know for sure that she's safe," Elric said.

"Oh, I'm not too worried about her safety. I'm just disappointed that she didn't speak to anyone before she left," Mia said, hiccuping.

"You really trust Romulus that much?" Elric asked.

Mia laughed. "You'll forgive me, Your Highness, but I grew up with them. There is no one more protective of Thali than her brother."

"Even more than Prince Tariq?" Elric asked.

Mia grinned. "It's hard to believe, I know, but yes. In all the time I've known those siblings, Rommy's always had one eye on Thali, making sure she was all right. He would die a hundred times for her."

A knot loosened in his chest. If Mia, Tariq, and Ambrene all said Thali would be safe with Rommy, then he would have to trust in that at least a little. A knock on the far door turned his attention back to his responsibilities. "Have a good day, Mia, and do something fun for me," he said. He didn't really understand how or why she was always sewing but left her to her work.

Outside his rooms, he found Avery waiting patiently for him in the hallway. He hadn't told Avery that Thali was missing, but he was sure she knew. Though he hadn't let anyone except the guards, Tilton, and Daylor into the rooms he shared with Thali, palace rumors spread quickly.

After leaving the palace through his usual side exit, he found Master Quinto waiting for him in the inner courtyard. It was a private training area for the monarchy, and Elric was using it now though he usually didn't because he hadn't wanted to attract too much attention while Thali was missing. He was surprised to see Isaia standing there with his father, Master Quinto.

Isaia bowed and Master Quinto handed Elric a practice sword. Isaia had gone to school with Thali, though he'd been two years ahead. They'd only overlapped for one year, but not only had he worked for her family after finishing school, Thali had saved his life at sea. They were close friends now. Elric had been pleased when Isaia had joined her personal guard. As a Quinto, his family was legendary, almost as famous as Thali's mother.

A few minutes into their training session, Elric realized Master Quinto was working them hard. Elric found he had to focus on their sparring more than usual as Isaia fought him and Master Quinto coached.

By the end of practice, Elric sat on the ground dripping with sweat, having been beaten a half-dozen times. Isaia definitely hadn't taken it easy on him.

"Your Highness, I have some news," Isaia said as Elric wiped his brow.

"Yes?" Elric asked, panting.

"Alexius and I have been scouring the library for any information on Etciel. And we've discovered that while Alexius can't go through, he thinks he might be able to open a door for someone else to go through," Isaia said.

Elric stood up suddenly. "Why is this the first time I'm hearing this?"

"Well, we've just learned it might be possible. We're still missing a few pieces, but Alexius has been living in the library, trying to fix this. He's torn up that she disappeared without him knowing," Isaia said.

Elric hadn't seen Alexius much since Thali disappeared but was glad to hear he'd been productive. He still blamed the dragon for not knowing Thali had gone, for not alerting him.

"Let's go talk to Alexius then," Elric said, nodding to Master Quinto, who was pretending not to listen. He supposed a family like the Quintos probably knew as much about palace goings on as he did. The family had lived on the palace grounds for three generations and had never broken the royal family's trust. He trusted their discretion and appreciated their service, especially with Thali gone. But thanks to Isaia, he might just be able to go to her.

CHAPTER FOURTEEN
Garen

G AREN STEPPED OFF THE boat, nodding to his man before strolling down the dock and into the city. He rounded a few corners, always looking for the tiny symbols that told him where to go, and nodded to a few more folks he recognized before he came upon a grandiose hut. Its bright-pink walls and white roof made him roll his eyes as he went around back and climbed the back wall to enter through the uppermost right window.

"Little brother, how nice of you to drop in." Joren smiled.

"Love what you've done with the place. It really blends in," Garen said, dropping his bag and sitting on a tiny chair. He took the already-filled cup of tea and looked at his big brother. Joren looked tired. Even through the makeup and the bright clothing that he always took to extremes, his older brother, the prince of thieves in these lands, looked tired.

"You know," Garen stated.

Joren said nothing but nodded his head.

"And?" Garen asked.

Joren bobbed a fluffy yellow slipper on his foot and crossed his leg over his other knee.

Garen noticed Joren had tea for two set out on a children's table in the empty room. The tea was hot. So, he'd gotten word of Garen's arrival quite quickly then.

"You need to work on your stealthiness," Joren finally said. A vine next to Joren's head dangled over the teapot and refilled Garen's cup after he'd taken a few sips.

"Apparently." Garen snatched a cookie from the tiny plate and sniffed it before eating it to make sure it was real food. Joren had set up a little girl's tea party, and Garen wanted to make sure what he was eating was actually food. "So?" Garen asked.

"I've been looking," Joren said as he shrugged.

"Anything?" Garen said.

"It's tougher than you think to find something when you don't know what you're looking for," Joren snapped back. He was definitely tired.

"It's called Etciel," Garen said.

"That doesn't help me much. I'm not looking it up in a book," Joren said.

Garen rolled his eyes. His brother was the king of snark and sarcasm.

"Did she at least leave a note?" Joren asked.

"Yes," Garen said. "She promised. After that first time."

"You mean after that time you almost destroyed the city looking for her." Joren sipped from his tiny cup, pinky out. Somehow, none of his pink lipstick ended up on the cup.

Garen rubbed his thumb along his teacup's edge. "I was worried."

"We know." Joren opened his left hand to a vine, and a leaf reached out. He stroked it. "You weren't followed, by the way."

Garen rolled his eyes. "Have you had problems with magical animals lately?"

"We did, but after a few run-ins with some of my babies, they don't dare enter the city," Joren said. He gently ran a finger down the vine as if petting a small animal. "Have you thought about what you're going to do when we find a door to the other world?"

"I don't have much information at my disposal," Garen said.

"You know that other prince, the handsome one with all the jewels, Tariq?" Joren asked.

Garen nodded.

"Rumor is that his family guards a portal that leads to a different world. A world of ancient magic," Joren said.

Garen's eyebrows knit together. "If Tariq has a portal, why does he not use it?"

Joren looked at his little brother's face for a moment. "Tariq believes Thali is safe. Why would he need to use it?"

And why would he not tell anyone about it? Garen wondered. If Tariq had told him about it, he could have used it to go find Thali. At the same time, part of Garen wasn't sure Thali even wanted to be found since she'd left of her own volition with someone she cherished dearly: her brother. He sat in silence, letting his conflicting thoughts simmer.

Chapter Fifteen
Tilton

T ILTON COULDN'T SLEEP; HE was worried. He had been worrying for days while he and Daylor had split their time between seeing to their duties and pretending to work in Thali's rooms. They were still pretending that Thali was redecorating, and as her friends and secretaries, they would of course be helping her with it, but he knew that certain people in the palace—those who knew them from school or worked closely with them—wouldn't be fooled for long.

"You worry too much," Daylor said, tousling Tilton's hair.

Tilton turned away from the window he'd been staring unseeingly through to look at Daylor. "The whole palace is upset. Have you seen Alexius lately? He's a mess. He looks like a bird that's been pulling its feathers out. Do dragons do that? Do they pull their scales off when stressed?" Tilton asked.

"I'm not sure. Maybe we should ask Alexius."

They were quiet for a moment, each absorbed in their own thoughts as they stood shoulder to shoulder. Tilton knew that Daylor was as worried as he was; he just hid it better.

"She'll be back. I know she will. She just needs some time with her brother," Daylor said, wrapping his arm around Tilton. Daylor tucked his thumb into Tilton's belt.

Tilton eased into the embrace. There was a comfort there he could use right now. "But what if he's been compromised? What if something or someone turned him evil?"

"Evil?" Daylor chuckled.

The rumbling in his chest made Tilton smile. He tilted his head to look up at Daylor. "You know what I mean. What if Xerus, or even Romulus, is behind all this?" Tilton asked.

"Why would you think that?" Daylor asked.

"The way Alexius looks, the way he's acting. He clearly doesn't trust anyone in his family, maybe not even Romulus," Tilton said.

"That may be, but you've seen how Romulus and Thali are together." Daylor gave Tilton's hip a squeeze. "There's no way he would harm a single hair on her head."

"As long as he sees her as his little sister, yes. But what happens when he sees what she's become, how powerful she is? What happens when she resists him?" Tilton asked, unconsciously leaning into Daylor's muscled chest.

"Maybe he won't see that part of her. Ever. You don't give Thali enough credit. She's smart. She'll be smart enough to play along if she does discover he's not the brother she once knew."

Tilton wondered if Daylor was trying to convince himself of that or if he truly believed it. "I hope you're right," he said. He was still worried, but he knew Daylor wouldn't budge in his conviction. He couldn't. Daylor wasn't like that. He had to have hope that their friend was safe.

They stayed that way in silence, resting against the windowsill, Tilton nestled in Daylor's arm and Daylor resting his head on Tilton's, until the sun disappeared behind the hills and the moon took its place in the sky.

Chapter Sixteen
Bree

"Tariq. Tariq ..." Bree tapped his shoulder repeatedly as he hunched over a table with multiple books spread out before him. "Tariq," she said a little louder. When he still didn't respond, she got fed up. "TARIQ! STOP!" she shouted as she waved her hands in the air. The couple had returned to Bulstan a few days ago. Tariq had gone straight to the private library and hadn't left since.

"I'm close, Bree, I know I am," Tariq muttered. His hair stuck out at odd angles, and he still wore the same clothes he had arrived in. Bree had left him alone, hoping he would work it out of his system, but after four days in the library and her lady's maid telling her this morning that he hadn't eaten his supper last night or breakfast this morning, she decided she had to knock some sense back into him.

Books lay open on every surface: floors, desks, atop stacks of other books. Tariq had built a perimeter around him, and he dashed from one book to the other as he flipped through them.

"Tariquin," a deep voice said from behind Bree, and Bree and Tariq both froze. The voice was gentle, but Mupto Shikji was the kind of man who could command a room without effort.

Bree had never heard so much emotion in her future father-in-law's voice. Mupto weaved through the stacks of books, somehow not stepping on any of them as he glided through the mess. King Shikji had always been strong and stoic, serious and full of joy at the same time. He enjoyed a good laugh, but when it came to his children, he had always been very strict.

"Tariquin. It will be all right." Mupto put his hand on his son's shoulder, and Tariq broke, sobs racking his body as he turned and dove into his father's chest. Mupto enveloped him in his arms and squeezed him tight. Tariq had grown to be a large man, and though he was a head taller than his father, Mupto still held him. Tariq curled into his father just like he had as a little boy. Mupto patted his son's back and absorbed all his tears as he held him.

Bree was glad that Tariq had finally faced the emotions she knew he had been storing since they had thought Rommy was dead. Rania had crumbled, but Tariq had stayed stoic for her and strong for his father. Then, Thali had suddenly grown up, and Bree watched him worry about his friend's heart and how quickly she'd gotten herself involved in global politics. And then they had discovered Rommy wasn't dead. The final brick on Tariq's heavy pile of emotions was Thali leaving without saying goodbye after he had blamed her for Bree's injured arm, though he certainly hadn't meant it. That weighed on him the most.

Bree slowly backed out of the room to give father and son some time alone. She went instead to check on Rania, who mostly slept now. She didn't know if Rania would even want to know that Rommy was alive. Rommy had left again, and the whole family worried that she would sink further into her grief if she knew he hadn't come back for her. A little voice inside Bree wondered, though, if Rania would cheer up just knowing he was alive.

Bree knocked softly on her door and poked her head in. Rania was where she was most days when she wasn't sleeping, sitting by the window and looking out at the ocean. Bree walked in and nodded at Rania's lady's maid sitting in a chair nearby. At first unsure of what she could do for Rania, Bree glanced around the room before noticing a strand of hair had come loose from Rania's braid. So, Bree picked up a brush and gently undid Rania's hair, brushing it softly. Rania had the finest wavy hair. Bree took her time brushing each strand carefully and fully to the floor. Rania closed her eyes briefly as Bree took great care with each stroke.

"We love you, Rania," Bree said, separating Rania's long hair into sections to rebraid it. Rania said nothing. Bree didn't mind. When she was done braiding Rania's hair, she nodded at Rania's lady. Mupto had posted round-the-clock companionship for Rania, worried she'd do something rash. Rania just continued to look out the window, toward the ocean, and Bree tied a ribbon in her hair before quietly leaving the room.

Chapter Seventeen
Thali

"Rou?" Rommy poked his head into the magical library.

Thali was curled up in the window seat, reading a book about objects that could enhance magic in places where magic was scarce. She looked up and saw her brother glance at the magical shelves that brought you any book you wanted to read without having to ask for it. It was one of Thali's favorite things about the palace, and she never ceased to be amazed by its ability to know all the things she wanted to read about and how perfect its selections always were.

"It's suppertime, Rou. You coming?" Rommy asked.

"Oh!" Thali uncurled her limbs from under her and folded the blanket that always sat on the window seat. Tucking the book under her arm, she walked with her brother to the smaller dining room.

Supper was casual at the palace, but the family always ate together. It reminded her of how her family had always insisted they eat together, and as awkward as it was with Xerus, Jaxon, and Aexie, she enjoyed the time with Rommy.

She left the book on the table by the door. Rommy held her chair for her and tucked it in as she sat. Jaxon, Aexie, and Xerus were already seated. Xerus sat at the head of the table, Jaxon and Aexie were on one side, and Thali and her brother sat on the other side. "I'm sorry to have kept you waiting," Thali said, looking at Aexie, Jaxon, and Xerus in turn.

They all nodded at her, and as soon as Rommy sat down, dishes were served. Thali let everyone else start before helping herself to small samplings of each dish. She was still getting used to the colorful food they had in Etciel, though it all tasted relatively similar to what she was used to. In front of her was a pile of what looked like purple mashed potatoes, but it tasted like roast meat. On the next plate Rommy handed her were perfectly round slices of ham, but they tasted like squash. It was strange that what she saw did not correspond with what she put in her mouth, and she could only imagine what it was like for Alexius and Aexie to come to her world and experience the same thing in reverse. "Aexie, was it strange when you came to my world and had to eat our boring-looking food?" Thali asked.

Aexie smiled. "It was definitely a unique experience eating food that was all the same color, or mostly the same two colors—brown and white—with only the odd splash of color. I'm sure you're experiencing something similar."

"What about vegetables? Are they all brown or white?" Jaxon asked.

"Not always. Some are green, some orange, red, or yellow, but when they're cooked, they have more of a brownish tinge to them," Aexie said.

"Strange," Jaxon said. He grinned at Thali. "Do you even know what you're eating now, Thali?"

"Not at all," Thali said as she put another spoonful of purple mash in her mouth. She was raised to be polite and hadn't had stomach issues, so she simply tried everything and tried to catalog it all.

"You're very brave," Jaxon said in a mockingly solemn voice.

"When you've experienced eating the same thing for every meal for a fortnight, you'll try just about anything. Right, Rommy?" Thali said, cocking an eyebrow at her brother.

"That's very true," Rommy replied.

Jaxon's features darkened for a moment, making Thali wonder if there was some tension between Rommy and Jaxon. She decided it was best to change the subject for now. "Jaxon, I haven't had a chance to train today yet. Do you have some time tonight?"

Jaxon grinned. "Definitely." He started to eat a little faster.

"Give it at least an hour after you eat," Xerus said, finally joining the conversation.

"Yes, sir," Jaxon said.

"Routhalia, we will start again tomorrow morning, in the Jade Room," Xerus said. He was always quiet and somber. Thali wondered what had happened to make him so serious.

"Will you join me tonight?" Thali asked Rommy.

"No, I think I'll leave Jaxon to beat you to a pulp himself. I have some work to do in the library," he said.

While Thali wondered what work that could be, she thought it best not to ask at this moment.

Thali found Jaxon in the training space outside later that evening. After supper, she'd gone to change into different clothes while she waited the requisite hour.

"Tonight, I thought we'd focus on footwork," Jaxon said.

Thali groaned. Footwork meant fast movements and lots of ducking and running.

"Not the kind you're used to. You probably know most of the drills for that, anyway. I mean the magical kind," Jaxon explained.

Thali stood a little taller. She hadn't ever used magic in combat. She hadn't really ever needed to.

"You see magic in threads, correct?" Jaxon asked.

Thali nodded.

"Tonight, I want to work on a magical version of combat. You need to be able to use all tools available to you, and magic, though costly, is one of them," Jaxon said. "I want you to attach magical threads on yourself for now, here and here." He pointed to his ankles.

Thali's brow crinkled. She unspooled some of her magic and did as Jaxon asked, feeling strange as she connected to her own ankles. For a moment, she could see the layers of skin and the tendon in the back of her leg, then the bones of her ankle. She wrapped the magical thread around the biggest bone.

"Good," Jaxon said, smiling. She didn't know how, but she knew that Jaxon, Xerus, and Aexie could detect and maybe even see other magic.

"Now, slowly, pull one of the threads backward," Jaxon instructed.

Thali took hold of one and willed it to move backward. Her foot moved immediately, and she was thrown forward as her foot moved out from underneath her. Jaxon's arm shot out to catch her. He'd obviously been expecting that to happen.

"You're not moving your foot with your own nerves. It'll take time to get used to it," he said, trying to hide a smile.

Thali looked down at her foot again and reached out ever so slowly to move it with her magic. Even though she was in control the entire time, it felt alien, like someone else was moving her foot. She tried the other foot and accidentally pulled at both rather suddenly. She landed face first in the dirt.

Jaxon howled with laughter, doubling over with the force of it. "Maybe we should try a different method," he suggested when he finally caught his breath. "Let's attach another thread to each hip and shoulder, the big bones only. You don't want to risk snapping your smaller bones by accident."

Thali did so, seeing four threads in her mind's eye plus the two attached to her ankles. She gathered them all together in a bundle and pulled ever so gently. She looked down and watched the ground move as her body slid backward. It was such a peculiar feeling that she stopped, pulled gently again, then stopped. Next, she imagined the threads were stiff and pushed, this time propelling her body forward.

"Good. You're getting the hang of it. Feel strange? Like someone else is moving your body?" Jaxon asked when she returned to him.

Thali nodded. She was a little unnerved by how easy it was to move someone—even herself—with magic.

Jaxon interrupted her train of thought. "The answer is yes. There have been some who have used magic to control others, to make them do things like jump off cliffs and buildings or drown themselves." A shadow passed over his face. "It takes serious concentration to move someone else's body, though. You have free access to your own, but the body has natural defenses. It would take someone quite powerful and practiced to move another intelligent being. And even then, the mental shielding we learn, and our magic, protects us from someone taking hold of our bodies, so it happens rarely."

Thali nodded her acknowledgment.

"Using just your magic, can you get your body to step up on this and walk across it?" Jaxon patted the bench behind him.

Thali moved the threads. It was painfully slow, and she moved awkwardly, but she approached the bench and suddenly realized she didn't have to step up on the bench. She could just lift her whole body up onto it. However, she yanked a little hard, and her head spun a little as she landed hard on the raised surface. She blinked a few times and saw Jax hiding his mouth behind his hand. Even she had to admit it must be quite entertaining to watch someone jerk their own body around.

Walking across the bench took a lot of concentration as she watched what her feet did and adjusted how she manipulated the threads. She raised her arms triumphantly when she finally made it across.

"That took an excruciatingly long time," Jaxon said.

Thali's face fell. "Of course it did. It's like relearning how to walk."

"Yes. When you do it that way it is. You're still moving mechanically in the real world and forgetting you have magic. What if you pour your magic onto the bench? Don't use your eyes, use your threads," Jax said.

Thali's brow crinkled again as she thought about that.

"It's like finding your way in the dark," Jax said.

Of course, Thali thought. She realized she could spool her magic out, find the bench using the threads, and pull herself up and along them. Before she knew it, she was on the other side of the bench, blinking as she tried to figure out exactly what she had just done.

"That's more like it," Jaxon said, clapping. "Now, go over the bench."

Thali imagined her threads stretching away from her and then up and over, draping over the bench. Then, she took the bundle of threads attached to her body and guided them along the threads she had laid out. Slowly, she felt herself gliding up and over the bench.

"Yes, that's it," Jaxon said. "Now, sit down for a minute. You can detach your magic."

Thali sat on the bench and physically swung her legs over it, feeling strange doing so as she detached and rewound her threads. She tucked the magic back into herself, becoming aware of her actual body as she did. Her ankles and shoulders and hips were sore as if they had been yanked on. She pulled the collar of her shirt down over her shoulder and saw a bruise blossoming where she had attached a magical thread.

"And that's why it takes time to get used to," Jaxon said. He put a silver tin on the bench next to her. She opened it as he pulled another bench closer. Thali twisted the top off the tin and breathed in the soothing minty smell mixed with notes of things she didn't recognize. She started to rub the salve into each point on her aching body with a grimace. If it hurt this much now, it would hurt a lot more tomorrow.

"Why would someone choose this method instead of physically moving?" Jax asked.

"If their body is incapable or injured. Because it's faster," Thali replied.

Jaxon nodded.

Suddenly, he looked up and Aexie appeared out of thin air. Thali always forgot that the female dragon could make herself invisible.

Aexie glared at them from a distance, and Thali tried not to focus on the dragon as she took some more salve from the tin and rubbed her bruised shoulders. Aexie stomped back up to the palace.

"I don't think she likes me very much," Thali said after Aexie had disappeared into the palace.

"It's not you. It's me. She's mad at me for teaching you what she thinks should be kept a secret," Jax said, rolling his eyes.

"Why *are* you teaching me?" Thali asked. She guessed maybe Xerus had asked him to teach her, making her wonder why. What did he want in return? They didn't have to teach her their secrets.

Jax shrugged but didn't look at her. "You're not like him," he muttered under his breath.

Thali wondered why it would matter that she wasn't like Xerus.

Jaxon clapped his hands then and turned to put away the few things he'd taken out. It was clear he was done talking.

Thali pulled her shirt back over her shoulder. She'd have to rub the salve into her other parts in the privacy of her own room. She and Jax walked back up to the palace together in silence, Jax catching her when she misstepped as she readjusted to using her physical body and almost fell to the ground.

Chapter Eighteen
Nasir

"**Y**OU KNOW, HER BROTHER is a formidable warrior," Nasir said.

Elric was drenched in sweat as he sparred against Nasir. "What do you know about her brother?"

"I was a palace guard in Bulstan until I came here. I watched Routhalia and Romulus grow up alongside Prince Tariq, Princess Rania, and Lady Ambrene," Nasir said.

"And how do you know I'm thinking about Thali's brother?"

"Because your face does this twisted squishing thing when you're thinking of him." Nasir tried to imitate Prince Elric's angry, thinking face. Then he continued. "Thali has been in Romulus's shadow since the day I met them. Thali has improved since Romulus's absence, but Romulus is the gifted warrior. Maybe even better than his mother." Nasir started to hit Elric's weaker blocks a little harder.

Elric matched Nasir's efforts. "And how do I compare?"

Nasir stopped abruptly, Elric following suit. They were in the private training room, and Nasir was grateful. "Do you want an honest answer, Your Highness?"

Elric nodded. "Yes, Nasir. You will not be punished for speaking your mind here." His face twisted again, Nasir assumed he was bracing himself for the blunt reply.

"Your skill equals Thali's when she was ten. Romulus's when he was eight. Tariq's when he was also eight," Nasir said, his face serious.

"Really?" Elric drooped. He sat down on a bench. "My skills are that of children."

"You must remember their mother is *the* Lady Jinhua. She grew up with a staff in her hands and was training before she could walk, and for hours a day. She put her own children—especially her daughter—through the same rigorous training. Plus, they lived aboard a ship full of sailors. Yes, many were family, but there was always the chance they would have to put down a mutiny or fend off a hijacking. They were always prepared," Nasir explained.

"Guess I should train more," Elric said, "if I'm ten years behind my own wife. Thali always makes combat look so effortless."

"If you trained an extra hour a day, I think you'd catch up faster than you think. Especially with me and Isaia training with you," Nasir said.

"Isaia's better than I am too, isn't he?" Elric said.

Nasir looked hesitantly at Elric before nodding. "You have great potential though, Your Highness." He looked nervously around.

"It's all right, Nasir. I said you wouldn't be punished, and you won't. I asked. I should have been ready for an answer I didn't want to hear." Elric stared off into the distance. "I miss her so much."

Nasir sat down on a bench adjacent to Elric's. "I do too."

They sat in silence for a while, then Elric asked, "Do you really think she's safe with her brother?"

"Yes, I do." Nasir pulled his legs up on the bench and sat cross-legged, pushing on his knees a bit to stretch his hips. He smiled. "There was one time, I think Thali was eight and Romulus was twelve. Usually, the moment they arrived in Bulstan, they'd split up: Romulus would go off with Rania, Thali with Tariq. Romulus would always go and find Thali in the middle of the day to check on her, but one time, Thali had broken her arm on the ship before they arrived. So, Romulus made Rania do everything Tariq wanted to do so Romulus could be with Thali. And Romulus and Tariq would fight each other in training every morning to decide who would cut her meat up and who would help her climb the tree. It's not as if Thali had absentee parents, but Romulus has always kept Thali tucked closely under his wing. She's precious to him. He would die for her," Nasir said.

"How old were you when you went to work for Tariq's family?" Elric asked.

"I was orphaned shortly after I was born. In Bulstan, orphans can choose to be a soldier, a cook, or palace staff. We grow up learning our trade of choice."

"Interesting." Elric looked far away.

A cough interrupted their silence. Avery appeared in an archway. Nasir stood and bowed to Elric, walking away so Avery and Elric could speak privately.

Nasir lingered and paced the edge of the courtyard though, still on guard duty. He was too far away to be within earshot, but he didn't need to hear them to know what they said. He had long suspected Avery of having feelings for Elric, and Nasir's first allegiance was to Thali, so now he watched closely as Avery rested a hand on Elric's arm as she spoke.

Elric didn't react to Avery's touch, only listened quietly before replying. His face turned serious, and he stood to leave through the other door. Without a second glance for Avery, Nasir slipped around the edge of the room to follow Elric.

CHAPTER NINETEEN
Thali

THALI SAT ON A bench on the balcony. She'd been looking for a peaceful, quiet place—not that the palace had become busier—because she'd needed some time to contemplate. When she'd wandered into the Jade Room and saw the door to the massive balcony that looked out onto a forest and a field with a herd of sheep, she knew she'd stumbled on just the right spot. The sheep looked wild and like they were the only defense against a possible out-of-control grass problem. She watched as the sheep grazed, wandering this way and that. She didn't know why, but she was fond of them. As such, she left their minds alone. Then, she suddenly thought of Alexius. Thali felt guilty that she hadn't at least gone to wake him and tell him she was leaving. Maybe he knew of another way to hold the defenses up and could have come with her. She couldn't help feeling like his siblings were angry with her, and she wished Alexius was with her to explain or maybe even help her convince them to like her.

"So, this is where you are," Rommy said. Thali jumped. She hadn't even heard him approach. Turning around, she saw Rommy standing there with a tray, upon which rested two cups, some cookies, and a teapot. Thali used her magic to pull a small table and a second bench over to the edge of the balcony so Rommy could put the tray down.

He raised an eyebrow as the furniture moved. "You're getting better at that," he said as he placed the tray on the table. When Thali didn't say anything, he quietly served the tea and sat down on the bench she'd pulled over for him. She took the teacup in both hands and curled up with it.

They sat quietly in the cooling afternoon air for a little while. Thali knew her brother would ask her soon, but she was grateful for his patience.

"Am I going to have to tickle it out of you?" he finally asked.

Thali smiled at that. She thought of all the times Rommy had made her tell him how she was feeling by tickling her when she refused to say.

"That's better. You had an 'I feel terribly guilty, and my world is crumbling face.' on," Rommy said.

Thali lowered her legs to cross them instead of bringing them up to her chin as she'd been going to. "I was just feeling guilty that I didn't even tell Alexius I was coming here. I could have at least conveyed a message to his siblings for him."

Rommy tilted his head in her direction but stared out beyond the balcony. He kept quiet as she continued.

"And ... and I miss Elric. Maybe I should have woken him up before I left. As much as I like the peacefulness here, I miss the hubbub of the palace. Plus, I'm wondering how Bree is doing and if her arm is feeling better. I left Tariq badly, and without saying goodbye. He was so angry with me, and I don't know if he's still angry or ... or if maybe he's even more angry because I abandoned my duty. I wish I could talk to ... well, a friend of mine in town, and ..." She turned to look at her brother. He only raised his eyebrows, patiently waiting for her to continue. "What's the point of training in this world when I can't, but need to, use it in our world?" Thali finished quietly.

Rommy didn't say anything. He took another sip of tea, waiting for her to continue.

"I mean, I love all the things I'm learning. But I don't know how much of it I'll be able to use when I get home," Thali said. "What if I'm so weak, I can't help anyone?" She stared into her teacup now, feeling empty.

Silence filled the air for a long while before Rommy spoke. "It's wonderful here, isn't it? Even I can feel the energy that fills the very air here. It's ... invigorating."

Thali nodded. She did enjoy using magic here. Instead of draining her like it would in her world, it seemed to make her stronger. It was like magic was just begging to be used in this world, and it surrounded everyone and everything.

They were quiet for some time again before Rommy finally said, "I've been doing more research on a way to store magic and bring it with you."

Thali spun her head around to look at him. "Really?"

"I came across some papers in Xerus's office. I didn't want to tell you until I could find something substantial, but maybe you'll be more resourceful than me. After all, you've managed quite well without me these last few years." He grinned at her. "The papers talked about before, when everyone could move freely between our worlds. Individuals used to take things with them that they could fill with magic."

Thali turned to her brother fully now. "Like how the apothecaries from our world use amber to draw out disease and such?"

"I'm not sure. The text was vague, but it mentioned specific objects that could store specific magic, like the carriage crystal," Rommy said. He crinkled his brow.

Thali assumed he was rereading the text from memory. "That would be amazing. I wonder how much magic you could store in them. How it would travel to Adanek. I wish I could ask Alexius."

"You could ask Xerus. He'd tell you," Rommy suggested.

Thali nodded, turning back to the horizon as the sun began its final descent behind the indigo hill. The siblings sat together on the balcony in silence, watching the sun set and finishing their tea. Rommy stood up to pour another cup for Thali, removing his jacket to place around her shoulders. He moved the tray to the bench so he could sit on the stone table closer to his sister. Thali felt peaceful in that moment. Even though she still had many questions, this one moment was familiar and comforting. This was how she and her brother had once ended many a day: together, watching the sun set—usually from the bow of a ship or from the crow's nest—but he was the person she trusted most in the world.

"Is there a normal place where I can go swimming that won't create new beings?" Thali turned to Jaxon after a particularly grueling training session. Now, she had to work with him twice a day, once for physical combat and once for magical. She had just finished a physical combat lesson, and in her sweaty state, she missed the lake by the school where everyone had once gone swimming.

Jaxon turned to her, one eyebrow raised. "There's the moat." He made it sound as if it was the strangest thing for someone to want to go swimming.

"Are there carnivorous crocodiles-dolphins or some other creatures that'll try to eat or attack me in there?" Thali asked.

Jaxon's eyes rolled up in thought. "There might be. I'm not sure."

"Arrgh," Thali growled before stretching out on the stone bench. She closed her eyes. At least the bench was cool. She tried to imagine just absorbing all the coolness so she wouldn't be as sweaty.

"You know we have a lake underneath the palace, right?" Jax asked.

Thali sat upright. "What?"

"How have you been bathing all this time?" Jax asked, looking confused.

"The tubs in the bathing room attached to my chamber. You know, that room that's sunken into the ground," Thali answered.

"Oh right," Jax shook his head. "You don't have a bigger form to bathe."

"How big is the lake?"

"Big enough for a few full-sized dragons."

"Would you show me?" Thali felt a thrill of excitement at getting to swim again.

Jax pushed his lips together. "Don't see why not." Without another word, he turned and started to walk back to the palace.

Thali ran to catch up.

"So, you have to wash both your forms?" Thali asked.

Thali woke up a few mornings later to find the palace abandoned. She found breakfast in her sitting room, but when she poked her head out into the hall, all was quiet. She looked out her window and didn't see anyone in the training rings. Her footfalls were oddly loud in the plush carpet stretching down the hall, and she narrowed her eyes, listening hard for any sounds from the other rooms.

She wandered into Xerus's room and found it quiet and cold. Not wanting to snoop, she left quickly and went to the library. Walking in, she looked around expecting to find Aexie or Jaxon or Rommy, but no one was there. She finally wandered to the Jade Room and found a note on a table.

We had some pressing matters to deal with, nothing of great concern. We'll be back. Enjoy your quiet time.

—R

Thali looked around, frustrated with having to wait. Every moment here was costing her time at home.

Her gaze shifted to the balcony. The sun was starting to rise above the forest, and Thali felt compelled to walk out. She glanced at the bench that always appeared, but it didn't look particularly comfortable. Instead, she sat on the rail, pulling her knees to her chin and using magic to ground her so she wouldn't fall accidentally. She'd come so far magically, and she was excited to bring her talents back to Elric and her kingdom, if she could. She thought for a moment about *her* kingdom. Because she was only a princess right now, she had a hard time imagining that one day she'd be sitting in the chair that Elric's mother sat in. That particular station put her so far beyond her friends and family it often made her uncomfortable.

Thali let her gaze wander over to the sheep that roamed in the field beyond the palace. She thought it strange that so many sheep gathered in this field when they could easily roam the forest. For that matter, why were the sheep and that tiny cottage behind the palace while all the other farms were situated in front of the palace? She wondered if one of the royal dragons had a little side hobby. Did one of them keep sheep? And were these sheep different from the sheep in her world? Oh, her questions were endless. Thali sighed and wrapped her arms around herself, hugging her legs closer to her chest. She could feel her magic ties keeping her in place, so she watched the forest quietly as the sheep came and went, most opting to stay in the field of grass and graze.

Then, Thali looked within herself. She could feel her spools of magic at the ready. There was so much to learn, and yet there was not enough time to learn it all. Already, she'd been gone for weeks in her world. She needed to learn more before she went home though. She had to be useful. She had to be able to help. But how would she know when it was time to go home? Could she bring magic with her? Would Rommy be able to go back with her? Would Aexie come? Or maybe Jaxon would come if she asked him. And at the same time, would Xerus allow Jaxon to come with her?

While Aexie was all right, Thali preferred that Jaxon come with her. He had taught her the most about combat, and it was easy to see his vast knowledge of war history. Besides, after Alexius, she got along best with Jaxon. He understood what it was like to put your body through a hard day's work and go to sleep tired and weary. She wondered what it was, exactly, that Xerus was trying to achieve. Why was this place so abandoned? Not just today, but she'd barely seen a soul in or out of the palace. Back home, Elric's palace was always filled with people, often overflowing even.

Thinking of everyone back home made Thali take a deep breath. Then, she let it out slowly, counting to eight. She held onto that moment without air before giving in to her diaphragm's need to expand, to bring breath back into her lungs and body. She breathed out and this time, counted as she breathed in. At the peak, she held her breath and restarted the count until she couldn't hold her breath any longer before letting her diaphragm push it all out again.

She recognized the foul mood she was sinking into at having been left behind. Thali had started feeling like one of them, a member of the family of dragons. Suddenly, she realized she wasn't. Despite her recognition of her mood, she let her thoughts spin downward into a spiral of doubt.

She didn't belong anywhere. She wasn't magical enough for this world, but she wasn't normal enough for her own. She was too experienced for school but not noble enough for the palace. She was too Adanekian for her mother's family but not quite Adanekian enough for her own kingdom. She hadn't been enough for Garen, and now she wondered if she was enough for Elric. Before she'd left, she'd tried. She'd always managed to scrape by at formal events but was always being watched by dozens of people and had Elric subtly trying to correct her posture or the way she held her knife. She especially hated having to always stay one step behind Elric when they walked among guests and other nobles. Every noble lady had to follow their lords perfectly and with poise, always a step behind them but still with them. She didn't understand how they managed to stay upright walking that way with all those skirts!

The cloud that had been hanging over Thali had fully descended. It enshrouded her like thick fog, and she started finding it hard to breathe. She gasped for air, needing to stand up but forgetting she'd magically tied herself down. She splayed her limbs and thrashed for a full two seconds before realizing what held her down. Grabbing the cool stone balcony behind her with both hands, she wrapped her feet around the edges and focused again on breathing. She counted again, slowly, to eight ... then backward to one. She continued like this for a while until the beating of her heart slowed. Then, she pushed all thoughts away and stared at the sheep, counting those in groups of eight, too.

Finally a little more relaxed, she slowly reached into her magic and untied herself. Letting a strand drop over the balcony, she teased it out until it reached the edge of the field where the sheep were. She let her body glide gently along the thread until she reached the field and stood quietly at the edge. Three of the nearest sheep looked at her with curiosity. She was at first surprised they weren't flighty, but then, seeing dragons fly by all the time probably set a different standard for normal. They approached her carefully and put their heads softly in her hands, and she obliged them with a scratch. She stopped suddenly, wondering if that's actually what they wanted, but they butted her hand, so she continued. She let her magic wander into their heads and confirmed their enjoyment of the affection. They leaned into her, and Thali had to put her body weight behind her arms as she scratched them vigorously.

More and more sheep started to surround her, and when one had its fill of scratches, it would move and another would take its place. She marveled at how they waited their turn. Sheep in Etciel were a lot more patient than the sheep back home. They would have all pushed their way in until someone started a fight.

She laughed at their persistence and continued petting the sheep until late afternoon began to blossom and she was sprawled in the field among the sheep, one even edging its way under her head to be used as a pillow. Thali could feel her dark mood hovering in the back of her mind, but she felt the happy satisfaction of being around animals and let her mind wander instead to the clouds above. The yellow clouds in the green sky formed strange shapes as she watched, and she wondered if she saw dragon shapes only because the sky was green.

Then, some of the sheep started heading toward the palace, and Thali knew everyone had come back and someone was coming to get her. She stayed where she was though, wanting to prolong this blissful state.

"So this is where you are," Jaxon said. But instead of pulling her to her feet, he petted a few of the sheep and lay down next to her, nudging another sheep under his head. It obliged him, so Thali realized that Jaxon must visit the sheep, too.

"Are these your sheep?" she asked.

"No," he said, shaking his head. The sheep made a noise to show its displeasure at the movement, but Jaxon laughed it off.

"Did Alexius ever tell you about his dragon mate?" Jaxon asked.

"No," Thali said quietly.

"Hmm," he said, probably wondering if he should tell her.

She waited silently for him to decide.

Jaxon began the story. "Every dragon has one mate. Some dragons spend several lifetimes finding their mate. Some are lucky and find them young. My parents found each other quite young. Xerus's mate, well, he found him when he was quite old but Xerus was very young. Alexius and Brixelle were young. Their bond was immediate. The original sheep in this field were hers. She was a sheep farmer."

Thali had never heard of Brixelle. "What happened to her?"

"She died. A long time ago," Jaxon said, not elaborating.

"The mating bond isn't as strong as the blood oath?" Thali asked.

"No. Mated dragons have in the past taken the blood oath but ..." He was quiet for a moment. "... but most don't. Mostly because if they have children, they don't want to orphan them if something happens to one parent. You do know that if one dies, the other dies?"

"With the blood oath, yes, I do. Does Alexius have children?" Thali asked.

"No. It's tragic really, how little time he and Brix had together."

Many things started to make more sense to Thali then, especially some of the things Alexius had said in the past. "Was it his fault?" she asked. She wouldn't have dared ask Alexius, but she knew she'd get an honest answer from Jax.

"She died protecting him, so he probably thinks it's his fault. But could anyone stand by if they had an opportunity to save the one they love?" Jaxon asked.

Thali's brow crinkled as she took all this in. She looked up to the sky and squinted as some black dots appeared while the green sky turned to purple.

"We should go back in. Your brother is wondering where you are." He stood up and offered Thali a hand. They petted the sheep as they walked back to the palace. "He's in the casual dining room," Jaxon said as he turned down a different pathway.

Thali found her way to the small dining room where she and Rommy often ate breakfast together if no one else was joining them. She pushed the door open and was once again struck with wonder. If nothing else, this palace was beautiful. Rommy wasn't there yet, but she took her time looking at the walls. This room was round, so the walls were curved. Even the doors looked curved on the inside despite seeming flat from the hallway. Scenes depicting what Thali assumed was the history of dragons were carved in the wall of blue wood. She'd never seen wood quite like it. It was the same blue as the ocean and a certain pair of eyes. She stood close to each vignette, carefully inspecting the wood, and wondered what the person whose eyes this color reminded her of was doing. She hoped he was well. And what would he think of all this? What would he think of these dragons? Would he and Rommy have gotten along? Rommy and Elric seemed to get along all right, though they'd not had more than a few interactions with each other. The scenes depicted in each panel blurred as her mind wandered.

"Ah, sorry, Rou. I was trying to finish something for Xerus," Rommy said as one of the panels opened and he came through.

"That's all right. All these rooms are so beautiful, I don't mind spending time in them," Thali said despite her now-buried frustration. She let Rommy take her arm as they strode to the middle of the room where a table was set with a covered pot and three dishes, also covered. As Thali sat down, she uncovered the two dishes closest to her and Rommy did the same with the last. Then, he grabbed two smaller bowls and placed rice in each before handing Thali hers and sitting down with his. Thali smiled at the sticks on her napkin and used them to fill her bowl with some red vegetables, purple meat, and something that looked like tofu but with a blue tinge.

"This almost looks like the same stuff we eat back home," Thali said.

"I prepared it myself. I thought you might like a little taste of home, or at least as close as I could get. If you ignore the color, it should taste nearly the same."

As he helped himself to the three dishes, Thali grabbed a veggie, closed her eyes, and took a bite. Memories of all their family dinners together came rushing back, as did the memory of Rommy always making sure she got food first before he filled his own bowl. "What did you all do today?" she asked.

"This and that. Sometimes we talk at length about human customs, and other times, I help him do some research or write things out for him. But today we went out to The Gathering, then north to check up on a few projects."

"Do you like working with the dragons?"

"It's fascinating. Did you know that all royalty are dragons? Xerus and them lived here in Etciel as royalty since the beginning of recorded time. I mean there are *some* dragons that aren't royal, but not many. They used to live in harmony with griffons, unicorns, and pegasi, among others, as their loyal, content subjects." Rommy paused to shovel food into his mouth.

"Interesting. So their society was like ours? Is it by bloodline like ours too? Or by family? Or are they appointed or elected or something?" Thali asked.

"By family, but their lifespans are much, much longer than ours, so there is often a singular ruler for a very long time."

"Do they have kingdoms here? So multiple dragon royals?" Thali asked.

"Oh no," Rommy said. "Etciel is its own world, so they have one ruler here. It used to be divided among their family into separate kingdoms, but that was a long time ago. I've heard rumors of other worlds, but they're much more difficult to get to. You can't just walk there or ride a horse there or even fly there," Rommy said. He dove into finishing the rest of his bowl, so Thali gave her brother a chance to chew and swallow as she focused on the items in her own bowl.

Her brother always inhaled food so fast, she had barely chewed her first vegetable by the time he was done. He'd always been like that, in private at least. Her parents had given him the stare often enough that he knew to eat at a glacial pace in front of others, whether guests or hosts. Apparently, she didn't count as either. She grinned as they continued to eat in silence, only muttering a few words between bites. Rommy ate a second and third bowl before she finally finished hers.

CHAPTER TWENTY
Tariq

TARIQ HADN'T BEEN ABLE to find anything truly useful in the library. He'd given up on literature and decided just to try bashing his way through the portal and make the rest up as he went. Then he'd finally taken a long rest, and this morning, he woke, trained as usual, and returned to his room to see Bree, fully healed and standing there dressed in pants and a loose shirt like Thali might wear.

"I'm going with you," she declared.

Tariq smiled. "Are you sure? I'd prefer you stayed here."

"I know that, but she's my friend, too. Not only do I feel responsible, but you need someone to watch your back. You rush in too fast. These are *dragons* we're talking about, and who knows what other creatures we'll encounter?" Bree said. She strapped on her backpack, and Tariq felt a flutter in his stomach at this side of his future bride.

"I love you so damn much, I can't stand the thought of anything happening to you," he said as he wrapped his arms around her, backpack and all.

Bree batted him away gently, coughed, and straightened her outfit. "Now you know how I feel every single time you leave me behind." She held her chin high to emphasize her point.

"I'm sorry. I know you can handle yourself," Tariq said.

"Thank you. Now, shall we?" she asked and signaled toward the door.

Tariq grinned and grabbed his pack. It seemed a little heavier than he thought it would be if he had packed it, but he shrugged it on as he chased Bree out the door.

Their horses were ready, and they rode out to the portal, the gate to the other world. It was nothing but a clearing in the forest. If you flew over it from above, you'd see it clear as day, but when traveling by foot, it was completely hidden but for an engraved stone.

"How are we going to get the guards to let us by?" Bree asked.

"Umm ... well, I think since I'm the crown prince, they'll let me through," he said.

Bree rolled her eyes, and they hopped off their horses. "Go home, sweet horses," Bree said, and they turned and trotted away.

Tariq and Bree walked the rest of the way to the edge of the treeline. The meadow itself wasn't particularly large, but it felt large. Bree had only been here once, and she blinked as they approached. "This place. It was important," Bree whispered. "It's so ... shiny," she said, squinting.

"Father?" Tariq asked. His eyesight had settled before Bree's. He took Bree's arm as they walked up to the intricately carved stone sphere. But Tariq could only see the top half of it as before it stood his father and five dozen guards. "Father, what's going on?"

His father, in a bright gold-and-green tunic, stepped out from the line of guards. "Tariquin, I know you want to go after Thali and Rommy. But you cannot. This gate does not lead to Etciel. It leads to Vancel. You know this. You cannot risk letting in more creatures from another land."

"But Father, we can sneak in. I can get to Etciel through Vancel."

"Our family is charged with guarding this portal, to prevent anything from coming out or going in. That includes us."

"But it's Thali, Father."

"I know, son." King Shikji's eyes shone, but he held his chin high. He was resolute.

Tariq looked at each guard in turn as they all stood there in formation and avoiding eye contact. They weren't siding with him as he'd originally thought they would; they were there to protect the gate from him. His colleagues and friends, people he'd grown up with, would fight him. He was struck suddenly with the realization that he was the one on the wrong side of this.

"But it's for Lili," Bree pleaded.

He turned and sighed. "They're right, Bree. We can't. Even for Lili." Tariq clenched his jaw. His insides were tearing in two. He wanted so badly to go through. But a small part of him recognized this was not a good opportunity. He could find a quieter time so fewer people would get hurt, though he'd still have to fight through some of his friends to get to his best friend.

King Shikji gently put a hand on his son's shoulder. "We'll find another way to help."

Tariq swallowed and the rings of guards relaxed. He knew there was no way he'd get through them all, get to the gate with Bree, and figure out how to activate it before the guards pinned him down and put him in chains. No, he would have to find another way.

"Come, let us have some tea," his father said.

Tariq pretended to acquiesce as they walked back through the forest toward the palace. He looked back once only to see that none of the guards had moved. They stayed in their layered rings around the great sphere. As he wondered if they would be posted there night and day, Lari shrieked her falcon's cry as if saying she would watch for him. She flew around, found a tall tree to settle in, and perched there. While Thali was the one who could communicate with animals, he swore that bird read his mind.

The trio continued walking for some time before Tariq glanced at Bree as she conversed with his father, likely to give him the freedom to look around, to plan, to think. Bree was the most intuitive person, and he knew that she knew his mind better than he did sometimes. He would ask her later if she had any ideas about how he could get to the portal with enough time to figure out how to open it. And perhaps he should learn more about Vancel instead of Etciel. His father had slipped up there. He had told him where this gate led. Tariq hadn't known before now which world the portal went to, so now he could learn how to get to Etciel from Vancel.

As they entered the palace, his father insisted they sit for some mint tea.

"Tariq, your father asked you a question," Bree said as they sat.

"I'm sorry, Father. I was trying to think of the next best way to help Thali."

"I've sent a letter to her parents. They may need our support. And they may know better what measures the prince is taking to recover her."

"She doesn't need recovery. She's safe. It's not like she was kidnapped. We just need to convince her to come home," Tariq said.

A soft sigh caught their attention. They all turned to the open archway to see Rania standing there. She still looked impossibly thin, but her eyes were brighter. They looked human for the first time in a long time. She was finally present, not lost in her head.

"Rania, please, sit and join us." Bree stood up and guided her to a seat.

His sister looked stronger than she had in a long time. "You're talking about Thali," Rania said. "Rommy took her to teach her how to use magic."

"You've been in contact with Romulus?" King Shikji asked.

"He comes to me in dreams sometimes, but only recently. It makes me want to sleep all the time, but he said that I need to get healthier, get stronger. For our life together," she said as she stared at the wall behind

Tariq's head. Tariq found it unnerving, though Bree would chastise him for being unkind.

"How often has he come to you?" Tariq asked.

"Only twice. The first time I thought it was surely my imagination for he said all the things I was hoping he would say. But the second time, I heard Thali with him. I heard her call for him, and he told me that she's learning so much. She's happy. But then he had to go, and I woke up," Rania said. Bree pressed a warm teacup into her hands and Rania brought it to her lips. After taking a sip, she turned to Bree. "Tomorrow morning, Bree, will you walk with me in the gardens?"

"Of course, Rania. Name the time and I'll be there," Bree said, her eyes sparkling, for this was the most present Rania had been in a long time.

Rania nodded. Then, she rose so suddenly that only Tariq's quick reflexes saved the ornate glass teacup from crashing to the ground. Thankfully, the tea was lukewarm. He put the cup back on the table as Rania went over to their father, King Shikji, and kissed his cheek. "I'm tired now, so I think I will go to bed. But I'll see you all at breakfast," she said before turning and leaving the room.

Bree, Tariq, and Mupto all looked at each other and blinked.

"Well, there's one good thing that's come from this craziness." King Shikji smiled.

Tariq's brow furrowed. "Father, how is Rommy able to speak to Rania in her dreams?"

"I'm sure he isn't, not really. Rommy's never set off your magical detection, has he?" Mupto asked, turning to Bree. She shook her head. "Then she's coming around. I don't care if she has to have imaginary friends. She's coming back to us." King Shikji's smiled widely as he pushed up from the table. He winced as he straightened, and Tariq saw his father's arms strain as they took on most of the weight. King Shikji hobbled the first three steps before his gait smoothed as he left the room. Tariq's father was getting older in front of his eyes.

"What do you think?" Tariq asked Bree.

"I think it's concerning that Rania has been brought into all this. And I think we need to learn more about Vancel. And ..." Bree said as she looked at her hands folded in her lap. "I think I have to stay with your family when you go get Thali." She stared at the doorway Rania and Mupto had just disappeared through.

Tariq realized that while he felt a duty to go after his best friend, he could sense that his time to take over was closer than he might have thought. He should be stepping up to ease his father's burden so his father could spend more time with Rania. His heart was being torn in two. Thank all the gems he had Bree.

Chapter Twenty-One
Elric

E LRIC SAT AT HIS desk, his chin on his fist as he stared at a blank wall.

"Sir?" Avery asked, bringing his attention back to the pile of paperwork on his desk.

"Sorry, Avery, what did you say?"

"I didn't, sir. I just came in. You have a meeting with the captain of the guard in five minutes."

"Right." Elric stood and looked at the papers in front of him. They were already stacked by immediacy and involvement. There was always so much to do. There had to be a better way to accomplish it all. And then the grip on his heart squeezed, reminding him again of that someone who was not there, not in the palace, not within the safety of his walls. He swallowed.

Avery coughed.

He looked up at her and gave her a tight smile as he followed her. She silently led him to his next meeting, handing him some papers as she opened the door for him.

The captain stood stiffly in one of the palace's many receiving rooms. When Elric remembered that this meeting might offer more information about Thali's well-being, he focused and nodded to Avery to stay outside.

"Your Highness," the captain said.

"Captain, thank you for coming to me. I know you're a busy man."

"It's my pleasure."

"What news do you have of my wife?"

"The princess has not been seen by any of our search parties. And she is ... noticeable. So I trust this information."

"What of her family?"

"They seem to be preparing to leave Densria to trade earlier than usual."

Elric nodded. That likely didn't mean anything really. They were merchants, after all. "Did you receive another note?" He massaged his temples in frustration.

"Yes, sir."

"Why didn't you lead with that?" Elric's eyes flashed open, and he grabbed the note the captain held out to him. It was written neatly and was the second note to appear in the captain's window. The first note had simply said, "Don't trust Etciel." His scholars and soldiers had been working day and night since then to learn more about Etciel's history, about the ruling dragon family's history. That first note had come within a week of Alexius being unable to confirm he could trust everyone in his family or his world. Elric was beginning to think Thali had been kidnapped and forced to write her note or had been tricked into leaving as he had a hard time imagining that Thali had left all her duties behind for her brother, as much as she loved him.

He unfolded the piece of paper and read the title of a book. He stood and rushed to the door. Opening it, he found Avery off to the side doing paperwork in her lap. As soon as she saw him, she jumped up and ran over. "Yes, sir?"

"Find this book immediately," he ordered, showing her the note. She scrawled the title down and rushed away. He closed the door and turned back to the captain. "Any idea who's leaving us these notes?"

"I have an idea, but I don't think you'll like it," the captain said.

Elric nodded. "Speak plainly."

"It's said that the princess was once involved with someone she perhaps shouldn't have been. A thief."

Elric kept his face neutral.

"While they are only rumors, it does explain some things." The captain glanced at him.

"Like what?" Elric's interest was piqued.

"The princess's interest in the poor, for starters. How we never seem to encounter trouble when we're out with the princess, no protesters, no pickpockets, no thieves. While I would like to think the people love her, they haven't had enough time yet to get to know her. Not as our princess, anyway. Also, it explains why these notes are left anonymously. Why hide unless you have something to hide? And why help us in that case?"

"Interesting," Elric said.

"I mean no offense, Your Highness." The man swallowed, looking like he regretted being so frank.

"No, no it's all right. You make some interesting observations. Thank you for your candor. You'll let me know as soon as you hear anything else?"

The captain nodded and left through the servant's door.

Elric fell into the nearest chair. He had always thought that whoever Thali had been interested in before him would have been more … well, average. But a thief might seem much more exciting to the daughter of a merchant. He wondered how it was that she had been able to justify the moral implications if it was true. Then, he wondered how good, how important, a thief he really must be. Surely, she wouldn't have settled for a lowly, petty thief. No, the man would have to be someone spectacular.

He wondered if the man had a magical ability like Thali and whether he sat somewhere too, right now, feeling just as miserable as Elric did. There was one thing he knew, though. That man, that possible thief, still loved her. He wouldn't have put himself at risk to deliver notes to his captain if he didn't.

"Thank you for letting her go," Elric said aloud. He thought of how miserable she'd looked that day he'd gone to surprise her, how those smiles had slowly come back, slowly increased until she smiled every time she saw Elric. Then, those smiles were for him, because of him.

Knowing that he wasn't the only one feeling helpless and frustrated strangely made him feel a little better.

CHAPTER TWENTY-TWO
Alexius

WITHOUT THALI TO GUARD, Alexius had been added to the rotation on the wall. At the end of every shift, he found a spot high up in the tallest turret and sat on the edge. Hidden from view, he meditated. He spent an hour in quiet calm before trying to connect with the flame that was Thali. He gently shone a light down the beam, and still it stopped at a glass wall. She was still too far away and being blocked, probably by one of his brothers. It was frustrating, but still Alexius tried any spare moment he had. He wondered how his siblings were doing. It had been difficult enough to leave them to bond with Thali, but now it was doubly difficult and incredibly lonely to be without their shared connections, both his family connection and Thali's. For the first time, he felt as if he had no friends at all, no family to talk to. Tonight, he looked up at the sky and saw a star shoot across it. He smiled as he remembered his sister, Danxing, his dear sister who had left life too soon. She had moved as the star, shooting across every surface with brilliance.

Alexius then spent some time strengthening the barrier protecting the palace. He checked to see if it had been tested by anyone, and it had, by at least thirty different creatures of varying magical levels. He searched for thinning layers and strengthened them. He added layers to any areas that had been repeatedly tested. Then, he sat back and watched the stars. He should get something to eat and go to bed, but the stars were beautiful tonight.

"I thought I saw you come up here." Isaia's smooth voice floated up to Alexius as he climbed up to the roof. Alexius offered him a hand as Isaia had something in his other hand.

"I brought you some sustenance," Isaia said, handing it to Alexius as he sat down.

"Thank you," Alexius said. He took it and chewed on the proffered bread. It was stuffed with meat and cheese, and he appreciated the gesture. The dining hall wasn't a friendly place for Alexius right now, so he preferred avoiding it.

"I'm sorry that everyone blames you. But I don't and neither does Nasir." Isaia looked out at the town from where he sat.

"That's two of you," Alexius said.

"They're all more upset at themselves than they realize for letting her slip through their fingers and now having to pretend she's still here—even though everyone knows she's gone," Isaia said.

Alexius didn't say anything for long while. "Why *don't* you blame me?" he finally asked. If they only knew what he really was, what he was capable of, they too would join in the blame.

"I know you're not human, in a more powerful and magical way. And I also know that you've helped Thali become more confident and self-assured with her abilities than I've ever seen her before."

"I deserve your blame. I should have been more careful. I should have watched her more closely."

"Alexius, I have the exact same thoughts. Maybe if I had been on duty, I would have heard something, though Nasir's hearing is already eerily better than anyone else's. And he *was* there, and he still didn't detect anything. Do you really think even if you had the opportunity, she would have refused her brother for you?"

"Maybe."

"I don't think anyone could have changed her mind. Not even Elric. Rommy's her brother. From what I hear, they were inseparable until everyone thought he was dead. Plus, he's as much a parent to her as a brother. I know because I have an older brother just like that."

"Do you ever doubt she'll return?"

"I have no doubt she'll return. And when she does, she'll be a powerful magical wielder," Isaia said.

"How do you take it all in stride so easily?" Alexius asked. He'd never had a very long conversation with Isaia, though he'd always admired his combat skills.

"I have six brothers and sisters. Our house was never calm or quiet." He paused. "The forest became my quiet refuge, even from a young age. I was three when I was in the forest behind the palace one day, and I saw a stag run through the woods. It almost ran me over, except it stopped three feet away from me. As it walked closer and closer, it sniffed me. Suddenly, it took off in the opposite direction, and I ran down the hill into my mama's arms. That was the scariest thing I'd ever experienced until the day I almost died at sea and Thali saved my life."

"I don't understand how that has anything to do with me."

"After those experiences, nothing's really phased me. Nothing else is really that big a deal anymore." Isaia shrugged.

Alexius nodded. He was getting tired of Isaia's company, even though he'd been perfectly kind. He finished the stuffed bread, hoping Isaia would leave.

They sat in silence for a little while. Isaia didn't take the hint. "What does it take to hold the magical barrier to protect us?" he asked.

"Magic."

"Are there any other sources of magic? Besides within you, I mean," Isaia asked.

"With time and patience, magic can be imbued in objects in other worlds, but that's not easily done here, unfortunately."

"If we were to capture a magical creature, could you siphon its magic to feed the barrier?" Isaia asked.

Alexius turned to Isaia, surprised at the darkness in his thoughts.

"I'm no stranger to having enemies, Alexius. I also think you're our best chance of getting Thali back. Elric is falling apart at the seams. My father tells me that even the king and queen are getting worried. She needs to come back soon."

"And do what? If she doesn't train with her magic, then she can do no more than she could before. She needs time to learn," Alexius said, though it killed him not to be with her while she learned, to maintain the wholesomeness of her learning. He wondered if she realized that she was the only one not under her brother's control. And even that Alexius wasn't so sure of.

"What if it takes years? There might not be a palace, or kingdom, left to save," Isaia said.

"I don't think it'll be years. I just hope she's not too changed by the experience."

"What do you mean?"

"She hasn't seen her brother in two years. She was just getting to know herself without him and now he's back. I'm worried she's going to retreat into being the little sister and let him handle everything without thinking about what he's doing and why."

"You really don't trust her brother." Isaia scratched the back of his head.

"I don't. I can't say why, but he's not who he seems to be," Alexius said.

"Good enough for me," Isaia said. "Well, I'm getting cold. See you in the morning."

Isaia stood and climbed back down the wall, then swung into the window below before disappearing. Alexius's shoulders relaxed as he took in the night air, and the cool and calmness soothed his irritation like a temporary balm.

He stretched out on his back and looked up at the stars. Before he knew it, he'd fallen asleep on the turret. Suddenly, he was in the training room back home. Xerus was there and Jax was carrying a cage with a hornsnoad in it. They were dangerous toad-like creatures with wings, and he was surprised there was one in the palace.

He felt the cool floor beneath his feet and felt the confusion of seeing a small creature in a large cage. He felt the flood of confidence as Thali speared her way into the hornsnoad's mind. That had taken him a year to master, and here she was learning it in a single day. Alexius felt the flood of magic in his veins and recognized the consequences of it as she took magic freely from Etciel. She wouldn't ever see the true damage with Rommy around.

At that, Alexius woke with a start, nearly falling off the turret as he scrambled to grab the edge, climb down, and swing himself back into the tower window. There, he stood inside panting, his hands on his knees as he realized he'd made it into Thali's mind. Whether it was because she was open enough or strong enough or he'd found some kind of loophole, he could only hope he could do it again. He suddenly realized how much magic they were teaching her to wield and how easily she mastered it. Now it was imperative that he get to her.

CHAPTER TWENTY-THREE
Tilton

T ILTON LEFT HIS ROOMS as he did every morning and headed to Thali's office. There, he sat and organized and replied to what correspondence he could. Without Thali, he was at a bit of a loss of what to do. He tried to make decisions as he could, but there were some things he was not comfortable responding to. Thali had personal relationships with so many visitors that he couldn't begin to guess how to respond to the personal letters she received from them all.

"Tilton," Avery said, putting a hand on his shoulder.

He turned his head and pasted a smile on his face. He didn't like Avery. He'd observed enough to know that she used her good looks to get what she wanted and seemed bitter about not getting the ultimate prize, Prince Elric. "Good morning, Avery." He hoped his smile was convincing.

"I was wondering if you needed any help with your correspondences. I know it's difficult to adjust to palace life." She smiled, but it didn't meet her eyes.

"That's really kind of you, but I think I've got it," Tilton said. Thank goodness for all the helpful people in the palace that weren't her.

"Was that Daylor I saw leaving your rooms this morning?" she asked.

Tilton swallowed. "Sorry?" he said to buy himself more time.

"I thought I saw Daylor coming out of your rooms this morning."

"Yeah, we're good friends. We both know Thali from school," Tilton said.

"Of course." Avery looked at him closely. "I'd best get on with my day. I'm sure you're busy."

Tilton nodded as Avery left. As the door closed behind her, he wondered if Avery knew about him and Daylor. They'd never really talked about who might know of or suspect their relationship. They were strictly friendly in public, even though they spent most nights together. He knew there was no one else for Daylor, as it was for him. Tilton had struggled with the idea of loving a man, but the way he felt with Daylor was impossible to ignore. He hadn't really realized how he felt until he'd discovered he was jealous of all the girls who'd swooned over Daylor at school.

Tilton shook his head. He had to put the thought away for later. Right now, he had mail and correspondence to sort and forge answers to.

A knock at the door made Tilton blink. He was completely surrounded by papers. What had started as three piles had turned into five and then ten, and now he wasn't even sure how many there were.

"Hi. I thought you could use some lunch," Daylor said as he walked into the office. Ana and Indi strolled in behind him, giving a wide berth to the piles of paper and jumping up onto an empty couch.

"Don't move," Tilton said.

Daylor's eyes went wide, and he froze halfway into the room.

"Close the door," Tilton said. The last thing he needed was a draft to waft in and make the piles of paper fly all over the room.

Daylor closed the door softly, carefully picked his way to an empty couch, and placed the two plates down. He kept an eye on the tiger and dog, "Should I leave?" he asked.

Tilton saw the hurt on his face. "No, no. I'm grateful you came because I don't think I would have stopped. I need a break." Tilton blinked as he rose and the world started to tilt a bit, so he grabbed his chair before slowly making his way to Daylor. He slid his hand up Daylor's strong forearm to his shoulder, enjoying the warmth that spread through his body at the contact. Daylor turned his head, so Tilton took advantage of the moment and brought his lips to Daylor's.

"I should bring you lunch more often." Daylor grinned.

"Please do," Tilton said. They luxuriated in each other's lips a few moments longer. The tiger groaned and they separated, worried about their plates.

"What's all this?" Daylor asked as he looked around at the piles of papers and objects and gifts scattered around the room.

"It's mail. Most are letters building up that I have to forge a random polite answer to or keep for Thali to respond to when she finally gets back." Tilton sat down and brought the plate of lunch to his lap.

"Can I help?" Daylor asked.

"That's sweet of you, but you're already helping by taking Indi and Ana out. They like you more than they like me anyway," Tilton said.

A knock on the door startled them, and Tilton stood with his plate as he said, "Come in," and took a few steps away from Daylor.

A runner opened the door. "More letters, sir," he said and placed the letters on the table closest to the door. The runner glanced at Daylor, who smiled at him and nodded before he left the room.

When the door closed, Daylor put his plate down. He'd already inhaled everything piled on it. "Are you embarrassed of me? Of us?" Daylor asked.

"No. What do you mean?" Tilton asked.

"Just now, you jetted away from me like a shrimp would," Daylor said.

Tilton put his plate down as he moved to sit next to Daylor again. "I'm sorry. I ... I always expected to marry a woman, have children. I didn't expect to fall in love with a man."

"There's nothing wrong with a man loving a man."

"I know that."

"I'm sure Thali would be supportive."

"But she's not here right now. What if Elric doesn't approve? What if it makes him uncomfortable?"

"I don't see how my love for you and your love for me would make the prince uncomfortable."

"Royalty has killed for less. We have to be careful. Though I agree, I think Thali would support us and stand up for us, but she's not here."

Silence reigned at that thought.

"I wonder what dragons think of homosexuality," Daylor suddenly said.

"Alexius? I don't know. Do we want to risk a dragon thinking poorly of us?"

"Don't worry, I'll protect you." Daylor winked.

"As a roasted Daylor?" Tilton grinned. He crashed his head into Daylor's shoulder as Daylor wrapped an arm around him. "I just want to wait until Thali's back. Then we'll tell her. Then we can tell everyone. We have real jobs we need to protect, lives at the palace. Lives to live for that matter."

"All right then," Daylor said. He spun Tilton to envelop him in both his arms and kissed the top of his head.

CHAPTER TWENTY-FOUR
Garen

GAREN PACED BACK AND forth on the sandy rooftop. He didn't know why, but he enjoyed rooftops much more than rooms.

"Sweet brother, you are upsetting my afternoon tea." Joren, wearing a bright-pink dress with fluffy skirts and drinking tea from a fine porcelain teacup, tilted his head toward Garen.

Garen ignored him. They were waiting on news from Joren's people about magical creatures.

"You know you're going to have to go back to your lands at some point," Joren said.

"Yes, I know my duties. I'll be back next week. I just want to hear the reports firsthand before I go." Garen growled. "Give me something to do Joren, or I might tear your city down."

"Would having a peaceful cup of tea be too much to ask?" Joren asked as sweetly as he could. Red circles were painted on his cheeks, fat faux lips over his own, and exaggerated eyelashes all the way up to his forehead.

Garen sighed. He was about to answer when Joren suddenly interrupted him.

"Incoming." A vine reached up the side of the wall. "Come here, darling," Joren said, reaching out tenderly. He kicked his foot under the table. "Leave us." A man crawled out from under the table, making Garen roll his eyes and his cheeks flush hot as the man licked his lips and scrambled off the rooftop.

Joren unrolled the paper the vine had brought up to him. Garen went behind Joren to read over his shoulder.

"There are four gates. One was opened, and Bulstan has a second. The third is in Ming's territory, and the fourth is unknown," Joren read aloud.

Garen went and sat down in the tiny chair opposite Joren. This wasn't great news. The gate at Star Island, they had learned, was impossible to find if you weren't there exactly at the right time of year. His band of thieves was forbidden to step on Bulstan unless specifically invited, and if Tariq hadn't gone through the gate, then it would be more closely guarded anyway. And Ming was secretive and restrictive on a good day. He was not one to take risks. But Garen had no choice. "I have to go to Ming," he said.

"That's a bad idea. He might like Thali, but he doesn't like you that much. And he definitely hates me. There's no way that man will chance letting even more magical creatures into the world, even to rescue one of our own," Joren said.

Garen knew his brother was right. As Joren buttered a tiny scone and ate it in tiny bites, Garen closed his eyes to think. He sensed the vine before his eyes flew open and he reached out to grab it.

"Just keeping you on your toes," Joren said as the vine withdrew from Garen's face. "I know you can't think clearly because of your lovey-dovey stuff, but you should help her here. Well, not here, here, but on your own lands here, in this world," Joren said. He waved the butter knife at Garen before scooping clotted cream onto the other side of his scone.

"What do you mean?"

"I mean, do you trust Thali?" At Garen's look, he said, "I know you do. Don't scowl at me. This just feels like something she has to go through herself. Yes, I'll keep looking for another way to reach her because even I think something fishy is going on with her brother. But in the meantime, it's not all up to you. She might not need saving." He licked the clotted cream off the scone only to put more on. The pause was deafening before he continued. "Say you could walk through the gate and get to her. She's with her brother, whom she loves and trusts and has grown up with her entire life. Do you really think you could convince her to leave, to come back untrained to do what? See you in secret while she carries on as the kingdom's princess?" Joren only pointed the butter knife in his direction, but it was a jab to Garen's heart regardless.

Garen nodded. He knew Joren was right this time, too. He was getting sloppy if he had to depend upon his brother so much. He remembered how Thali had spoken of her brother. It would be monumentally difficult to get her to distrust Rommy. He was as much a third parent as he was a confidant and her first best friend.

"Have something to eat," Joren said, and he handed Garen a piece of scone.

Garen took it and ate it, chewing as he mulled over his options. He felt himself get sleepy, and his eyes went immediately to Joren.

"Nighty night, Garen. I'm sending you home because you have business to take care of," Joren said as he waved his fingers up and down as Garen tried to stand and failed. His head drooped to the side and then the world went black.

Damn my brother, was his last thought.

When he woke, he was in a lidless crate, and he felt the swaying of a ship. His eyes flew open as he remembered what had happened, and he jumped out of the crate. He was in his own small room. There was a bed and a desk and a door, and as he stood there, the floor tilted again, confirming he was on a ship. He should have known better than to trust Joren so much. He tried the door, and it was locked. Should he try to escape? Knowing his brother, waiting would likely be smarter.

Garen lay on the bed and waited. His heart cracked as he thought about Thali and what she might have to overcome before she could make it back to her kingdom and her people. She was friendless in that world without even realizing it.

At a knock at the door, Garen palmed a dagger before saying, "Come in," as he sat up. There was a crunch as someone broke the lock and possibly the handle, too.

Ilya stepped sideways through the door and Garen's head tilted. Ilya was supposed to be in Densria finding out what he could about Thali's brother.

"I got a note from you to meet you here," Ilya said.

Garen nodded. So his brother had sent for his captain. "What of Densria?"

"Only that Romulus kept to himself, that he was a quiet, responsible kid. He has a low boiling point and a taste for vengeance if you stir his anger long enough. Those are the top things folks had to say, that and he loves his sister above all else and trusts her completely."

Garen nodded. That corroborated his information and what he knew of Thali.

"Boss?" Ilya asked. Garen just looked at him, so Ilya continued. "I can't decide if our princess is in trouble or if she's taken a holiday."

"Both, Ilya. She went with her brother to learn new skills, but I fear she's in more trouble than she realizes."

"What are we gonna do 'bout it?" Ilya asked.

"Nothing. This is something she has to face on her own. Let's just hope it won't be too late when she finally does realize it." Garen's heart twisted as he said it. "What of magical creature attacks in Densria?"

"They're nonexistent. There's a large flock of fluffy white chickens that have taken residence in the town, but they're welcome and taken care of. Town's built a barn for them in the middle of the main square, and they wander freely. Nothin' chases them." Ilya pressed his lips together.

"Out with it," Garen said, seeing Ilya hold back.

"It's said the chickens can heal a person. Cuts, scrapes, whatever. Injured folks will sleep there and wake up healed the next day."

"Did you test it?" he asked.

"I did." Ilya rolled his sleeve up and showed Garen his left forearm. Garen raised his eyebrows as he took in the unmarked skin. Ilya said, "I sliced myself from here to here and pretended to be drunk as I leaned up against the barn for the night. When I woke up, not only was I healed, but the scars of old were gone."

Garen remembered Ilya's arm. He'd had scars that crisscrossed his arm from when he was learning knife fighting. He had a bad habit of using his forearm to block blades.

"You said 'can.' Have they chosen not to heal someone?" Garen asked.

Ilya leaned in closer then. "It's said that they only heal those of pure heart. It doesn't always work on everyone."

Garen was surprised that Ilya had decided to try it. "Keep this quiet."

Ilya nodded.

A knock on the door sounded as it swung open, and a surprised ship boy blinked at the missing doorknob and lock as he brought in two trays of food. Ilya took them and nodded to the boy as he left.

Ilya has a knack for uncovering information, Garen thought. He scratched his head and said, "Maybe you should have come with me to visit Joren."

Ilya shrugged as he ate.

CHAPTER TWENTY-FIVE
Thali

*B*AP *BAP*, *BAP BAP!* Thali focused on hitting each target Jax put in front of her. To exert control, she was to hit with fist, foot, foot, fist. And then she started all over again. Jax presented the targets at different heights, and she grinned as she felt her body reaching to meet the challenge. She relished the feeling of having to focus, especially when it came to the physical exertion. It was a sensation that combined muscle building, learning something new, and adding something to her catalog of skills.

And while she loved the physicality, she enjoyed the mental challenge, too. As she hit each outer target, she fought off small creatures with sparkly pastel pink threads with her magic. They were so numerous, it felt as if each one exploded into a dozen more when she struck it. Jax didn't stop coming despite her mental battle, but she had thrown up a magical barrier to protect herself from whatever Xerus had just released into the training room, so she was confident she could overcome both challenges.

"No. Offense, not defense," Xerus said.

"Thanks for not including me in your barrier," Jax said, and Thali rolled her eyes. They didn't stop sparring, but Thali took her barrier down as Xerus froze the tiny threads. She hadn't seen the creatures yet and didn't know what they were, but this time, she threw out a magical net with dozens of tethers on it so she could catch some of the creatures and infiltrate others.

"Better," Xerus said.

Jax stopped and Thali put her hands on her knees as she took deep breaths and turned her head to see what the tiny little pink threads were.

"Pixies," Jax said. He made a face as he swatted at them.

"Don't be rude," Xerus said.

Jax scowled. "You're done your physical training." He swatted at a few more pixies, then turned to the door. "I'll see you later!" he said over his shoulder as he hustled out.

Xerus sighed loudly.

Thali turned to look at the pixies. Surely they couldn't be so terrible. Her eyes grew wide as she saw a dozen tiny humanoid creatures with butterfly wings of various colors and shapes and decorated with unique designs. They weren't as pretty as she might have thought. Their skin was all bumpy as if they'd all had an allergic reaction. They hung in mid-air as Thali held them in her net and examined them. "I thought there were so many more," she said.

"That's the pixies' talent. They can clone and duplicate themselves as they wish. But each pixie has different wings, so that's how you can tell if they've cloned themselves," Xerus said.

They stared at the strange shape Thali had frozen them in. It looked like an imperfect sphere had enveloped the lot of them.

Thali could feel their threads. They were trying to get back into her mind, trying to regain control. Xerus nodded then and Thali released her control over them through the threads.

"You weren't kidding when you said you'd found a powerful human," the pixie closest to her said.

Thali noticed now that he seemed male, or at least he sent the idea of maleness to her. The pixies were indistinguishable in body to her eyes, and while they didn't wear clothing, they certainly didn't have the same body parts humans did.

"Your Highness, I am pleased to make your acquaintance. I am called Balthazar." The pixie bowed in mid-air, dipping his head so low that she could see the back of his head where two antenna protruded.

"It is an honor to meet you, dear Balthazar," Thali said. Jax had disappeared when Xerus had warned him not to be rude, so she realized that manners must be of great importance to pixies. She pulled out every bit of good manners in her arsenal.

"It is our honor to help with your training," Balthazar said.

Thali released the rest of her net, reeling it back into her mind.

"If I may be so bold, I can see magic as you see it. Threads, correct?" Balthazar asked.

As the rest of the pixies flew to a table that had been set with refreshments, Xerus and Thali took a seat. Balthazar hovered. Thali nodded her assent. She'd never met anyone who could see her magic as she saw it.

"It is my singular talent to see how others interpret their magic. Anyway, instead of spooling it, why not think of it instead like grass? Keep many threads at the ready like a field and have them grow. Then it wouldn't take as long to send your magic out, and you could take on many more pixies at once," Balthazar suggested.

"That's brilliant, Balthazar. Thank you for your insight," Xerus said.

Thali had never considered it. A field of threads instead of spools. As Xerus watched her expectantly, she thought of Joren, of how he must think about his magic with plants. It occurred to her she'd never asked him how he saw it.

"Focus," Xerus instructed.

Thali blinked. She went back into her mind, but instead of seeing spools of magic on imaginary shelves, she pushed threads out as if they were a field of grass. She held them there, then tried to send them out like threads but in greater numbers with greater purpose.

"Good. That's enough today. You'll want to drink some willow tea because you're sure to have a headache," Balthazar said. He bowed again and took off to join the others.

"Come, let us go for a walk," Xerus said as he glanced at the pixies feasting on a cake at the table. They tore into the food like ravenous beasts.

Thali didn't refuse or question him. She understood enough to know that if Xerus wanted to leave the room, the pixies must have really good hearing or there was another reason.

They turned at a hallway and descended some stairs. Thali had never come this way before, and when she reached the bottom, she was surprised to see a cavernous hallway. It was easily the largest and tallest hallway she'd ever seen, and she couldn't quite believe that she'd never seen it before.

"We're dragons, remember?" Xerus said. He stepped away and popped into his dragon form. Now, he looked like Alexius but longer, taller, and more slender.

You'll forgive me, but if you could climb onto my shoulder, we'll move much more quickly. Xenon spoke in her mind.

Where are we going? Thali replied. It was easy to slip between telepathic and spoken communication now.

Jaxon told me you wished for a place to swim.

That made Thali excited, and she eagerly climbed up onto Xerus's palm.

I am surprised at how well you handle my transformation.

Alexius has done it numerous times. I'm just glad you know your spacing.

Xerus didn't respond to that. He just started to glide along the hallway. In his dragon form, he filled the space better, and Thali wasn't sure if he was walking, gliding, or flying because the movement was so smooth.

The hallway was made of large stones easily three to five times her height. And while she chastised herself for assuming the dragon's area would be dark and gray, she was pleased to see that it was bright and warm with light-beige stones and a fire that filled the cracks between the stones. The ceiling was arched and Xerus had quite a bit of clearance, making Thali wonder how tall the tallest dragon was.

They turned down a hallway after passing a few giant wooden doors, and Xerus walked through another archway. Thali's gaze was drawn immediately upward when she saw the concave space sparkle. It looked as if the ceiling was completely covered with diamonds. It was so spectacular that it took Thali an extra few moments to notice the humidity. The space was the biggest she'd ever seen. Ten dragons could fit in this room easily, and there was one pool that spanned the entire length of the room. Steam curled above one-half of the pool, even here in the humid warmth, and the other half was still.

Hot and cold, Xerus said simply and lowered her to the floor. Then, he sank into the hot pool. The water barely rose even though she had expected his mass to set off a tidal wave. *There is much magic in these pools. They are as old as the land. It's even been said that the first of our family chose this spot for the palace specifically because of this pool.*

Thali walked to the middle where the two waters met. She wondered if hot for a dragon would boil her skin and cold would freeze her instantly. Deciding to play it smart, she tried the middle of the two pools as Xerus closed his eyes and leaned against the edge. Thali slowly dipped her feet into the mixed water and found it just right. She looked again at Xerus. He was naked, but dragons didn't really wear clothes in their dragon form, so that wasn't something new. She was, however, not wearing clothes that should get wet. She took a couple breaths to calm herself and then she stripped out of her clothes and piled them neatly on a dry spot. She climbed into the middle pool, and her body finally felt like her own again. Relishing the warmth of the water so much, she swam over to the hot side. She was only as big as Xerus's foot though, so she stayed close to the edge, ready to leap out should he suddenly move and send a wave her way.

The pixies are an old species, and while they have their tricks, they are incredibly polite and well-mannered. But to anger a pixie is to wedge a thorn in your side forever, for they hold their grudges forever and will not forgive easily, Xerus said into her mind.

Thali opened her mouth, and that noise alone reverberated in the huge space. She switched to letting her thoughts travel down the line that Xerus extended to her. *Do all pixies have unique magical gifts?*

Some do. It's more prevalent in their species than others, but it's nothing incredibly powerful. Small magic, if you can say it as such. I've known of pixies who can read minds when making physical contact or influence fire but not create it. Some can turn water to ice and gas, not within bodies but only with external water sources like ponds or a glass of water. Generally, their magic is limited by proximity, which is why they can be dangerous in combination with their ability to clone.

Are all the clones identical to the original? Thali's eyes were open, but Xerus had kept his shut this entire time. She tried not to think too hard about the fact that she was technically sharing a bath with Xerus.

Yes. Remember what I said about their wing color? And the clones are just as deadly as the originals. I think it's like they multiply themselves and then absorb each other's magic.

Thali nodded, and while she knew that Xerus couldn't see it, she also knew he'd felt her agreement in their mental conversation. Thali sank below the surface until just her nose poked out of the water as she let her body absorb the heat. Thankfully, she knew that dragons didn't have the same kind of aversion to nakedness as humans did, except maybe Alexius. She was grateful, though, that Xerus wasn't commenting or teasing her mercilessly. She knew Jax would have. And she wasn't sure she'd be able to do this with Alexius or Aexie.

His eyes still closed, Xerus flew up, then landed in the cold end of the pool. Thali braced herself for the rush of water that would carry her away as she gripped the stones at the edge, but the water remained in place.

Remember when I said the pools were magical?

Thali nodded again. She remembered another culture that regularly switched from hot to cold pools, but she was enjoying the feeling of all her aches and pains melting away too much to traumatize her body with cold.

When Thali looked over at Xerus, she saw that his eyes were still closed. She wondered if he could see without using his eyes and whether closing his eyes was really just a show for her.

She pushed into the middle pool then and started to gently swim back and forth, stretching her tight muscles and relishing sluicing through the water.

Xerus was quiet as he rested his head on the ledge. When Thali was tired, she moved back to the hot-water pool and noticed two tendrils like thick whiskers extending from Xerus's jaw that seemed to dance in the humidity. She wouldn't dare ask him but kept the question tucked away for Alexius. She suddenly missed Elric and her friends. Looking around, she could imagine Alexius in these pools. He must have loved swimming in a space designed specifically for dragons. She thought of the last time she'd really enjoyed swimming. She'd been with Daylor and declared her confidence that he could swim in the ocean should his ship ever sink. A thought suddenly occurred to Thali then. *Xerus, do dragons mate with others of the same sex?*

Yes, we have same-sex partners as well as opposite-sex ones. Our genders are more fluid than humans. My mate is male, and I also identify as male.

Oh, I didn't know you had a mate. Thali actually did remember that Alexius had told her Xerus had a mate, but she was hoping Xerus would tell her more. She was curious about dragon culture. Strangely, a memory of Xenon, her previous captor, popped into her head, but she couldn't quite grasp it.

I do. We are not currently on friendly terms.

I'm sorry. That must be difficult.

We've had more good memories than bad, and I hope one day he will return to me.

Thali swallowed. She'd tripped into something much more personal than she'd intended. She wondered if dragons chose their gender and whether that was represented with different anatomy or if dragon anatomy was all similar. Her cheeks warmed even as she sank into the hot water. She had to move on to a different subject because Xerus flew back into the hot water, and sharing the same body of water while thinking of dragon anatomy was just too much for her.

CHAPTER TWENTY-SIX
Elric

"JUST GET IT DONE!" Elric yelled at the ministers gathered in the cavernous room. His father's eyebrows shot up, and the ministers nodded as they hurried out of the room.

"A minute, son," the king said.

Elric stopped in his tracks. He knew that voice. He knew the command and kingliness of it, not to mention the fatherly, chastising tone. Elric knew he had taken things out on those who hadn't deserved it and would be writing apology notes for the rest of the afternoon. He sank into his chair. Avery poked her head in, but when she saw the king still there, she disappeared and closed the door softly.

Elric deflated as his father got up, then came over and rested a hip against the table in front of him. "I know. I lost my temper. I shall write the ministers and apologize," Elric said.

"How is the progress on the search for your missing wife going?" the king asked.

Elric swallowed his surprise. He hadn't expressly told his parents, but he should have guessed they knew. In fact, he guessed that most everyone knew and just didn't talk about it, not to him at least. "How did you know?"

His father crossed his arms and sighed. This was the father, not the king then. "Your mother once went to visit her sister on the Isle of Vail. Your mother left a day later than she had meant to because of some issues here, and the messenger she sent did not reach the Isle of Vail in a timely manner. So, because her sister didn't get the message and your mother did not arrive on time, your aunt sent a message to tell me that your mother had not arrived. At the same time, we were anticipating the southern lands mounting an ocean attack, so I could only send half a dozen ships to find her. With the lag caused by traveling messengers, it took three days for me to find out she'd landed safely on the Isle of Vail and all was as it should be. For those three days, I didn't know what happened to your mother, and I was frantic."

"So you know how I feel."

"I recognize it. Besides, I still have my informants," the king said.

"And what wise advice do you have for me?" he asked.

"Take time for yourself. You'll help no one by storming around the castle," his father said. He patted Elric's hand. "I can take back some of the duties you've so bravely taken on for now. I'll get Avery and Joudrey to work out the details."

Elric nodded and sank further into the chair. He added "failure" to his list of things to feel terrible about.

But his ever-intuitive father said, "This isn't failure, son. You can't run a kingdom by yourself. Everyone needs a little help sometimes."

Elric sighed, resigned. "I know." He rose then and started pacing. He had to move. He had so much anxious energy building up inside.

"What's really bothering you?" the king asked.

Elric stopped pacing and turned to his father. "It was supposed to be easy. Find the girl, woo the girl, get the girl, marry the girl, split the duties, and bam, a nice, settled life."

The king sat silently.

"And then magical creatures show up and start attacking people. Why couldn't they have arrived as allies? My reign was supposed to be easy and peaceful. It was supposed to be about creating alliances with other kingdoms, magical or no. It was supposed to be about growth and prosperity."

The king grinned then. "No reign is ever easy, son. There are always difficult decisions and unexpected conundrums. Granted, you're faced with the return of magical creatures, but your chosen partner is out there gaining skills to help take that on, no?" the king asked.

Elric's brow crinkled and he stopped and nodded. There was no use lying or hiding anything from his father. He wondered wistfully when the gift of being all-knowing would be his, too. "I didn't expect to feel so worried about everything. She was supposed to be here. It was supposed to be easier than this."

"Son, there's no use obsessing over what should have been. Things are different now. That's that. You have to move on and work with what you have."

"And what do I have?" Elric asked. He'd wanted to shout it, but this was still his father, and the king, he was talking to.

"You have your mother and me. You have a full staff ready and willing to help. You have a library of resources. We've always been great keepers of books. The magical creatures have not arrived but have *returned*. There must be something in the past to help bring us into the future." The king raised his eyebrows.

"How do you know they've returned? I've never heard of magical creatures in these lands."

"But you know *of* them. They've lived on in stories. You know what griffins are and what pegasi are. They are not completely foreign in name; therefore, they are old. Those stories had to have originated from somewhere," the king explained.

Elric was stunned at the obvious simplicity. His father was brilliant. "That's it! The solution to resolving this whole situation must be in the library!"

"I've already tasked the scholars with finding what they can. We'll meet with them this afternoon to see what they've unearthed. They send daily reports, but today we'll go speak with them, together."

For the first time, Elric didn't feel quite so alone. He walked over to his father, and as his father's arms encircled him, Elric let his emotions out.

Chapter Twenty-Seven
Garen

G AREN ALWAYS PREFERRED WALKING into his place at night, when it was lively and his people were celebrating or commiserating or reuniting as a family. Their work was often solitary and dangerous, and it was always a relief to see his family back in one piece at night.

The moment he walked in tonight, they noticed. He sat at his table in the corner and noticed there were no strangers among them this evening, no weary travelers wandering in, no citizens looking for a little excitement. Tonight, it was just family.

Ilya set himself up at the bar, but next to his table. Garen was glad Ilya was within earshot.

Fletch appeared next to Garen then, sliding in to sit next to him. Garen rubbed his thumb along his pants seam, calming his racing heart. Fletch constantly caught him off-guard. The man was so stealthy that even Garen never knew he was there until he made his presence known.

Launching into his report, Fletch said, "People have started to trickle into the city. I expect more will arrive with the magical creatures seeming to attack at random. My cousin works on a farm two hours north of the city and sent word that he's seen a lion with wings, the face of a hawk, and claws. And he's seen smaller, stranger creatures like a pig-toad and a cat-snake." He spoke quietly. Garen only heard him because of the man's strange ability to put his voice only where he wanted it heard.

Garen nodded.

"Also, there's report of a bandit stealing wagons as they near the city road. I've sent people to investigate. We await your direction about what to do with them."

"The usual," Garen said.

Fletch nodded and looked as if he wanted to leave, but he stayed an extra beat.

Garen, without looking at him, raised an eyebrow to ask what else he needed.

"Our princess, no one's seen her in three weeks. And then you take off ..." Fletch began.

Garen knew that the young Fletcher had once had a crush on the love of Garen's life, so his attention was a little more piqued than others, but the Prince of Thieves knew everyone was worried. "She's off traveling, learning new skills," was all Garen said. And he said it loud enough that the whole room, which had seemed to still as Fletch had asked his question, heard it and would spread it.

"Is she safe?" Fletch asked, more quietly this time. This was a personal question.

"I think so," Garen said. He gritted his teeth so he didn't swallow, didn't give any sign that he didn't believe his own words. Let them wonder what it was that sowed doubt in him. Let them worry a little, stay on their toes as they went about their day. But he couldn't let on that he was keeping something from them, that she was in another realm, a magical realm, because he would have an uprising on his hands if they found that out. They'd all want to go save her. They needed to think she was here in this realm, at least in one of their many territories. Then, they'd feel she was undoubtedly safe.

Garen surveyed the room again, expecting his captains to step up with reports after Fletch left, which he did just then. He tipped his head and returned to his post on the roof, moving through the crowd like a shadow.

Garen saw one captain missing. She worked nights so it wasn't surprising that she wasn't here yet. Ella would probably pop in once she heard he was here but only to report before returning to her work. Garen looked around the room again, then took a drink of the ale that had appeared before him. Business looked good tonight. His people were in good spirits, coin bags looked heavy, and his people had fewer bandages. He let out a breath and eased his shoulders.

Suddenly, the tavern door burst open, and his missing captain stumbled in, covered in blood and supporting two other women. Ilya was there in a flash, and Sesda in the next moment, all pretense of frivolity dropped. His people cleared two tables and laid the two women on them. Garen, rushing to the women, knew Fletch would have gone for the healer as soon as he saw them enter the tavern. Garen didn't have to say anything. His people were prepared and knew what to do, knew the protocol. Hot water, linens, and clean bandages appeared beside the women, and Garen's eyes widened at the sight of them. Their skin was covered in blood. It was as if their pores were weeping blood, like a sheen of sweat, but red. Then, Ilya draped some sheets over them; his people knew to give them space.

Garen turned to Ella, his captain. She looked terrified. He put his hands on her shoulders and turned her away from the two women. They were thrashing and moaning.

Ella's words came rushing out. "A foreign man came into the brothel. He paid handsomely for two women, and I listened to be sure they were safe. It was quiet. After some time, it was too quiet, so I peeked in, and they were both lying there as if they'd been drugged. And ... and his hand had become a talon, and he was carving into their skin with it. I rushed to get in, and when I flung the door open, the man turned into a whirlwind of smoke and disappeared. I wrapped the girls up and brought them here immediately. I didn't know what else to do. The foreigner, he didn't speak, just gestured, and when he disappeared, so did the money—the coins he offered up—like they were made of smoke, too."

The door slammed open, admitting Foxall. He was an old man with strange white—almost blue—hair, and he toted his satchel over to the two women on the table. He peeled back a sheet and dabbed at one woman's arm with it. "Did the man speak?" he asked.

Ella shook her head, her red, blood-coated curls shaking, too.

"Did he vanish?" Foxall asked.

The captain nodded.

"Damn griogeos," Foxall murmured.

Garen had no idea what he was talking about. But Foxall opened his bag and started to rummage through it. Garen couldn't help but notice that the healer dug a lot deeper than the depth of the bag.

The tavern's owner appeared beside Ella. "May I take the captain to get cleaned up?" At Garen's nod, she led Ella gently to the back rooms where a bath was probably waiting.

"Aha!" Foxall took a vial from his bag that looked like it was covered in dust. "Two glasses of ale, the oldest ale you have." The barmaid rushed to get them.

"They must be in glasses, not cups!" Foxall said, struggling to uncork the vial of blue-green liquid. Then, he tapped the side ever so gently as the barmaid brought over the two glasses of ale. Foxall grabbed them, placed them on the table, then spilled two drops of the liquid into each glass. The ale turned a dark green, like the darkest moss in the forest. "Garen, come."

Garen stepped up.

"We must get them to drink the entire glass. One each," Foxall instructed.

Garen nodded. Two more people stepped up to help. Garen took a glass of dark, mossy green ale, and as Ilya supported one moaning woman, Garen brought it to her lips.

"It should taste sweet, so this should not be difficult. But they must drink every drop." Foxall pressed the second glass to the other woman's lips, and she seemed to take it happily.

Garen again brought the first glass carefully up to berry-stained lips. This was one of the new women. He'd interviewed her himself to see if she was fit for the life she'd wanted to choose. She enjoyed physical pleasures and had offered her services with open eyes, so he'd felt confident hiring her. Now, her skin was almost orange with the blood seeping out of her pores.

As Ilya supported her, she sat up a little, moaning, so Garen tipped the glass a bit more. She swallowed and then seemed to awaken with terrible thirst, so she drank more and more. She even licked the inside rim, so he tipped it upside down for her. Once she'd had the last drop, she sank into Ilya as if she'd immediately fallen asleep.

"The griogeo pierces only the top layers of skin," Foxall explained. "As they sleep, let us wipe the blood gently from their skin and apply this salve." He handed Garen a tin of salve.

Garen opened it but was interrupted as four women stepped over and said, "We can do this part." He backed away. Ilya also moved away, and even Foxall let the women take care of their own. The women got to work, gently removing the sheets and wiping the women down with clean towels and hot water. As the blood cleared, Garen noticed that there was a specific design to the shallow cuts.

The tavern emptied, leaving only Garen, Foxall, and Ilya to sit at a table. Even Fletch had returned to his post, and Sesda had disappeared, likely out prowling the streets looking for the griogeo.

"What's a griogeo?" Garen asked as they sat down.

"A griogeo is a creature made of air. They like to appear as smoke, ash, or dust by picking up and swirling the small particles around them," Foxall said. "They believe themselves artists, and their preferred canvas is skin. By observing people, they can create the illusion of being a person but cannot speak or truly see. They use air to knock their victims unconscious, and then they get to work on their canvases. They do not kill, but they will draw intricate designs in their victims—in fact, some realms deal with them by asking for volunteer subjects. Strangely, the designs are beautiful," he added though his expression was grim and thoughtful. Almost to himself, he said, "They shouldn't have been able to get through the barrier."

Garen had assumed as much. Alexius had hinted the city was protected, and for them not to see the number of creature attacks as other villages, Garen had guessed that Alexius must be holding a kind of protective barrier against the magical animals.

"If you encounter a strange client that cannot speak, banish them from the premises. They will be offended enough not to return," Foxall instructed.

Garen nodded. "What of the women?"

"They will need a couple days to heal. The salve should remove any aches and pains. They will be all right," Foxall said. "I will contact our mutual acquaintance, and you will hear from one of us in a day or two." Then, he closed his bag and left the tavern.

Garen nodded his chin in the healer's direction, and one of his men went to make sure that Foxall arrived home safely. The two women were moved to a bedroom to sleep and recover, leaving Garen to wonder what they would be left to live with.

He stood then and headed to his own room here. There, he threw his cloak on. He knew Alexius would be the only other person who knew as much of magical creatures as Foxall. While Garen's jealousy at Alexius's closeness with Thali still made his stomach roil some, he reminded himself that he had no right to that. Thali was married to the golden prince, and Garen should be grateful that she had a friend like Alexius who was knowledgeable in these matters.

After slipping through the window, he made his way from rooftop to rooftop, being more careful when he neared the forest. At the palace, he scaled the wall to the tallest turret, the one he knew Alexius preferred, and waited for him to show up.

"Garen," Alexius said as he slipped onto the turret moments later.

"Alexius." Garen sat down in the shadows. He'd only ever met the dragon twice, once when he'd given the dragon the galinka Joren had grown for Thali to free her from her imprisonment in her mind and then earlier when Thali had introduced them in the forest. Garen knew though that Alexius had taken a blood oath to Thali, that he'd done it to save her. There was a time when Garen could not keep the jealousy from rearing its ugly head, but now that was no longer his business. "How did—"

"I cannot tell you yet how the griogeos came to enter the village, but I will investigate in the morning. Their imprint deepens in the air over time. They will be nearly undetectable, now, but will soon be obvious," Alexius said.

"How did you know?"

"Foxall sent word."

"Ah. Are you able to hold the barrier alone?" Garen asked bluntly.

"I am. Indefinitely. But I cannot travel anywhere outside of Adanek," Alexius replied.

Garen nodded. "Do you have any guesses about how the griogeo got through?"

"They might have taken human form and walked through that way. I've adjusted the barrier to prevent a certain measure of magic itself from coming through. Griogeos are much more powerful than any human magic wielder, except for perhaps our mutual lady."

"How will she return, then? And is she truly that powerful?" Garen asked, reminded of what the oracle had told him. Again, he felt the spear to his heart at those words. All he could do was watch things play out and help when and where he could.

"She is," Alexius said. Then he told Garen of what he'd seen. "There are few who can enter a hornsnoad's mind. If she is training to do that, then she is more powerful than she realizes. What worries me is that she has not been warned or given the time to consider the ramifications of her actions. Those hornsnoads will have died by now. When their minds are infiltrated, they consider themselves dirtied and will kill themselves shortly thereafter."

Garen's heart dropped for Thali. He knew her well enough to know that's not what she would want. She wouldn't want to harm something innocent.

They sat in silence for some time. Garen could feel the power that rolled off the dragon, like he could sense it in Joren and Thali, even the Prince of Bulstan. But this was different. It smelled different. It was ... older, like old parchment but magical. "How is Elric?" Garen asked eventually. It had slipped from his lips, and while part of Garen hoped the prince was miserable, he conceded that it would not make Thali happy to know her beloved was in pain. He swallowed his pride.

"He's managing. He's frustrated like we are at not being able to help, but he's also busy."

"Do you like Elric?" Garen asked. Alexius's answer had seemed ... indifferent.

"He is a good man. And while she does love him, I have my suspicions that their love was a happy accident. He's been ... slightly different since they married," Alexius said.

Garen's brow crinkled then.

"Like I said, he is a good man. But I think you should know she did love you. And this love with Elric, it's different. It's not the same as what you had with her."

"How do you know?"

"I know because when we first started speaking mind to mind, she had a lot of trouble controlling what I heard, so I got a good look at everything." Alexius stretched his legs out.

Garen watched Alexius. He recognized the look in Alexius's eyes. "Did it end well for you and your love?"

"No. It didn't. I'm grateful for the short time I had with her, but she died protecting me. And cowardly as it may be, I would give anything to have died for her instead."

Garen was quiet, wondering if that would be his role too, to die for Thali.

"You need to prepare your people. This is only going to get uglier before it gets better." Alexius laid down and rested his hands behind his head.

Garen was surprised Alexius wasn't cold. His own toes and fingers were getting chilled.

"Once I know more, I'll send some instructions to Foxall to help keep your people safe," Alexius said.

Garen nodded. It was all he could do. This was all beyond his realm of understanding.

"I know this isn't fair, but she's going to need you," Alexius suddenly said, head turning to look at him.

Alexius studied Garen as if he knew what he was asking of him, and Garen nodded. Garen would always be there for Thali. For him, there would never be anyone else.

CHAPTER TWENTY-EIGHT
Thali

THALI HAD FOUND THE pools empty after training this morning, so she dulled her body's aches with the hot and cold waters. Once refreshed, she was excited to have an afternoon to herself and went to the library to dive into some reading. She dashed into the library and found Xerus, Aexie, and Jaxon talking. They stopped when she walked in.

"Sorry, I didn't mean to interrupt. I'll go—" Thali began as she started to back away.

"The library is open to all who live here," Xerus said.

Thali froze. Jaxon threw himself onto the couch with a sigh as he opened his book, and Aexie disappeared. Thali still didn't know why Aexie hated her so much.

Xerus invited her over to the magical bookshelf in the middle of the room. "Our mother was adamant about all her children reading. She was also an advocate of sharing books, knowledge, and stories," he said.

Thali approached the bookshelf, and it occurred to her that Xerus was using this as a test to see what books would come up for her. She was not ashamed of her reading choices though, so she stepped up, and seven books appeared on the shelves. She grabbed the romance off the top.

"Hey, Jax, even she has seven come up," Aexie said from nowhere.

Jax grumbled something unintelligible and turned away as he settled deeper into the couch. When Thali looked to Xerus, even he was hiding a smile behind his hand.

"What does it mean?" Thali asked.

"Nothing, perhaps," Xerus said.

"How many do you get?" Thali asked Xerus.

"Eleven," he replied.

"Aexie?" Thali asked.

"Eight. And Alexius has nine. Jax here can't get more than three," the disembodied voice said.

"Maybe he's just intensely focused on one subject?" Thali offered.

Everyone laughed and Jax made a rude gesture before bringing his book back to his face. It was a strange moment of camaraderie for Thali. They were just beings in a library, reading. She knew Aexie liked to read in the window seat because there were often romance books laying there. Thali didn't want to accidentally sit on her, so she went to sit on an enormous pile of cushions and pulled her book into her lap, arranging the pillows to get comfortable. Xerus settled at a desk, and the room quieted to just rustling fabrics and pages. It reminded Thali a lot of quiet afternoons on her family's ship. Some of the sailors had learned their letters alongside her, and she'd taken it upon herself to teach new sailors who didn't already know their letters. But on some sunny afternoons, they would pull a sail across the deck to create some shade and spread out to read. Some even drew. They were more talented than you'd expect.

On this afternoon, it wasn't long before Thali got sucked into her book. Her parents had never really approved of her reading romance novels, but Mouse, one of her family's sailors, had always slipped her a couple when her parents weren't looking. They felt like guilty pleasures, like savoring a rare piece of chocolate.

"Thali, if you'd like to join us for supper, we'll be convening in fifteen minutes," Xerus said. He switched off his desk light, and Thali came up for air. She was just reaching the end of the story but knew her brother would be upset if she didn't make an appearance at dinner.

She stood up and looked around, surprised at the length of the shadows in the room and that she was the only one left. Aexie might still be there, but Thali was never sure.

She tucked her book under her arm as she walked to her room. She freshened up, leaving the book on her night table, and changed her clothes to something a little nicer before going in search of dinner. Thali followed her nose to the formal dining room. She pushed the door open to find only her brother and Xerus inside. Even Xerus had switched his jacket with a more intricately embroidered one. He'd worn it to dinner before, but with his back turned to Thali now, she saw the design was an image of two dragons, one that looked a lot like Xerus and one that looked like her captor, Xenon. A shiver crept up her spine, but even she had to admit Xenon was beautiful, a slim argent dragon, more snakelike than Xerus. The two dragons were entwined like they were one, and Thali looked away, for even the embroidered picture looked intimate.

"Thali," Xerus said as he moved to sit at the end of the table.

"Hey, Rou. How was your day?" Rommy asked. He turned his full attention to her, and she smiled. He'd always been like this, always giving her his full attention, always asking her how she was before telling her how he himself was.

"It was lovely. I got to read for the entire afternoon without interruption," Thali said.

"Like those afternoons on the ship," Rommy said.

Thali nodded. "Exactly what I'd thought of, too!"

"Wow, those were beautiful days. I read so many books that way," Rommy said.

"My favorite kind of day," Thali said. Rommy held Thali's chair out for her, and she slid into it. He pushed her chair in. Then, Jax arrived looking tidied, hair still damp from bathing.

Aexie appeared in her chair, her hands folded in her lap, keeping a surreptitious eye on Xerus. Jax also watched him, but Xerus watched Rommy. Ordinarily, Thali would have looked to Xerus for cues. He was definitely older, and he seemed to be the wisest, the crown prince amongst dragons. So why did he look to Rommy all the time?

Rommy smiled at everyone, though Thali noticed only tight smiles in return from Aexie and Jax, smiles that didn't reach their eyes. Rommy then sat down and started the meal. It was not lost on Thali that Xerus waited until Rommy had filled his plate before filling his own. "How was everyone's day?" Rommy asked.

"Relaxing," Aexie said.

"Boring," Jax said.

Thali grinned at that. She understood how being motionless felt boring. She had a rare appreciation for both physical exhaustion and mental satisfaction.

"It was illuminating," Xerus said. He was elegantly slicing his meat, so much so that it reminded Thali to take her time slicing and eating her own food.

"How about you, Rommy? What did you get up to today?" Thali asked.

"Oh, you know, exploring the woods, doing paperwork for Xerus," Rommy said. He tucked his thumb under his fingers. It was such a small gesture, one that he knew to easily hide by putting his hand under the table. It was usually missed by everyone. Except Thali. Thali had known her brother her whole life, and he was good at lying. But he had one tiny tell. He always tucked his thumb under his fingers. It was why he often kept his hands in his pockets during conversation or together on his lap with his thumbs tucked into his hands. He just couldn't help but tuck his thumb in when he withheld some part of the truth.

She wondered why he would lie about exploring the woods or catching up on paperwork. Was he hatching a plan to get away from the dragons and Etciel? She still hadn't figured out what was tying him here. He'd been able to survive in her world, the human world, for some time despite telling her he'd die if he left Etciel. She hadn't asked him again after he'd brushed her off the last time she'd asked why he could suddenly come back. Thali stayed silent now, too.

Rommy and Xerus kept conversation light, and when the meal was done, Jax excused himself to leave for training and Aexie followed soon behind him. Xerus left to review some more paperwork before bed, and finally, it was just Thali and her brother in the dining room sipping mint tea and popping crumbly cookies into their mouths.

"Rommy, how did you survive in the human world when you came for my wedding?" Thali asked.

"Has that been on your mind this whole time, Rou? Xer found a way to contain enough magic that I could exist off it for a few months. If you hadn't come back with me, I was going to have to leave soon," Rommy said.

"So, you could go back again? If we fill something with magic again so you can feed off it for a while? You could come and visit?" Thali asked.

"Xerus is looking into ways for me to siphon magic more directly so I can come and live forever in the human world again."

"Is that what you want? I mean, you seem pretty happy here sometimes."

"Have you ever fallen into a dragon pit?"

"Sorry?"

"The other day, I was walking and I fell into this pit. I looked around and realized it was a dragon footprint," Rommy said.

Thali couldn't help but laugh. "How did you get out?"

"I climbed a tree, almost breaking the branches." Rommy grinned.

"I haven't climbed a tree in at least a couple years."

"Why not?" Rommy asked.

"It's not exactly what a princess ought to do," Thali said. She remembered all the palace rules and courtesies that she hadn't had to think of in a long time.

"What's the matter?" Rommy asked.

"I was just thinking about the palace. It's been nice to be here, where I don't have to be the princess." Thali thought about putting her feet up on the table, but this wasn't just her and Rommy's home. This was the residence of the royal dragons. She settled for putting her elbows on the table instead.

"While I can appreciate your needing to follow certain traditions and protocol, you need to be you, Rou." Rommy leaned back in his chair in that way he always did, balancing on a single leg of the chair. It always made Thali nervous, though he'd only ever fallen over twice and only broken one chair.

"But which do I know to follow and which to break?" Thali asked.

"Ask which ones are the most important. Follow those and then be yourself with the rest." Rommy shrugged.

"You make that sound so easy. I can't. They've literally hired tutors to teach me all the rules, manners, houses, and gossip of the court. I have a gossip teacher, Rommy," Thali said. She put her head in her hands and took a deep breath. She wanted to run back into the library or her bedroom and dive into her book instead of talking about this.

"Surely Elric isn't making you do all that?"

"No. No one's making me do anything. But I wanted to learn, and they just dumped everything on me."

"You know how to *appear* before royalty, so how much harder could it be to *be* royalty? You don't have to appease, you get to be appeased," Rommy pointed out.

Thali looked at him, incredulous. "Did you know that the queen plans forty-five parties a year? That's almost one a week. And then she holds court for the ladies of the realm. It's as uncomfortable as a sauna or steam room *and* as hostile as bringing the wrong merchandise to a deal."

"There are ways to handle such things."

"Which I've never mastered." Thali thunked her head on the wooden table, and Ronimy placed a hand on her shoulder. He traced "R," "O," and "U" on her shoulder blade. Things would be all right. That's what he was saying. She couldn't count how many times he'd drawn those letters on her back to ground her.

Chapter Twenty-Nine
Tilton

TILTON LOOKED AROUND THE room. After her marriage to Elric, Thali was expected to redecorate her public office and her personal study, even her receiving room. While he was pretty sure Thali didn't care that much about what her rooms looked like, it was all part of the guise that she was making herself at home instead of going to her appointments for now. Tilton had even been instructed to redecorate her bedroom if he needed to so he could buy more time for Thali to come home. However, that meant that the rooms open to the public needed to look different. And with how long Thali had been away, they would have to look drastically different.

Tilton went in search of Mia. She was nowhere to be found in Thali's rooms. So, he went off to find the seamstresses. He hoped she'd found company amongst them. It could be lonely to be by yourself all day.

Once in the wing opposite Thali's, he followed bits of thread and tiny pieces of fabric on the ground to a set of double doors. He opened the doors to see swathes of colored fabrics draped over a dozen tables in a large room filled with chattering ladies.

No one stopped on his account, so he looked around to see if he could spot Mia.

"You are assistant to the princess, yes?" Someone with bright-red hair and wearing a charcoal gray-and-black dress approached him.

"Yes. I was looking for Mia," Tilton said.

"Ah yes, the loner. She's usually in one of those plant rooms out back. I can help if you need something specific, though." She smiled at him and fluttered her eyelashes. Tilton just thanked her and backed out of the room.

It was strange for Mia to be called a loner. She was always the center of attention. Suddenly, he was glad that he'd decided to go search for her. He followed the humidity to the greenhouses and smiled as he saw the odd bit of fabric here and a piece of thread there until he found Mia sitting on a bench facing the window, watching the sun rise as she hummed to herself.

"Hi, Mia," Tilton said.

"Oh hi, Tilton," Mia said. She moved some fabric aside so he could sit.

"How are you doing?" Tilton asked.

"Oh, I'm all right. Maybe a bit more worried. Thali's been off on adventures many times, but she always came back." Mia stopped talking then.

Her full stop was so abrupt that Tilton looked up, waiting for more. He'd never known Mia to be so reticent. When Mia still didn't continue, Tilton put a hand on her knee. "Mia, what's wrong?"

"Is it that obvious?" Mia asked.

"I've not known you a terribly long time, but Mia, you usually like to talk a little more," Tilton said. He didn't want to say she talked too much.

"I ... I just don't know what to do," Mia said.

"You're worried about Thali?"

Mia gave him a strange look. "Well, kind of. She's with her brother, and there's no one she'd be safer with—"

Tilton opened his mouth to say something, unwittingly making a pop sound. Mia noticed and instead of continuing, she raised her eyebrows to encourage him.

"How are you so sure that she's safe with her brother?" Tilton asked.

Mia blushed, her cheeks turning the same bright-pink color as the flowers behind her head. She looked down at her hands before stabbing her needle into her fabric. She rubbed at the fabric absentmindedly. "When I became a woman, many of the boys in my town noticed. It was a lot of fun at first, getting that much attention. But then I got myself into some trouble one night when I was stupid enough to fetch water after the taverns had been open a few hours. Three scoundrels surrounded me, and out of nowhere, Rommy showed up and gave them a beating—nothing awful—but enough for them to never try it again. He told me it just wouldn't do for his sister's best friend to get into trouble and spent a few days teaching me how to get out of a dire situation and how to protect myself. He also taught me that it's as much, if not more, about the posturing than the actual fight. Ha." She smiled and shook her head. "I had a crush on him at the time, I mean, all the girls in town did. And he was kind to me because I was Thali's friend. Anyway, if you'd seen them together as often as I have, you'd know what I say is true," Mia finished with.

"Everyone who knows them seems so confident, but people change. Thali's been without her brother for three years. Can you say you're the same person as when you walked up to those school gates?" Tilton asked.

Mia contemplated that before replying, "No, I guess I can't. I thought I'd open my own dress shop and take orders from all the famous ladies thanks to my connection to Thali, who would bring me all the finest textiles from around the world. I even thought about going with her once or twice just to see the different fashions of the world."

"That's funny. I thought I was going to start sourcing materials from different cultures too, bring them back for my family's shop. And look at us now," Tilton said.

"So, why did you decide to enter into the princess's service?" Mia asked.

"At first, it was our friendship. Then, it was the prestige. My family is common. We own a very small shop, so it's an honor to be a cog in the wheel that runs the kingdom. But I think I also want to witness history. Thali is going to be queen one day, the same Thali who dove into that river to save Daylor, the same Thali who flicked a paper ball across a table and hit me right in the mouth. That and I'm realizing I enjoy organizing chaos, making sure everything's in the right place or scheduled correctly, squeezing things in when need be. It makes me feel like I'm a part of everything. What about you?"

"I never realized I'd like working in a team so much," Mia said. "Someone always knows a better way to do something, and I keep discovering things I never would have thought of. I love imagining something and working with others to make it happen. And while Mistress Lily can be horribly cruel with her words, the other women are wonderful. Even the amount of work required is inspiring," Mia added. "Did you know that they've even given me money to commission a bigger version of the little sewing machine I invented with Aron at school?"

Tilton hadn't realized all this had been happening, and he scolded himself for not having asked or paid closer attention. "If you like working in a team so much, why are you out here by yourself?" Tilton asked.

"They call me the loner because I won't give them any dirt on Thali." Mia rolled her eyes. "I love working with them, but not all the time. There is way too much nasty gossip in that room, so I come out here for some quiet. Mistress Lily always says it's a shame that the cloth will be covered in dirt, as if I roll around in a compost pile with it, but dirt can be brushed off. Not that Thali really cares about that."

"Is that all that's really bothering you?" Tilton asked. He suspected something else was on her mind.

Mia's shoulders suddenly drooped. She looked around, then lowered her head. "I've been craving more and more quiet time alone lately. At first, I thought it must be because I'm so worried about Thali. But now, I've started feeling queasy no matter what I do or do not eat ..."

Tilton's eyes grew wide. He knew enough women to know what Mia was hinting at. "Have you seen a healer?" he asked.

"What for? I've not yet missed my monthly reminder. I can't be sure of anything yet."

"Aron? Have you told him?"

"I'm scared, Tilton. He has a position among the blacksmiths, but he's not as skilled as the others, so he works so hard to learn and succeed. I'm scared he's going to run the other way."

Tilton chewed the inside of his cheek. "Daylor and I are here for you, and I think your best friend will want to know too and help. No matter what happens." Tilton smiled. He missed Thali for Mia now. He wondered what Daylor thought of babies and children. It wasn't unheard of for a same-sex couple to adopt.

Tilton took Mia's hands. "If you're having a baby, then that baby will be the luckiest baby in the realms. They'll have so many parents looking out for them, and at the very least, an uncle that will spoil them rotten." Tilton smiled.

Mia's shoulders relaxed. "Do you think not being married will stigmatize the baby? And me?" she asked quietly.

"I think this baby will have an auntie who is the future queen of the kingdom, and she won't care that her parents are unmarried. And she sure won't put up with any negativity from anyone else, either," Tilton said.

Mia's eyes shone.

Tilton sat with Mia for a while longer, convincing her to visit the healers just to make sure she knew what to look for in the coming days and weeks. When she was back to her normal chatty self, he was glad he'd gone in search of her, that he'd helped her in some small way.

"I should get going. I was going to meet some of the other ladies for our midday meal," Mia said, so they walked together back to the main halls, Tilton helping her carry all her fabric.

Tilton continued back to the royal rooms. Mia had agreed to come find him that afternoon to help with Thali's rooms. He smiled at the thought of a little baby coming into the world, the luxuries it would have growing up in the palace.

Suddenly, a troop of guards ran by him, and he had to leap aside as they barrelled past. He waited until the last one had gone by and then followed them at a safe distance.

Nasir appeared at the top of the staircase. "They've caught a winged creature flying above the palace," he said before running to join the others.

Tilton stopped, wondering if he should stay away or if he should go see what was going on. He didn't really have much to offer as far as help went, but he was curious. He heard soft, lilting music and followed it to the courtyard between the guest wings. There, he saw about a dozen guards with ropes all trying to hold down a flurry of pink feathers.

He stayed well out of the way—he was smart enough to do that—but tilted his head as he tried to see what was struggling under the nets. Tilton wondered how it was they'd been able to capture it. It was the first time they'd had one make it through the barrier, as far as he knew.

In a space between two guards, Tilton saw a dark slit amongst the feathers. It opened to a golden, pupil-less eye. There was just a ring of silver within a golden orb.

"Close your eyes! Don't make eye contact!" Alexius shouted. Tilton slammed his eyes shut, but the silver ring in the golden orb was imprinted in his mind.

Finally, the guards' shouts and grunts lessened to nothing, and Alexius shouted, "It's safe! You can open your eyes now!" When Tilton did open his eyes, he saw only pink feathers under a net. There was nothing left. It had disappeared. The guards were left holding ropes attached to empty nets. They looked around in confusion.

"What's happening here?" Elric stomped into the courtyard, his guards in a tight square around him.

Alexius looked around the courtyard, eyes narrowed. He examined every face. Tilton ran up to join Avery at Elric's side. He hadn't quite thought to do that, but suddenly there he was, next to Avery, jogging alongside her as Alexius looked around and joined them.

"Your Highness, that was a signat," Alexius said.

"What did it want? Where did it go?" Elric asked. He looked around frantically as if it would appear somewhere in the courtyard.

"Is there somewhere more private we can continue this conversation?" Alexius asked.

Elric nodded and they continued to the guest wing where people were starting to gather.

Avery ran ahead and opened a door in what had looked like a wall. "It's a shortcut," she said. They followed her down a hallway, then through another door. They were suddenly in the hallway adjacent to the royal family's private wing. The guards there nodded at them as they continued into a parlor set up for entertaining guests.

Two guards melted out of the room, and Elric leaned up against a bookcase, glancing out the windows into the courtyard. "You may speak freely here."

Alexius looked around, noting the guards', Avery's, and Tilton's presence. He didn't ask them to leave, but Tilton had the feeling he was being watched ever so closely. "The form of a bird was just a ruse. A signat can appear as many things, but its main purpose is to find a host, a disguise, to use its eyes and ears. It is a spy."

Elric turned and crossed his arms. "How does it report back?"

"The signat lays an egg before a mission. When the egg hatches, the signat dies. But before then, whoever holds the egg can see and hear the things the signat hears and secs."

"I assume then that when it disappeared, it found a host," Elric said.

Alexius nodded.

"Does it control the host?"

"It only gives suggestions. The egg holder might try to direct the action, but the host can fight it." It seemed to Tilton that Alexius looked right at Tilton as he spoke.

"How do we find the host?" Elric asked.

"It will take time, and there are no real guarantees we will. The person holding the egg can also hatch it, ending the signat's life before we figure it out." Alexius's gaze roamed around the room. Tilton swallowed.

Elric continued grilling Alexius. "Will it kill the host?"

"No."

"So, we're at the mercy of whoever is spying on us," Elric stated.

"Not necessarily. Signats are rare. Very, very rare. They all went into hiding because they were so sought after for a time. You can see why. And to be separated from their young is torture," Alexius said as he strode closer to Elric and motioned to the far corner.

Elric nodded and they huddled there, disallowing Tilton from hearing what they were saying. The guards surrounding Elric stared at Tilton, making him feel uneasy, as Avery turned to him.

"Here are a couple of schedules, and there's a few correspondences and letters that you might want to look at, though I'd like the letters with a folded corner back," she said.

Tilton nodded. Avery moved to leave the room, but Tilton felt the urge to stay. She stopped and waited for him to join her, so he forced his feet to follow her out the door. It felt strange to want to stay and have to think of moving his legs just to send himself out of the room. His brain was a little fuzzy, like it was taking longer to do the things he normally did without really thinking about them.

As they walked, they discussed some of the practical items needing addressing. He found himself in front of Thali's rooms. He went in and found Mia standing there.

"Ah, finally. Have you eaten lunch yet? I brought you some food because Daylor mentioned you always forget to eat your midday meal."

Tilton thanked her and ate his stew as Mia looked around and examined the walls and furniture.

"She'd like this one, but do you think she'd prefer this darker blue color or the green? Both look like the ocean," Mia asked when she pulled out some little painted squares.

"Blue," Tilton said. He hadn't even thought about it, but it had come out of his mouth anyway.

"I think so, too. What about these? Do you think she'd prefer an image of little ships on here, a big ship, or perhaps no ships at all? Would it be too painful a memory for her?"

"A big ship," Tilton said. "I think she would like to be reminded of being aboard a ship. Not be surrounded by tiny little ones that look like toys."

"You're very decisive today, Tilton. I'm surprised you need my help at all," Mia said. "I know she definitely prefers a darker wood for furniture, though it will have to be hardy. She tends to throw her weapons around and bash into things more regularly than she'll admit. Plus, it'll have to hold up against a tiger, a dog, a snake, and whatever other animal she might collect." Mia absentmindedly put her hands on her belly.

Tilton tilted his head, wondering whether that was just maternal instinct or if it was a conscious thing women did once they started their motherhood journey.

"Tilton, do you know if these books are ones she brought from home, or are they palace books?" Mia asked as she moved into the study.

Tilton looked around at the titles. "They're from the palace," he said. He wasn't sure how he knew that.

She nodded. "Well, as much as these books might be great, I feel like she'll want to do this a little differently. She'll have books from home she'll want to put here, plus space for more books. I'm actually surprised she hasn't ordered more yet."

"She has. I believe she has a massive order over there in the corner," Tilton said. He knew that answer as he'd been the one to submit the order and tote all the books into the room.

"Ah, good. I don't know if we'll be able to decide what goes back to the main library from here or not, though. We might have to leave that for her, unfortunately."

"I suppose so."

Mia looked around again. "I do feel like perhaps we should add some white to this room. It seems so dark. Or perhaps we could paint some yellow to brighten it up."

"Sunflower yellow," Tilton said. He knew that was Thali's favorite flower. Really, who could forget the sunflower birthday when Elric had filled the school with sunflowers for her?

"Yes! And I'm sure we could get sunflowers in here regularly. I've already asked the gardener to continually grow them. Of course I had to tell him why, so he told me of his difficulty finding sunflowers that one time Elric wanted thousands."

"Speaking of Elric, I should go find him," Tilton said. He wasn't sure why he wanted to go see Elric, but those words had spilled from his own mouth.

"Oh, all right. I think we've got this well underway though. Would you like to make notes, or shall I?" Mia asked.

"I will," Tilton said. He felt badly for having to leave so suddenly.

"Tell Elric I said hello," Mia said, and she bustled out the door.

Tilton followed suit. He found his feet traveling to Elric's office.

"He's in a meeting in the public wing," one of the guards at his door said.

Tilton could feel words in his mouth, but instead, he nodded and kept his lips firmly shut. He couldn't insist on waiting in Elric's private office. There was no reason for him to be in there alone, and he wasn't about to start raising suspicion. He walked instead back to the public wing and sat outside the meeting room, watching the people coming in and out.

"Tilton?"

A hand on his shoulder made him jump up, startled. "Daylor," Tilton said.

"You were asleep," Daylor said.

"Oh. That's strange, I think I was trying to find Elric, then decided to wait for him here."

"I think he's in a long meeting given the guards still standing there looking bored to tears," Daylor said, waving to the guards, who waved back. "Important business?"

"No. I can't remember why I wanted to find Elric," Tilton replied.

Daylor shrugged. "You've always been more of an observant type. Maybe you wanted to sit in on the meetings to help?"

If that had been the case, Tilton would have entered the meeting room. But he'd sat down outside it. He shook his head. Perhaps he was just tired.

"Have you eaten anything yet?" Daylor asked.

"As a matter of fact, I have. Mia brought me some stew," Tilton said.

"Ah," Daylor said. "Fancy a walk then?"

"Sure," Tilton said, and they walked out of the wing. This time, Tilton didn't feel any overwhelming pull toward Elric. Maybe he was just overtired and overly anxious?

Chapter Thirty
Alexius

A LEXIUS KNOCKED ON STEFAN'S door.

"Come in," Stefan said.

"You wanted to see me, sir?" Alexius stepped into the plainly furnished office.

Stefan was technically part of Elric's guard, but since they didn't have a clear captain yet for Thali's guard, Stefan was filling that position for now. "Have a seat, Alexius."

Alexius sat, waiting for whatever was coming. He'd been scrambling, both in his attempts to re-enter the state where he could connect with Thali and to uncover the signat's host.

"Alexius, you need to take a week off duty," Stefan said.

"What does that mean exactly?"

"It means that you have been taken off the rotation and have a week to yourself."

"Is this a punishment, sir?"

"No. We've all noticed this has been difficult for you," Stefan said, "I understand you feel partially responsible for what happened to the princess, and we can see it's taking a toll on you."

Alexius caught a glimpse of his appearance in a glass-doored cabinet. His hair was standing at odd angles, but otherwise he looked the same. Maybe there were dark circles under his eyes? *Why was the human body so ... expressive?* he thought in consternation. He hadn't popped into dragon form in months now, and he wondered if that was part of it.

Alexius turned back to Stefan. He had been planning to wait until he could do it again, but Alexius decided in this moment to tell him that he had somehow seen what Thali had seen.

"And you haven't been able to do it again yet?" Stefan asked afterward.

Alexius shook his head. He had to admire how well the human man was taking all the magical events.

"I'm going to put you on the princess's direct rotation after a few days rest then."

"What does that mean?" Alexius asked.

"I want you to use it as a way to dedicate yourself to finding that connection again. And to take care of yourself. Three days, take a three-day break and do what you need to for your own health. Then, report to the princess's apartments," Stefan said.

Alexius nodded and rose. He was still confused as to why he had been singled out.

"Alexius, where are you on that spy-bird thing?" Stefan said before Alexius reached the door.

Alexius turned around. "Keeping an eye on it."

They made eye contact and nodded at each other. Alexius had his hand on the doorknob when Stefan cleared his throat. "Alexius, we don't blame you. I've told the others all to stop. You're not to blame for her leaving, understand?" Stefan asked.

Alexius froze and nodded but didn't turn around.

"I really mean that, Alexius. It's not your fault, and you should take a break. Maybe go to the lake or deep into the forest to recharge. There's a large lake that's completely secluded in the forest behind the palace," Stefan said.

Alexius looked over his shoulder and nodded. "Thank you." He left the captain then and suddenly felt the urge to pop into his more natural form. He nodded to people as he walked out of the barracks. Then, he bumped into someone very familiar. He was a thin old man with frizzled white-blue hair that stuck out at all angles. But there was no mistaking his teal eyes. "Foxall?"

"Alexius, Your Highness," he said.

Alexius looked around. "Come with me," he said, leading them off the path so they would look like they were talking about some kind of ailment. He wrapped a bubble around them. "What are you doing here, Foxall?"

"I go where it is exciting, and this world, it is exciting. Ha, I knew I recognized the magic in the barrier. So I came looking for you to offer some assistance."

"Do you have objects to hold magic?" Alexius asked.

"I only have the one, and it will only hold for a day at most," Foxall said.

Alexius's shoulders drooped. There went his chance to go find Thali on his own.

"I *do*, however, have a few things to help you. I could feel your energy waning," Foxall said. He gave him a pouch with three vials in it. "Drink these before you pop into your other form. They will help replenish you."

"And what do I owe you?" Alexius asked.

"Nothing. Dark times are coming. I will present myself to the palace in its time of greatest need, but this is a gift for the prince who has put other species before his own needs." Foxall bowed then and Alexius was glad to have wrapped them in a bubble of privacy.

"Thank you," Alexius said.

"You are most welcome. Now, please take down the bubble so I may be on my way. I plan to slowly ingratiate myself with the guards for when the time comes," Foxall said.

For the first time, Alexius looked at the cart the old man was hauling and saw a large keg of what he assumed was ale. "Go around the back so the captain doesn't see you," Alexius said.

"Enjoy your flight," Foxall said before he toddled away with his cart.

Alexius was now more anxious than ever to pop into his dragon form. He nearly jogged straight into the forest, glancing around him before disappearing beyond the tree line and continuing onward in the direction Stefan had mentioned until he reached a meadow. There, Alexius took the three vials from the pouch and popped all three corks before tossing the contents into his mouth. He removed his clothing and hid it in the roots of a tree. The less magic he had to use in this world, the better. He walked into the middle of the meadow and popped into his dragon form.

Taking a deep breath in and giving a deep sigh out, he felt his real body for the first time in a long time. He made himself small enough for the trees to hide him, wrapped himself in some invisibility magic, and took off into the sky. He flew. He flew and he flew and he flew. The air streaming along his body filled a tank within that he hadn't realized was empty. It felt so good that he stopped circling the forest and flew over the ocean. Then, he flew south toward Densria as the sun set. The air currents allowed him to glide, but he ached to use his wing muscles, so he flapped to get there faster. He followed the sun as it started to sink lower and lower.

All at once, pain seared his wing, and he spiraled to the ground. He crashed in his dragon form and demolished a small group of trees as he landed.

When he looked at his wing, he saw a whaler's harpoon caught in a delicate part of it. Alexius roared with the pain in a pitch unrecognizable by humans. He could not turn back into his human form until the metal was removed from his wing, and he could not reach around with his other arm. Looking around frantically to find something that would help him dislodge the weapon, he finally saw a light bobbing toward him as darkness fell. At least he could still camouflage.

"Hello. I am not here to hurt you. I'm here to help." A small man with the same skin tone and hair color as Thali's mother held up a lantern.

Alexius sent his magic out to infiltrate the man's mind and saw that this was one of Thali's friends. He had known Thali his whole life and long admired her, perhaps a little inappropriately at times, but he cared for creatures like his father did. He had some vague memories of sleeping in a barn with the furry, the feathered and the scaly.

How did you find me? Alexius asked magically. He had been careful to remain invisible.

"You may be invisible, but the trees certainly did not break and explode on their own," the young man said gently out loud.

Alexius had been careless then. If whalers had seen him parting the clouds, he might as well have been visible. He removed his camouflage. *I am a friend of Routhalia's. I need to remove the metal in my wing.*

"Then we have that in common. Well, you are my first dragon. I hope you won't eat me as I approach and take a closer look at your wing." He sidled closer but stayed four feet away, which was silly because if Alexius had wanted to, he could have killed him when he'd seen the bobbing light. "I'll need some help getting this out. Can you walk with me to the barn? It's just over that way, in the clearing."

Yes. Holding his wing high above him, Alexius waddled through the forest, trying not to move the harpoon or destroy more trees. He was wary of this person. Even though the man knew and worked with his lady, that did not guarantee his motivations or true self. Alexius couldn't even be entirely sure he was who he said he was. But still Alexius hobbled along, moving gingerly and carefully around the trees, trying not to move his wing. It was much easier to walk around as a human than a dragon.

"Are you Alexius?" the young man asked. He was perhaps not quite so young, but then Alexius was so old that they all seemed young.

"How did you know my name?" Alexius asked.

"Thali's mentioned you. She always tells us about people we should trust should they come by. You made the list last time. She mentioned you right after we introduced her to our special creature, Chicky. Though a dragon was not what we were expecting."

"Who are you again?"

"My apologies. my name is Jito. My father is Deshi. We take care of the animals Lady Thali collects," the young man said.

That explained it. Thali had mentioned Jito in passing once, and he'd seen the barn and some of the animals before. Now Alexius had context, not enough to trust, but enough to continue following him. "Do you go out looking for injured animals often?" Alexius asked.

"I do. They tend to flock here. We're a lighthouse for injured animals, especially now that Chicky's friends have come." Jito walked into the open without a care and Alexius hesitated. He looked up and around the clearing before he followed Jito, waddling like a duck toward the large building.

The manor itself, Thali's home, was large for a human dwelling. It had two wings along its perimeter. Alexius knew one was a training ring and the other was the guest wing her parents had had to build when she'd become so popular. It was a castle fit for a lord, as her father had inherited it from his mentor when he'd been given the title of Lord of Densria. And the barn her father had built for her animals was just as impressive. It wasn't dark and dank as the stone castle was, but large with glass windows that allowed light in and kept all its occupants warm. Alexius also spotted the small house behind it where Jito most likely lived with his family.

Jito led him around the barn to the courtyard. "If you'll wait here a moment, I'll go get the tools I need," Jito said. "And my father will probably want to come and meet you." He looked like he was going to turn back a third time but didn't. He came back out a few minutes later with an older man who looked just like him.

"Hello. I'm Deshi." The man bowed to Alexius.

"Alexius." He liked how respectful the father was.

"Can you lower your wing, Alexius, so that I may reach it easier?" Jito asked.

Alexius lowered his wing so the bottom brushed the ground. Deshi went to hold the enormous arrow, and Jito approached with a wicked saw. Alexius shrank away from him, and he stopped.

"I'm going to cut the end off so we can remove it from your wing," Jito explained. He turned and looked at Alexius. He didn't move until Alexius nodded his head. Jito approached slowly, raising the saw to the arrow's shaft. "This is going to hurt," Jito said.

Alexius nodded and Jito clamped down on the head of the large arrow and sawed it off as quickly as he could. Alexius clenched his jaw as he tried not to roar at the pain that ripped through his wing with the movement.

Deshi yanked the arrow out. Blood started to spurt, and Alexius fought the instinct to retract his wing, his jaw clenching.

Jito dipped a cloth into a bucket. "This will sting but will clean the wound."

Alexius nodded, and through gritted teeth, let Jito wipe off the blood. He followed that immediately with a salve that Alexius felt the cooling effects of immediately.

"Do you have to stay in this form while it heals?" Deshi asked as they were tidying up.

In response, Alexius popped back into his human form. His shoulder started to ache, then feel cool again. There was a much smaller hole through his shoulder blade.

Alexius closed his eyes, using magic to heal the spot. He didn't want to disrespect their kind gesture, but he would be much more comfortable without the constant aching.

"Come, we should get you some clothes and then take you to meet Chicky," Jito said.

Deshi handed him a large towel, and Alexius wrapped it around his lower torso. Humans were weird about nudity.

Jito led the way as Alexius followed and Deshi brought up the rear. While he didn't like being sandwiched between them, Alexius trusted that Thali knew these two very well.

"I don't know the customs of dragons, but if you wouldn't mind washing just inside this door, then you can put on whatever fits best after. We try to keep the inside of the healing barn as clean and quiet as possible," Jito said.

"That's very clever," Alexius said. He watched Jito peel away his clothes, wash, then step into new clothes and boots. He watched Deshi do the same, then followed suit. He noted that there was a pair of well-worn, clean boots in Thali's size on the other side of the door.

"We always welcome Thali, however randomly or suddenly she may appear," Deshi said as he followed Alexius's gaze to the boots.

"I'll go barefoot," Alexius said. The ground was soft, so he didn't mind, preferred it in fact.

The healing barn was serene. He would say it was the most serene place he'd ever stepped into in the human world. All the inhabitants were calm and quiet and resting. This place was even more tranquil and hushed than a human healing room. As he got further into the healing barn though, he felt the why of it. "You have a caladrius," Alexius said.

"A what?" Deshi asked.

Alexius stopped where he stood. Caladrii were rare to begin with. He had sensed one protecting the town two years ago, but he assumed it would have taken off and hidden away. To have one still here and settled within their walls was unheard of. "It looks like a white fluffy chicken with very long tail feathers. Have strange things happened?" Alexius asked.

"Ah yes, we call her Chicky," Jito said. They continued then until they reached the last stall, where the caladrius was.

"These creatures are very rare. They appear only to heroes in times of dire need, and only in fables at that. It is surprising that one has come and stayed with you here," Alexius said.

"She's not wanted to leave. We've kept a window open for her," Deshi said, sounding a little defensive.

"We've also tried to offer her a bigger space. Usually, once an animal has recovered, we try to set them free or move them to the other building where there are no sick animals. But Chicky has become one of us. Sometimes she will follow us as we do our chores or tend to the sick, and she helps out once in a while. I was hoping she would heal your wing," Jito said.

"I have no need of the caladrius. But thank you," he said as he stepped up to the stall door. There was no netting around the stall, only the bird settling on a short stump of wood. Alexius kept his gaze downward; he didn't want to make eye contact with the bird given the judgment he feared from it. It was said that a caladrius looks upon a creature and judges its worthiness to be healed. Some are deemed worthy, and some are not. But those judged not worthy were doomed to a terrible death.

In all honesty, Alexius just didn't want to know if the good he'd done in his life outweighed the bad.

"Jito, please fetch Chicky's meal. She can't be expected to work on an empty stomach," Deshi said, and he shooed Jito away.

"The caladrius judges those she looks upon, doesn't she?" Deshi asked when Jito was out of earshot.

Alexius nodded as he stared at the walls around the stall.

"Age brings perspective." Deshi looked at Alexius. "If Thali trusts you, then I do too, but I understand your hesitation."

Alexius said nothing. He considered telling them her real name: Vitafera. But even in his mind, Vitafera seemed happier being called Chicky.

Deshi invited him down the hall for a tour of the rest of the building.

Alexius was surprised at how many animals they cared for. "Is it just you and your son that care for these animals?"

"Yes. Sometimes we have some help here and there, but mostly it is just Jito and I. My wife will help if she has to." Deshi smiled at that.

"You keep a great many creatures," Alexius said.

"It certainly takes some organization, but we have a system now," Deshi said as they arrived at a large room between the buildings filled with a plush set of couches, a table, a stove, a fireplace, and a pot of water.

"May I offer you some tea?" Deshi asked.

"That would be lovely," Alexius answered. He recognized the extra care Deshi took with his manners. His manners were not those of someone trained but of someone grateful.

As Deshi poured the tea, Jito walked in. Then Deshi brought three cups and the large pot to the table between the couches. "With your permission, Alexius, we would like to let the lord and lady know you are here," he said.

"Are they in?" Alexius asked.

"Only for another night, but I believe they would very much like to dine with you," Deshi said.

"Please, I would very much like to meet Thali's parents." Alexius played along, pretending that he would be meeting them for the first time as he took his teacup with two hands and took a sip.

Jito threw back his tea and jumped up. "I will go tell them," he said, and he was out the door before Deshi or Alexius had uttered another word.

"To be young again." Deshi raised his teacup.

Alexius grinned. Though may he look young on the outside—perhaps not quite as young as Jito—he recognized what Deshi was feeling.

Jito was back in mere moments. "Lady Jin would like our whole family to join them for dinner, with you as their honored guest." He bowed to Alexius.

"Thank you," Alexius said.

"And I'm also to say there is a room prepared for you at the main house," Jito added. "Would you like me to take you?"

Alexius finished his tea and thanked Deshi before following young Jito.

"I will be there in a few minutes with my wife," Deshi said as he bowed his head to Alexius.

Alexius nodded in return.

"Lady Jin asked me to bring you through the main entrance," Jito said as they walked alongside each other. "It's not like most houses around here, but kind of half Adanekian and half Cerisan from what my parents tell me." Jito was clearly trying not to run up to the main house.

"When did you move here?"

"I was born here. But my parents tell me a lot about Cerisa, like how it's common to have a fishpond inside the house. I love the fish," Jito said as he bounded into the house. Alexius was surprised that Jito was as comfortable as he was in the main house. Most help would be at least timid when entering their masters' house.

"Alexius." Lady Jinhua was resplendent in a light-blue dress.

As Alexius entered, he saw that beyond the entrance to the right was a large sitting room. Except it was more like an indoor garden than a sitting room with its large, glassless cutout windows with only shutters to keep the weather out and grand pond in the middle of the room. Seating options lined the perimeter, and a thick ledge surrounded the pond. Perhaps most surprising were the lithe fish that swam lazily within the "C" shape of the pond. The fish were all mostly white but speckled and striped with orange, red, and black. "This is beautiful. Even among the koi ponds in Cerisa, this pool outshines the others," Alexius said.

Lady Jinhua grinned, looking pleased with herself. For a moment, Alexius saw a flash of Thali in her face, in the joy. "Why thank you," she said. "It's lovely that you've come this way. Thank you for stopping by."

"Thank you for having me, and I apologize for the lack of warning. I just happened to stumble into the right place at the right time," Alexius said.

"Any time. Routhalia has told us how close you are and how important you are to her, so you are equally important to us," she said, easing Alexius's mind as she kept the ruse up for Jito's sake. He did wonder what she would say if she knew of Alexius's association with her son, Rommy. Then, she turned to Jito. "Thank you for bringing our esteemed guest, Jito. Why don't you go down the hall to clean up for dinner," Lady Jinhua said.

"See you in a bit, Alexius," Jito said before running from the room.

Alexius followed Lady Jinhua down the hall to what he assumed was the guest wing, where she pushed open a black lacquered door. "This is yours for however long you like."

"Thank you," Alexius said. He didn't want to volunteer more information than he had to.

Lady Jinhua closed the door behind her and glanced around the room before speaking. "We were not expecting a report so soon, Alexius. Is everything all right with the barrier?" Lady Jinhua asked.

"Routhalia is still away, and the palace still scrambles to make it look like she is not. I cannot go far or for long, but ... but I have been able to see some of her experiences."

"And? What do you glean from them?" Lady Jinhua asked.

"That she is being taught what she needs to be," Alexius said. He was forbidden to mention much about her son, so he stopped there.

Lady Jinhua narrowed her eyes and nodded. "What brings you here so suddenly then?"

"I was flying above when my wing was punctured by a harpoon."

"Damn those infernal fishermen. People are taking things into their own hands with all the creatures flying around, though none ever land here. I will see to it that it never happens again. But I'm glad that you had the opportunity to meet Deshi and his son, Jito." Lady Jinhua's forehead wrinkled as she thought of something else. Alexius recognized the same expression on Thali's face when she was putting lots of puzzle pieces together.

"Alas, I will leave you be. Thank you for the information," Lady Jinhua said before leaving Alexius alone to look around the room. The decor was a mix of the different kingdoms: trunks and furniture from Cerisa but a bed from Adanek, a table of Cerisa's famed dark cherrywood. Even the furniture in the sitting room was a mix of Cerisan chairs with cream silk cushions and an Adanekian plush couch in blush pink.

He was impressed with the large size of the guest room; it had a sitting room, a bedroom, and upon further exploration, a bathing room. The bath had two taps, so he pulled the one with the red ribbon, surprised to see hot water come out of the spout. He looked up, wondering where the water was heated and how it was brought about; he would ask later. He never minded a cold bath though as he could heat it himself.

Sinking into the bathtub, he paid attention to the new tissue in his shoulder. It was a little tender. As he relished in the heat of the water, he thought of the first time he'd been here, walking in through a side door under the cover of darkness. Thali's parents had summoned him into the human world, with permission of course. When he'd first arrived, Alexius had wondered if it had been all part of *his* plan. And Alexius had been angry, angry that he was under someone else's control, angry that he was to be a glorified babysitter, angry that he was so powerless. He'd even thought about trashing the place but had been under orders to mind his manners.

It was funny that Alexius had been given the same room now. He hadn't seen the koi pond back then, but he wasn't sure he would have really noticed, anyway. He eventually climbed out of the bathtub and dried off, then found fresh clothes in the closet, choosing a looser pant and longer tunic.

Alexius prepared for dinner, then opened the door and followed his nose to the dining room. It wasn't large like most noble houses, but finely decorated. The same cherrywood chairs with silk cushions—this time in light-blue silk—surrounded a cherrywood table. It was intricately carved with swooping vines, flowers, and even a few little dragons on the edges and legs. The table was set for six.

"Alexius, so good to see you again," Lord Ranulf, Thali's father, said as he shook Alexius's hand vigorously.

Lord Ranulf and Lady Jinhua nodded at each other as Deshi and his family came in. They sat along one side of the table, and Lady Jinhua, instead of sitting at the other end from Lord Ranulf, sat next to him. Alexius sat next to her.

"Alexius, this is my wife, Huiquin," Deshi said as he indicated the woman next to him.

She was tidy and clean, and Alexius could tell from the blisters on her hands that she was a hardworking woman. "It is an honor to meet you," Alexius said, bowing his head. He sensed something else then and his eyes narrowed, but he wasn't sure if the others in the room were aware of the lady's new state. He tilted his head, and she kept a smile plastered on her face. He would keep her secret. It was happy news, and he wondered for a second if she even knew herself. It was early.

They conversed lightly and pleasantly for the length of their dinner, even given how formal it was. Alexius much preferred this family style of eating like they used at home, where dishes were brought out to the table and everyone had equal access. It saddened him as he thought of his siblings, of how Jax was always the last to get food though he ate the most of any of them; he trained so hard so often. And Aexie was always granted first access as she was the pickiest.

"Alexius?" Jito's voice yanked him back to the present. He was looking at Alexius expectantly. "What do you think of Cerisan food?"

"Oh, it's delicious. All the different combinations and variety of ingredients are lovely," Alexius said. He chastised himself for not paying attention.

Deshi and Jito still had evening chores, so they were quick to leave once dinner was finished, Huiquin following her family. The whole family was clearly good friends with Ranulf and Jinhua, and Alexius appreciated that a lord and lady did not hold status above others.

"Alexius, would it be helpful to see her room? Would that strengthen your bond with her?" Lord Ranulf sounded hopeful. Alexius felt his sadness at his daughter's disappearance.

"Perhaps," Alexius said.

Lord Ranulf grinned widely and pushed his chair back at that, so Alexius followed him and Lady Jinhua through the hallways into the family's wing and into Thali's room.

He looked around. It had changed some since he was last there. The bed was just as tidy as it was before, and the items on the desk were the same, but it was the wall that most intrigued him.

"When she was eight, she tried to put daggers into the walls to climb them. That's when my wife decided the children were only allowed one dagger for emergencies in their room. Otherwise, no sharp weapons," Ranulf said, laughing.

Alexius's gaze roamed the shelves on the wall. They were filled with items from all over the world: bowls, statues, masks, a bracelet, a mug, all from different cultures and obviously of significance to Thali. He saw a few trinkets from Elric and recognized others that smelled of Garen. He smiled to see a little statue he'd given her two birthdays ago.

"I'm at a loss, Alexius," Ranulf said as he sat on Thali's bed. "I understand that you cannot go in search of her, that you're maintaining the barrier against magical creatures and that the royal resources aren't enough to bring her back. But do you at least have any idea *when* she might come back? You mentioned time works differently in Etciel."

Alexius nodded. "I got a glimpse into her training the other day. I'm not sure how, but I was asleep and dreaming and saw what she saw, I think. Her training is quite advanced. More than I would be able to do here. I believe she'll stay for about a month there, which may be more like a few months in our time."

"Romulus is with her?"

Alexius nodded. Even after taking his blood oath to Thali, which broke the magical control over him, he still wasn't able to say much more.

"She will be safe then. And does Etciel ... change humans? Romulus seemed strong when he returned, if not a little ... different," Lady Jinhua asked.

"Etciel as a place does not change someone, though the magic flows freely and is much more easily accessed. The experience, I dare say, may change her though," Alexius said. It was strange for him to be reporting to her family in her rooms.

Lady Jin exchanged a look with her husband. Thali's mother leaned toward him. "What is it that you're not saying, Alexius?"

"I cannot say everything that I wish to, but I am a little concerned that she's not getting the whole picture there. They aren't showing her all the consequences of the actions she's taking," Alexius said carefully. He couldn't say much more.

Lady Jinhua scrutinized him and nodded. Alexius could only hope that she was starting to pick up on what he was trying to say without being able to say it or even allude to it. At the same time, he wondered if parents were really ever able to see their child in a negative light.

CHAPTER THIRTY-ONE
Thali

THALI SAT ACROSS FROM Aexie in a room, an odd room with no name and seemingly no purpose. It wasn't a room with books or beds or food, desks or maps or weapons. There were only two chairs and a table in this room, and it was the least ornate of any she'd seen so far.

Thali was afraid of what it would be like to train with Aexie. She felt that Aexie was more dangerous than anyone really let on, and she suspected Aexie had a temper.

"Ah, thank you both for coming," Rommy said as he came through the door.

"When Xerus and I discussed court politics and navigating your way around people without violence, he said that Aexie would be the best to coach you through that," Rommy said.

"Do we have to stay here?" Aexie asked.

"No. I just wanted to give you a place to start, or a place to record things if you wish," he explained.

"Record?" Thali asked, looking around. She didn't see paper or quills or anything else.

Rommy chuckled. "The room. It records everything. You can ask for it written on parchment or etched in a rock."

"A rock?" Thali wasn't sure she believed him.

Rommy moved aside a curtain that Thali had thought was hiding a servants' door, but there instead were shelves and shelves of rocks lining the wall.

"Each is a memory, or a moment, that was chosen to be recorded," Rommy said as he brushed his hands along the rocks.

"That's incredible." Thali jumped up and went to look at the rocks.

"I think better when I'm outside," Aexie said.

Thali already sensed Aexie's annoyance. "I don't mind going outside," she said, not knowing why she was so desperate to please Aexie.

Rommy was irked, Thali could tell, but he smiled anyway, his polite, political smile. "Whatever you ladies prefer."

"Let's go," Aexie said as she jumped out of her chair and walked away.

Thali ran to catch up to her, hoping and praying that Aexie wouldn't just disappear, or worse, walk into the middle of the odd-colored woods and disappear. Thankfully, once out of the palace, Aexie's pace slowed. Thali continued to follow Aexie into the field of sheep. While Alexius's sister didn't seem to mind the sheep, they didn't approach her like they did Jax. A few called out to Thali though, making her smile. Aexie just kept walking and walking, but Thali was at least glad to be walking outdoors. It had been a while since she'd spent any time in a forest, and she followed Aexie as closely as she could without tripping.

As they got further and further into the woods, Thali saw Aexie relax. Her shoulders lowered, and her pace eased and slowed. Finally, she slowed enough that Thali could walk next to her as the path widened, making Thali wonder if that was what Aexie had planned all this time. They were now walking at a much more leisurely pace.

"You are weak," Aexie said.

"Thanks," Thali said. She wasn't at all surprised that the first thing out of Aexie's mouth was an insult.

Aexie continued walking for a bit before continuing. "Court politics is all about appearance. You must be aware of how you are seen. And then you must have spies to know what is truly going on at court."

"How do I find spies? And I don't know if my court is as ... volatile as what you've experienced," Thali said. She was surprised to find herself defensive of the Kingdom of Adanek.

"Doesn't matter. You need spies. You need to pay people, not always with money but with persuasion. Gain their favor or collect compromising information to hold them accountable. Those people will be your eyes and ears."

"What people? You mean servants?"

"Servants make excellent spies," Aexie said.

"What do I ask them to tell me? When and how do they tell me?"

Aexie ignored Thali's questions. "Start with Mia. You should employ her as your spymaster. She's good with people and moves easily among crowds. The prince of thieves, it would be good to ask him about spies too, if you still trust him. I bet he already has spies in the palace."

Talking about Garen with Aexie made Thali uncomfortable. "Whatever for?"

Aexie stopped dead in her tracks and looked at her. "Please tell me you're not that naive."

"I mean, I guess it would be good for him to have fair warning of palace happenings or to know if rulers are making changes that affect the whole kingdom."

"Or maybe because he's still in love with you," Aexie said.

Thali's cheeks heated then. She was with Elric now, married to him. There was nothing between her and Garen anymore. She hadn't even seen him in some time. "He's moved on, I'm sure," Thali said a little too quickly.

"Or not," Aexie said, narrowing her eyes.

"Anyway, Mia already takes care of my appearance. I'm setting trends," Thali said. She stuck her chin out because she was proud of her friend.

"She takes care of your clothing, yes. You may be a trendsetter, but what you look like is only part of it. How you act, with whom you engage, all matters. You know this. But now, think of how you would behave knowing there are spies everywhere. The ladies and lords of your court have motives of their own and spies of their own. Flowers being delivered to your door, for example. Spies will see that. They will report it. Who did they come from? Why? Did you react when you saw them?" Aexie looked sidelong at Thali. "The only time you have true privacy is when you're alone in your room with the curtains closed."

Aexie suddenly started to run. Thali ran to catch up and was nearly out of breath by the time Aexie stopped at a bright pink river. Her run turned into a walk as she slowly picked her way along the riverside. The shore was a dark blue. They walked closer and closer to the roar of a waterfall.

"You're out of shape!" Aexie shouted over the noise. Thali knew it was the truth. She couldn't even say it was an insult. She'd been so focused on magic, her body had been a second thought.

They approached a drop-off, and Thali wondered what Aexie would do next. They stood there in silence, Thali feeling more and more unnerved.

"Time to do something reckless," Aexie said. She grinned and stripped out of her clothes. She bundled them and tossed them over the cliff, where they landed on the sandy shore next to the foot of the waterfall. It was strange to see sand on the shore of a quiet lake. Before Thali could blink, Aexie took a swan dive off the side, and Thali crept up to the edge and saw her hit the water in a neat blip. Thali had half expected her to pop into dragon form and fly up, up, and away, abandoning Thali, forcing her to find her own way back to the dragon's palace.

"Coming?" Aexie shouted up. Thali swallowed. She realized this was the sort of thing she used to do all the time. She stripped her own clothes off, looking around to make sure no one was watching. She bundled them as she'd seen Aexie do and tossed them to the same spot Aexie had. Thali stepped gingerly along the rock, her toes curling over the edge. She looked below; the water Aexie was swimming in was a darker pink than the river. Thali gulped and jumped as Aexie had. Thali felt as if she was flying through the air ever so slowly like she was slipping through gelatin.

Landing in the pink water felt the same as it did at home, except she started rising more slowly. Was the water pushing her back to the surface? It felt that way. When she broke the surface, she gasped for air and realized how exhilarated she felt. Aexie was floating, and though Thali wanted to do the same, her nakedness made her stay vertical.

"The funniest thing about humans is how awkward you are with nakedness," Aexie said.

"Perhaps," Thali said. But she felt the challenge in the words, and still feeling the rush of jumping off the cliff, she decided to be daring and float, too. They were surrounded by bright-yellow trees very different from the blue ones at the top of the cliff. It was unlikely anyone would see her.

"Aexie, what's the difference between the trees here and the ones at the top of the cliff?" Thali asked.

"This is the beginning of the Forest of Whispers," Aexie said.

"What's the Forest of Whispers?"

"It is said that each tree is a soul from the human world."

Thali sat up, splashing water everywhere.

"So, when human souls die, they come here, to Etciel, and become a tree?" Thali asked.

"Well, some do. I don't think they all do as there would be way more trees. And don't ask me how because I have no idea."

"Can you talk to them?"

"I don't know. I never have," Aexie said.

When Thali looked over, she saw that Aexie had popped into her dragon form and was floating on her back, her wings spread out. Sometimes Thali forgot that they were dragons first, humans only in appearance. She supposed that having a forest of human souls would be like her having a forest of ant souls nearby.

Aexie didn't talk much for the rest of the afternoon, but Thali was grateful for the respite. They floated in the lake for some time until Aexie stood suddenly. "Xerus calls us back," was all she said as she leaped out of the water and picked her clothes up, bundling them again. Thali climbed out and dressed, despite the discomfort of putting clothes on when she was wet.

"It'll be faster if we fly," Aexie said. She hovered with her wings flapping and opened a clawed hand so Thali could climb on.

Thali swallowed at the sharpness of the claws but obliged and climbed up. Then, they were off, over the forest of yellow trees. She saw blue trees to the north and more to the south, but most trees were yellow. She wondered if the blue trees were uninhabited and the yellow were those that had taken a soul—and what happened to the soul if a tree was chopped down.

They landed in the courtyard, Aexie gently placing Thali on the ground before popping back into human form, donning her clothes, and strolling by Thali to walk into the palace. Thali's hair had dried on the flight back, and she followed Aexie straight into the dining room where the others were waiting. Many platters laden with food covered the table. It made her miss her own family. Sharing food and having dinner together was something her family always did, no matter how long they had to wait or how early they had to have it. They always ate together.

"Thali, why don't you go first?" Aexie asked as everyone sat.

Thali grinned as she nodded and filled her plate—before the picky Aexie. It was an honor to go first and Thali took it as a sign that maybe Aexie hated her a little less now.

CHAPTER THIRTY-TWO
Tariq

I T TOOK TARIQ NIGHTS to find any mention of Vancel in the library. He was only going to the library at night now so as not to draw suspicion, but during the day he read and researched in his room when he could. His heart had dropped when he had found information that corroborated his father's words. Vancel was not to be trifled with. It was a wild and lawless world without rulers. Bulstan's fighting style had come from them a long time ago. He found an account of someone who told of a strange bear-man who had come to them and taught them how to fight and defend the gate. He stayed to train them all. That training was to be passed down through the generations for the time when a gate was opened. Because one day, a portal *would* open. A creature smart enough, surreptitious enough, would find a way. The person who had written the account spoke of how one day, the bear-man had just walked into the woods and never returned. Because Bulstani forces had been protecting the gate, they'd known he was in this world but hadn't known where he'd gone, and no one ever saw or heard from him again. The author of the entry suspected the bear-man had gone off to the woods to die.

That part stuck out to Tariq. A bear-man had disappeared one day on their small island. He hadn't stolen a boat and sailed away; he hadn't gone through the portal but just disappeared into the woods. Tariq knew what he had to do. He wondered if the bear-man was the sort of creature that might still be alive.

Tariq returned to his rooms and put a few things together into a bag: rations and jewels and whatever else he thought a bear-man might want. Then, he paced until the sky started to lighten. He went to Bree's room and knocked on the door softly in the way he always did to let her know it was him.

Bree opened the door, and on instinct, he breathed her in deeply. He loved her smell. She ushered him inside quietly. It took him a moment to realize that Bree was dressed for riding.

"Are you going riding this morning?" Tariq asked.

"I am. And I wondered if you wanted to come with me." Bree finished buttoning the vest she'd put on over her shirt and trousers.

"Where are you going?"

Bree looked up, glanced at the door, then looked out the window and smiled. "I feel like a ride in the woods today."

Tariq narrowed his eyes. Was it just a coincidence that Bree wanted to go where he was planning to go?

"What did you find out?" Tariq asked in a low whisper.

"I'll tell you later."

"I found something, too." Tariq showed her the bag on his shoulder. Bree raised her chin. Then, she rubbed her arm. She did that nowadays when she was thinking about something.

"Let's go for a ride, my love," Bree said, holding her hand out to him. Tariq took it, and they walked to the stables. After the stable lads brought their horses out, they mounted them and, with a small contingent of guards, rode into the forest.

They rode in silence for a bit until the captain of Tariq's guard, Naseem, cantered up and stopped his horse to block their paths. "What are you two cooking up? We can smell it," he said.

Tariq looked around at the guards surrounding them. "Nothing," he said.

"Naseem, what you smell is the love between us. Let us ride to the clearing on the south side of the forest and break for lunch," Bree said. Naseem's eyes narrowed, but he let them pass, though he followed more closely. Bree was not one to deceive as often as Tariq, so the guards trusted her words more than his.

They stopped in the south clearing, far away from the gate, for that was never their destination and dismounted. Tariq helped Bree pull out the picnic she'd ordered packed and sat on the blanket with her. They put their heads together as they smiled, and the guards melted further away to give them their privacy.

"I found the mention of a bear-man who helped train our people eons ago, a possibly ageless bear-man. One day, he walked away from everyone and into the woods. I think he's still in here. He could be immortal," Tariq whispered.

"What a coincidence. I found something new on a map. It's been in front of us the whole time. Do you remember how we used to laugh at the strange animals on the map in your father's office?" Bree asked.

Tariq nodded. Those animals didn't seem so strange now.

"Do you remember what animal was by the caves, near the shore on the other side of the island where no one ever goes?" Bree asked.

Tariq's brow furrowed in thought. "It was a two-legged bear," he said after a time.

Bree's eyes widened, and she waited for Tariq to put two and two together.

"You're right! It's been there the whole time. We used to make fun of that drawing. We said they'd never finished drawing the bear. But what if they did it on purpose? Because it *was* a two-legged bear, a bear-man!"

"If I'm right, he lives in the caves on the other shore, where no one is supposed to go," Bree said.

"How did you think to look for a bear-man?" Tariq asked.

"You're terrible at remembering to put your books away. I went looking for you last night to see how you were doing and bring you some cinnamon milk, but I found the book open to the page of the account you mentioned, and it reminded me of the map in your father's office."

"How are we going to get away from the guards?" Tariq asked.

"We won't. We'll keep riding. My horse will suddenly get away from me and you'll chase after me. Then I'll fall off by the caves, and you'll bring me inside the caves to take shelter while you take care of me. When the guards keep watch outside, we'll go explore, see if we can't find the bear-man. Maybe we'll get lucky and not only find him but also find out what he knows before the guards even suspect anything," Bree said, smiling triumphantly.

"Do you have to fall off?" Tariq paled.

"Thali taught me how to fall off a horse safely. Don't worry. I can do it. And I'll make sure I do it on sand. It'll be a soft landing."

"The water might be a better choice," Tariq said. "Sand is pretty hard, and it'll get everywhere."

"Well, I'll make that decision when we get closer," Bree said. She squared her shoulders, obviously proud of her plan.

"It's a good plan," Tariq said. He kissed her temple, earning him one of her beautiful smiles. He was impressed his beautiful lady had such a devious plan.

"All right, ready?" Bree asked.

"Yes—" Tariq started to say.

Bree suddenly rose. "I can't believe you would say such a thing. Tariquin, you are being a worm, and I will not stand for it!" she shouted, then stomped away, swinging herself onto her horse and urging him into a gallop out of the forest toward the beach.

Tariq stood stunned for a moment, wondering what he'd done wrong. It also confused the guards, and he ordered one to clean up as he leaped onto his horse to pursue Bree. Only then did he finally remember that Bree was just putting on an act. Thankfully, his horse was a little bigger and stronger and caught up to hers easily as they galloped down the beach. Bree flailed her arms out wide and directed her horse toward the ocean. There, the horse refused to get in the water, and Bree went flying head over heels, landing in the deeper water beyond the sand shelf. Two guards went in pursuit of the horse as it continued to run away, and Tariq leapt off his horse and rushed to Bree, his heart pounding. He knew this was part of the plan, but it still scared him to death to see the love of his life thrown from her horse. His mother had died because of a horse, and it unexpectedly brought out his worst fear.

Bree's head bobbed at the surface until Tariq got there. He scooped her out of the ocean. As two more guards ran up to them, he looked at the caves. "She needs shelter. Go scout out the caves," he ordered, and one guard ran off. Tariq had no doubt that someone who had been hiding for so long would keep quiet and out of sight.

"My love, my darling, my everything, are you all right?" He nuzzled Bree's face.

"I am, my darling. You played your part beautifully," Bree said, her eyes shining.

"Does anything hurt? Your arm? Can you wiggle everything from your toes up?" he asked.

"I'm alright. I can wiggle everything, though my bottom is a little sore," Bree said.

"How did you know there was a drop-off there?" Tariq asked.

"I know it's not allowed, but it's not my first time here, Tariq."

"Well, I'm glad you're all right because my heart stopped for a minute there," Tariq said. Then he muttered, "It seems there are things you don't tell me."

As they neared the cave entrance, Bree turned her face into his chest without answering.

"The caves are clear, Your Highness," the guard said.

"Then, go stand at the mouth. The lady will need to remove her clothes to dry, so allow no one to enter," Tariq instructed. The guard nodded and strode to the mouth of the cave. Tariq strolled further in, around the bend, and then Bree leaped out of his arms.

Since they were around the bend and out of sight, Tariq twirled his fingers and a warm breeze dried them, clothes and all.

They didn't dare speak, so they moved further into the cave. At first, there was nothing but wall and floor. Bree, showing Tariq a whole new side to her, started to run her hands along the edges of the rock walls. Suddenly, she stopped, turned, and smiled.

"This is a boulder and not a wall," Bree whispered. They pressed on it together, Tariq using some wind to help them move the giant rock inwards.

When it moved enough for them to slip through, Tariq went first. He would face any danger first. But what he found inside was not quite what he had expected. There was a roaring fire warming the space, which was furnished with a dining table and couch, plus a bed in the corner. Before the fire sat a bear, not the hunched back of a bear who walked on four legs but one that sat upright, like a human. His body was mostly human though perhaps thicker and hairier. However, his hands were paws, and his neck up was all bear.

"I wondered how long it would take for someone to find me," the bear-man said, setting an empty bowl of stew with a spoon still in it on the arm of his chair.

"Hello, I am Lady Ambrene, and this is Crown Prince Tariquin," Bree said. She stepped within grabbing distance. It made Tariq nervous, so he stepped up next to her.

"Well, it's nice to know that someone has remembered their manners," the bear-man said. His accent was hard to place.

"How have you stayed hidden all these years?" Tariq asked.

The bear-man huffed at him and turned instead to Bree. "I have stayed hidden by treading softly, not speaking, catching fish, and learning to act four-legged."

"We've come to find you because we need your help. The world will need your help," Bree said.

"Ah, how I've heard that before. And then, after you are done with me, will your children also surprise me in the middle of the night and torch my home so I must run and hide again?"

"I'm sorry that happened. We did not know. Our children will be brought up to respect the extraordinary," Bree said.

The bear-man harrumphed. "And how can you be so sure?"

"Because their aunt has magic, their father has magic, and their mother has magic. There are creatures in the sky that were once only in my wildest imagings, and still we move toward the unknown, not shy away from it," Bree explained.

Tariq grinned ear to ear. He was so proud of his love. This bear-man was responding to her much more favorably than to him, so he waited and let his beloved introduce their wishes and steer the conversation. Half this island would be hers soon; she was his partner through and through, and he trusted her completely. He also knew she was better at winning strangers over.

"You have magic?" the bear-man suddenly looked back and forth between Tariq and Bree.

"Mine is very slight. I can detect magic in others, and sometimes I see into the future," Bree said, then turned to Tariq.

"I can control the weather, mostly wind," he said.

The bear-man narrowed his eyes. "Show me."

Tariq decided on a peaceful demonstration. He picked up a breeze and wrapped them all in it. He made the spoon rattle in the empty bowl and the fire roar.

"And this sister?" the bear-man asked.

"She is our best friend, the princess and future queen of Adanek. Her magic is more than ten times stronger than ours combined, and she was tricked into opening one of the gates."

The bear-man's eyes widened, and he asked, "Which one?"

"Etciel," Tariq chimed in.

"The land of dragons." The bear-man shook his head.

Bree continued where Tariq had left off. "We know nothing about the other lands. But she and her brother have been taken to Etciel, and she is being taught to use her magic."

"By dragons." The bear-man looked suspicious.

Tariq and Bree nodded. "Why does it matter that dragons are teaching her?"

"Dragons are snobs. If they have accepted your friend, the dragons are either truly special, or they have been enslaved. Though enslaving a dragon is difficult. Do you know who teaches her?"

"No, but one of them, Alexius, is a friend of ours, and hers," Tariq said.

"Alexius, the mourning prince," the bear said.

"You know him?"

"I know *of* him. That family of dragons is relatively honorable. I personally do not like dragons, but that is my own bias."

"What is your name?"

"My name is Tobias," the bear-man said.

"It's nice to meet you, Tobias," Bree said. She extended her hand to shake his paw.

He bowed instead. "You humans have very thin skin."

Bree nodded and Tariq was grateful for the bear-man's consideration.

"Will you come with us? Be our guest and help us navigate our new circumstances?" Bree asked.

The bear-man looked around. Tariq wanted to ask how long he'd been here, but it must have been hundreds of years. There was no need to count.

"You swear on your children that I will be treated well? Not like a monster?" Tobias asked.

Bree nodded. "On the heads of my unborn children, so long as you behave kindly and respectfully, we will do the same."

Tobias narrowed his eyes suspiciously. He stared at Bree for a long minute, and just as Tariq was about to open his mouth, Tobias nodded. He grabbed a few things and shoved them in a bag. "I will meet you at the boulder down the shoreline. Be sure no archers shoot at me."

Bree nodded. She backed away and held Tariq's hand as she led him out the same way. Once they had backed out of the opening, which closed behind them, Bree turned to Tariq, eyes alight with excitement.

"You are amazing. And incredible. And I'm not worthy of such an incredible woman," he said as he held her to him and showered her head with kisses.

"That was so exciting," Bree said. "Come, let us warn the guards and send word back to your father that there will be a guest for dinner."

They walked out of the cave hand in hand. When they reached the mouth, it took them a few blinks for their eyes to adjust. The sight before them took the air from their lungs. Standing along the beach in rows was half the royal guard.

"Oh, children. Why would you go and do such a thing?" King Shikji asked sadly.

CHAPTER THIRTY-THREE
Elric

"ALEXIUS IS MISSING," STEFAN said.

Elric had requested Alexius's presence to ask him more about whatever it was he couldn't talk about, thinking maybe he could find a roundabout way to get to the heart of it. "What do you mean, he's missing?"

"I gave him time off, Your Highness. I told him to go decompress for three days. That same day, he sent a note to Nasir saying he would be back by the end of the day, but that was two days ago," Stefan explained.

Elric combed his hand through his hair. "Do you think someone abducted him? Or is it more like he got distracted? Or he has left us?"

"I don't think he's left us. I feel like he might be delayed by some accident, or perhaps he's been taken," Stefan said.

"You trust him?" Elric asked.

Stefan paused a moment. "Yes. He has proven himself more than loyal to Her Highness. He stays to protect the things she loves even though he has his own home, his own family."

Elric nodded. He sank into his chair.

"Would His Highness like to talk about it?" Stefan asked.

"I've prepared my whole life for this role, for being king. I learned politics and court etiquette, and I fostered relationships. And now it's like we showed up to the party not knowing it was a masquerade ball. I feel so out of my element. I can't prepare for anything, I don't know anything, I can't *do* anything."

"I know something," Stefan said.

"Oh? Please do share because I am lost."

"I know we have you at the helm. You, who thinks of his people before himself. You, who cares about all creatures. Besides, our weapons have proven useful against the attacking creatures."

"Oh! I didn't even think about that. What if we encounter a creature our weapons are powerless against?" Elric's eyes widened, and Stefan cringed. Elric sat back and rested the back of his head on the chair. "Do you think this will end in war?"

"I think, at the very least, we will have to defend. Many of those coming from the other worlds are beasts. They are not all like Alexius in that they can see reason and speak reason. We will, at some point, have to defend ourselves against creatures that want to eat us or take our home," Stefan said.

Elric wasn't so sure. If only he could figure out what they wanted maybe they could avoid war. But Stefan had made a good point. He wished he could ask Alexius.

There was a knock on the door. "Come in," Elric said.

A hunched man in the robes of a scholar walked in, staring at the floor.

"Hello," Elric said. Everything about the man told Elric he was afraid.

"Your Highness." The scholar bowed so low, the papers in his hands touched the floor and almost spilled out. He rose abruptly to prevent the papers from falling and then dipped back down into the bow as if he'd made a wrong move.

"Easy now. It's all right. What's your name?" Elric asked.

"I am Scholar Kivu ... Your Highness," he said, remaining bowed.

"Please, rise. What have you for me today?" Elric asked.

"I have some reports summarizing our research," Kivu said.

Stefan approached the man with a smile and reached for the papers. Kivu thrust them forward, startling Stefan and causing him to back up before grabbing them. Kivu bowed immediately.

Elric intervened. "Kivu, thank you for the reports, but could you tell me about your most surprising findings?"

Kivu's voice shook a little as he started to speak, and he still wouldn't meet anyone's eyes, but he squared his shoulders a little. "There are multiple realms. Etciel is just one of them, as is the human realm. There is also Vancel and two others we have no name for yet. Etciel is the most powerful, however. Each world has a gate, or portal, that connects them to our world, though we think one may have been destroyed. However, there is one in Cerisa, though we have no idea where. Nor do we know where the other gates are. But each world is populated by different creatures, from small ant-like ones to large ones like dragons. No matter what kind of creatures they are though, we think they have societies much like we do."

"Do you know which are the most dangerous creatures?" Stefan asked.

"From what we know, dragons, without a doubt. There are a few others that are dragon-like but less intelligent and easily manipulated. They usually make up the dragons' armies."

"Dragons have armies?"

"We only saw mention of it once or twice, but yes," Kivu said.

Elric thought back to what Alexius had said about Gabol, the griffin in his unit. "So, they have societies as we do. Do you know how they're organized?"

"No. Only that dragons often lead them," Kivu said.

Now that Kivu had settled into explaining the research and presenting the facts, Elric noticed that he had relaxed.

"Do you know anything about the weapons in those worlds?" Stefan asked.

Kivu's eyebrows went up. "All those creatures *are* weapons."

Stefan nodded.

"Do you know why and how they were sealed into their own worlds?" Elric asked.

"We have found very little about that event, though it seems to require a lot of magic and a very specific individual," Kivu replied.

Elric nodded. "If you can learn more about that, I would greatly appreciate it."

Kivu bowed at the dismissal. He backed out of the room while still bent over, and Stefan sank into a chair. "I'll have to refresh the staff on proper protocol." Stefan rubbed his temples as Elric started to read the papers Kivu had left. "Why do we seem to be the idiot version of dragons?" Stefan asked.

Elric nodded. "I know what you mean. Alexius knows more than we do and is more capable than we are, yet he's the youngest in his family."

Stefan swallowed. There was silence between them for a while until Elric took a sip of his cold tea.

"It's a lot quieter around here without her," Stefan said.

A slow, sad smile spread across Elric's lips. "It's definitely calmer, though I'd give anything to get her back and have the palace buzzing again. I know she's her own person and has a unique ability to help the kingdom, but I just want her here, safe, with me."

Stefan opened his mouth, then closed it.

Elric waved him on.

"This might not be the safest place for her," Stefan said.

Elric nodded. He put the papers down and took another sip of cold tea. "You could be right. Alexius has to protect her with a magic barrier everywhere she goes so creatures don't attack her. I'm sure she's freer in Etciel." He sighed. "At the same time, I don't know if she actually would, but I feel like she'd know what to do right now better than I do." Elric placed the teacup down with a clatter.

"Perhaps. But would you really give up anything for her safe return? The safety of this kingdom? Of its people? Because you could send Alexius to retrieve her, but they might return to ruins," Stefan said.

"Almost anything, then," Elric said. It felt like acid in his stomach, but he realized his life, his feelings, came second to his kingdom.

CHAPTER THIRTY-FOUR
Garen

G AREN TOOK LONG, HURRIED strides to the brothel. His captain had urgently sent for him, so Garen was there in minutes. The women were all huddled in the corner, but Marisa was calming them. His captain, Ella, her red hair immaculately groomed, looked grim.

"We captured one," Ella said.

He nodded and followed her to one of the back rooms. "Whose room is it in?"

"Anette's. I think the crystals trapped it."

Garen nodded, and Ella pushed the door open. On the bed, surrounded by crystals of various shapes and sizes, was a humanoid creature of black shadow. It looked like black mist forming a human shape without features. Garen assumed had it dropped its more human features when it realized it was trapped.

"Send for Foxall," Garen said as he stood in the doorway. The creature tried to leap at him but couldn't get past the crystals.

"We moved the crystals closer to keep it contained on the bed," Ella said.

Garen nodded and watched as the creature glided—or slid?—back and forth in the small space. It moved like a cloud but faster, with determination rather than just drifting like a breeze. It had ceased its attempt to escape after just two tries, and now, after a few more laps up and down the bed, it halted. It floated in the middle, molded into a pyramid that seemed to curl up and down, then up and down again.

"Um, thank you, miss ... I ... uh," Foxall's voice reached Garen's ears. The apothecary sounded flustered. The shadow suddenly expanded then, like it was blowing up. Then it shrank itself as small and flat as a bug on the bed itself.

Foxall poked his head into the room. "Ah, Garen, thank you for sending for me." He turned his attention to the shadow creature. "Ah, you've trapped it with crystals." He turned and said over his shoulder, "Lovely. Good work ladies." When he turned back, his eyes flashed gold.

"It is one of the creatures that attacked the ladies the other day?" Garen asked.

"One of the same, I believe. Alexius fortified the barriers, but any already inside would be trapped within. He thought there might be two inside, but we'll continue searching for more. I'm afraid they'll be much more difficult to find as they are of one mind in some ways. The others will know what has happened to this one and will stay far away from this place."

"We'll keep watch. Which crystal keeps them imprisoned?" Garen asked.

"Any crystal. The rigid structures in a crystal prevent them from moving past when they're close enough together."

"What do we do with this one, then?" Garen asked. The shadow had moved to cower as far back as it could. Whatever creature Foxall was, the thing was terrified of him.

Foxall rustled around in his bag. "Well, we can bottle it, or I could eat it."

"Did you say, 'eat it'?" Garen asked.

Foxall nodded. "Strange, I know, but I have an excellent digestive system. If we leave it in a bottle, it can still communicate with the others, who will attempt to free it. If I eat it, the others will be easier to catch," he explained.

"How do you eat a shadow?" Garen asked. Now, he was intensely curious about what kind of creature Foxall was.

"Oh, I just pour this solution here on it, and the liquid turns it into a gelatin consistency. Much easier to swallow," Foxall said.

"And it is normal for your kind to eat this?"

Foxall tilted his head back and forth as if he was pondering the question. "Not really. However, we are ... like your goats."

"Foxall, I've known you for years now. May I ask what you are?" Garen asked.

"Ah, my boy, I'm surprised you haven't figured it out. Especially knowing what Alexius is," Foxall said.

"Are there many creatures that can take human form?" Garen asked.

Foxall tipped his head side to side, "Only a couple without help, and I am most definitely not slimy." He grinned.

"You're a dragon? That's why this shadow creature is afraid of you?"

"Yes, my dear boy. Now, may I eat it?"

"In a second. Do the shadow creatures have the ability to communicate with us?"

"They can, but only rarely and with difficulty."

"I bring warning," said a whisper of a grating voice like fingernails on a chalkboard. The voice made Garen turn quickly toward it.

"What warning?" Garen asked. Apparently letting Foxall eat it was enough encouragement for it to speak.

"We are not ourselves," it said.

Garen ground his teeth together as he resisted clapping his hands over his ears. This was not a pleasant sound.

"Huh," Foxall said. He looked from the shadow creature to Garen. "See, it speaks, if it really wants to."

Garen realized then that Foxall had only said he would eat it to get it to talk. It made him wonder if Foxall had ever threatened humans in the same way.

Foxall tossed a vial of powder onto the shadow. The powder settled on it, turning the cloud to a small tendril of smoke. Foxall grabbed it with his fingers and dropped it into a vial. "If your friends come to find you, I'll eat you all. I promise you that," he threatened. He pressed a cap onto the vial and tucked it into a padded sleeve before dropping it in his bag.

"Were you actually going to eat it?" Garen asked.

"I was prepared to. Dragons can eat nearly anything," Foxall said.

Standing in the now empty room, Garen realized it almost felt hollow without the shadow creature here.

"I assume you have questions," Foxall said.

"Can you hold the barrier so Alexius can go to Etciel?" Garen asked.

"I cannot. I became an apothecary because my magic is limited. With all my potions and tricks, I might hold the barrier for a few minutes, but I alone would not be able to hold it long enough for him to get there and bring her back."

Garen's shoulders sagged.

"I'm sorry, boy, but your lass is quite formidable. She can take on the strongest of creatures," Foxall said as he rummaged in his bag for something.

"She's not mine," Garen said automatically.

"All right, if you say so."

"She's married to the Prince of Adanek. There's nothing to suggest she still has feelings for me."

"Just because two people *can't* be together doesn't mean they don't *want* to be."

It was traitorous. Though, truly, what was the king going to do to a dragon?

"What do you know about Alexius's family?" Garen asked.

"Let's get more comfortable for this one." Foxall snapped his fingers, and suddenly they were sitting in Garen's private rooms at the tavern.

Garen blinked as he acclimated to the sudden change. "I thought you said you didn't have magic."

"I said I don't possess a *lot* of magic."

Garen stood up suddenly, went to the door, and opened it. He waved a surprised Sesda over. "Send word to the captain that all is well and safe at her home now."

Sesda nodded and Garen closed the door. He sat back down in a plush chair and wondered how powerful Alexius must really be.

Foxall must have sensed his thoughts for he said, "I can only speak to what I know. I have known Alexius since he hatched. He is a royal prince of my home realm. He has two brothers and had two sisters, but one passed at a young age and it changed Alexius as they were very close. His sister was the youngest, but now he is the youngest. Their father and mother were not just royalty but also mated. These are two very different things in our world. If I may be so bold, I would say you and a certain someone you don't want to talk about are mated, but she and Prince Elric are royalty." Garen was about to protest, but Foxall continued. "Alexius also had a mate. She was a farmer, but there was an incident and she died protecting him. He blames himself for it forever more." Foxall's voice trailed off as he stared out the window.

Garen opened his mouth but closed it. The story brought so many questions that he didn't know where to start. "How many kinds of creatures live in your world?"

"Oh, boy, it has been many years since I lived in that world, so long I'm not sure I can call it mine now. I tend to go where I may be needed. But I can tell you there are many. Just as you have ants and pigs and horses and people here, they have a whole world of creatures there. Some similar to the ones you have, and some not."

"Are all the creatures intelligent?"

"More than here, but not all. We have your average ant and slug, as well," Foxall said.

"Who is the king?"

"When I left, it was Alexius's father and mother. But it seems there may be something troubling going on there," he said.

"Why would you say that?"

"Because they never wanted to come to this world," Foxall said. "They were happy there in their own thriving realm. They, at least, did not possess the greed so commonly found here."

"So, you think there is someone else controlling the Kingdom of Etciel?" Garen asked.

Foxall shrugged. "I'm not sure. It has been much too long since I have been there. I just have my suspicions. Of all the dragons I know, Xerus's mate is ambitious. Perhaps he's turned Xerus, Alexius's oldest brother, in that direction as well."

"Is there a way for a human to influence or control a dragon?" Garen asked.

Foxall thought. "There are two. Both very dangerous. But yes—oh my, I must return to my shop." A puff of blue smoke appeared, and Foxall was gone.

Garen blinked, wondering what had just happened.

CHAPTER THIRTY-FIVE
Alexius

A LEXIUS HAD DECIDED HE would walk to town. Thali's parents had generously offered him a horse, but horses were generally too frightened of him to let him ride them. And his wing would still need a couple days to recover, so walking it was. He had been told to take some down time, so he supposed spending it in Densria wasn't so bad. Besides, Mia's family lived here somewhere, and maybe he could check on them for her.

As always, he got a few stares as he walked down the main road from the manor. His stomach growled, and he was amazed yet again at how often human bodies needed nourishment. He smelled yeast and bread somewhere nearby, so he followed his nose. He stepped into an empty bakery. Being midday, the morning rush was over and a blond woman with bouncy curls quietly restocked the trays.

"Hello, how can I help you?" She smiled brightly at him.

"Hello, um, I'm not sure," Alexius said. A sugary scent filled his nostrils, as did the smell of yeast and strawberries. He looked around at delicious-looking strawberry tarts, a ham and cheese sandwich, and loaves of bread.

"Hi, mister! You should get a strawberry tart. They're Momma's favorite." A small toddler with the same blond curls as the woman popped out from under the display case.

"Is that so?" Alexius asked with a smile. He was a fan of bold children.

"Mareth, come back over here. What did Daddy tell you about surprising people?"

"That people don't like to be surprised. But I didn't mean to!" Mareth said.

"I'm sorry for my daughter. We live just above and sometimes she forgets this is not part of her house," the woman said.

"It's no problem. Bold girls are brave girls." Alexius smiled again at Mareth, who grinned before running off into the back.

"You must be a friend of Lady Thali. Or I mean Princess Thali. That just sounds so strange. Please forgive me."

"I am indeed a friend of Thali's. How did you know?"

"Word spreads faster than wildfire here. Everyone knows there's a guest at the house, and if you're a fan of brave and bold girls, then you must be a friend of the lady, er, Her Highness."

Alexius couldn't help but grin. These were definitely Thali's kind of people.

The woman started to put a few things in a basket. "Are you from the palace?"

Alexius nodded. A large burly man appeared from the back. "Mareth just charged me with a baguette. Got me right in the guts," he said as he patted his belly. He looked up and smiled. "Good afternoon, sir."

"Marcus, this is one of the lady's, I mean Her Highness's, friends. From the palace," the woman said.

Marcus nodded. "Thank you for being kind to little Mareth. She is bolder than we know what to do with."

"We're going to need all the bold we can get," the woman countered.

"Have there been many attacks here?" Alexius asked.

The baker bustled around putting together what looked like a big order as she spoke. "Mostly flybys, thankfully. I think the reason they don't attack has something to do with the chickens. But mostly the creatures just swoop. They don't attack. The fisherman are too quick to fire their harpoons, though. Last week, they put one right through the house down the street," the woman said. She finally closed the box and slid it on top of the counter.

"The chickens?" Alexius asked as he rolled his injured shoulder.

"Oh! Have you not seen them yet? We have over a dozen silky chickens. The town practically worships them. They have their own home in the middle of the square just a ways down. Sick or injured folks go visit them, and sometimes they're healed. Mareth had a cut from slipping off a bench and they healed it up like new," Marcus said.

"I'll have to go take a look," Alexius said. Could it be a whole flock of caladrii had chosen to live here?

"Here, to bring back to the lord and lady." Marcus slid the box toward him.

The woman placed a small, wrapped bundle on top of the box and winked at him. "And that's for you, now. Her Highness's favorites." She smiled proudly, and Alexius wondered if it was because she'd remembered Thali's title properly for the first time or if she was just proud of her product.

Alexius dug into his pocket, grateful he had remembered to bring coins on his outing.

"Your money is no good here. We only ask you bring these to the lord and lady. We have much to be grateful for, and the lord and lady are the cause of it. And Thali is a friend, er, I mean Her Highness," the woman said.

Alexius smiled and nodded. "Thank you." He left the bakery and cut through an alley between shops on his way back to the manor. These pastries wouldn't do well in the sun, and he could come back to town after he had delivered them. But that didn't mean he couldn't try one of his own sweet treats. His stomach rumbled yet again as he slipped a strawberry tart out of his little bundle.

He felt her before he saw her. She appeared right in front of him just as he bit into the strawberry tart.

"Thank you, brother," Aexie said as she took the other half of the strawberry tart from his fingers and pranced down the alley.

"Aexie, what are you doing here?" Alexius asked.

"Eating," Aexie said.

Alexius rolled his eyes. He followed her as she finished the tart, then turned invisible as they walked out into the street again.

He remembered then there was something of great interest to be seen in the middle of town, and he switched direction. It would only take a minute. A few quick turns later, he found it. In the middle of an open space was a small building with a tiny door cut within a large door and glass windows along two sides. Around the building, a dozen caladrii were sunning themselves in the afternoon rays that reached one side of the building.

"Are those caladrii?" a disembodied Aexie voice asked next to him. He was careful not to respond too overtly as there were people in the main square. They might not think well of a stranger talking to himself. He was careful not to look the caladrii in the eye as he watched them through his peripheral vision for a few minutes. A woman came and set a little boy down on the ground next to the building's door. He had sliced up his knee and his tears were dry, but his cheeks were still red.

"Can you sit quietly next to the magic chickens for Mama?" the mother asked.

The little boy nodded and one of the chickens walked up to him.

"Hands on your belly button now. We don't know if the chickens want to be petted or not," the mother said.

The little boy looked at the chickens, then at his mother, and nodded. He tucked his hands under his coat and on his belly button.

A caladrius walked up to the little boy and looked into his eyes. Moments later, the knee started to sew itself together. The blood was still there but the slice was gone. The caladrius flew back to the flock and settled in for a nap amongst the blankets and cushions set out for them.

The mother came back to get the little boy. She put her hand to her heart and bowed. "Thank you," she said and sprinkled some grain on the ground. A few chickens came to explore the grain, but the one who had healed the boy was huddled among a few others, fast asleep.

"I've never seen so many before," the disembodied voice next to him said. Someone turned to find the owner of the voice, but Alexius turned on his heel and strode toward the manor.

They were climbing the dozens of stairs when Aexie finally popped back into sight. "Is that why you came here? To see the caladrii?" Aexie asked.

Alexius shook his head. "This is Thali's home. I came to try and strengthen our connection but was shot in the wing as I flew. It's not quite healed enough for me to leave yet."

"Who shot you?" Aexie asked as she turned to him. She was already preparing for a fight.

"It wasn't malicious."

"Right, because people shoot living creatures to show their appreciation for them," Aexie said as she rolled her eyes.

"No, but they do shoot in self-defense. It's fine. It was barely a nick."

"Big enough to keep you grounded for a few days," Aexie shot back.

"You haven't been here for months, so don't get all big sister on me now," Alexius said. He hadn't intended the bitterness that had come with that.

Aexie stomped up the stairs, and when they reached the top, Alexius headed into the house as Aexie disappeared. He brought the pastries into the kitchen and then went to his rooms so he and Aexie could speak in private.

He closed the door, and she reappeared as soon as they were alone. Then, she wrapped a sound barrier around them. He missed feeling his siblings' magic and closed his eyes to enjoy the light wrapping around him. "So, what are you doing here?" Alexius asked.

"Checking up on you. I'm the only one who can go back and forth without much notice," Aexie said.

"I'm surprised you're allowed to."

"Some of the restrictions have ... lifted a bit," Aexie said.

Alexius was sure that Aexie had engineered a way to bend the rules.

"How is everyone?" Alexius asked.

"Xerus is tired, Jax is Jax, and Thali is ... strong. Really strong," Aexie said.

"I saw a little bit of what she can do. I'm not sure how I saw, but she's being taught without knowing the consequences, isn't she?"

"You saw?" Aexie said as she nodded.

"I can't explain it. I fell asleep, and it was like I got a glimpse through her mind."

"Your blood oath," Aexie said.

Alexius nodded. It was the only thing he could think of that might explain it.

"I'll ask Xerus if I get the chance," Aexie said.

"Thanks."

"She feeds off Etciel's magic. We're not allowed to say anything or interject," Aexie said.

"She wouldn't make the same choices if she knew," Alexius said.

Aexie looked at him sideways. "I still don't get it." She plunked down on the couch and looked at him sideways again.

"Get what?" Alexius asked.

"I don't understand why you decided to tie your life to a mortal. You won't live beyond her lifespan, and humans don't live very long. Why do you want to help her so much? Do you love her?" Aexie asked.

Alexius swallowed and shook his head. "I do, I guess. Not like Brixelle, but she is very dear to me, more than I realized. She is a refreshing human. She wants to be kind, to be good."

"So help her, but did you have to tie your life to hers?"

"It was the only way out for her and for me."

"Was it truly necessary? This ..." Aexie waved her hand in a circle. "... time will pass. Eventually, humans die. We'll have our realm, our kingdom back again once they do."

"But will we? What if there's nothing left after the war? Are you suggesting I should have hidden until it all blew over? Like Xenon?" Alexius asked.

"I think that would be a better choice than giving your life an expiry date," Aexie said. She looked upset.

"That's not a life. I've lived a non-life for years since ... since Danx and then Brixelle. I've been a shell of a soul. But now, now I have lived. I have sailed on the ocean and laughed among friends and tasted delicious things."

"You are selfish to think only of yourself. What of us when you die?" Aexie asked.

Alexius shut his mouth then. Images of his other sister, Danxing, floated into his mind, and the sharp pain of her loss lanced his heart.

"That's a low blow," Alexius murmured.

"Well, it's true. You didn't stop to think about what your death would do to Xerus, Jax, and me—and Papa, if he's still alive," Aexie said.

"You don't need me, No one does. Xerus was running the kingdom long before he needed any help from me. Jax is ... well, Jax, and you, you've always found your own entertainment," Alexius said.

"We thought you needed space. Danx first, then Brixelle. We wanted to let you grieve."

"For three hundred years?!" Alexius roared.

"We're dragons. That's a blink of an eye for us," Aexie said. She crossed her arms.

Neither said anything more. It was an old argument. "Will you stay here while I go back and retrieve Thali?" Alexius finally asked.

"I cannot. If I am gone too long, it will be too suspicious."

"You cannot or you will not?" Alexius asked.

"I cannot. And will not. It's your decision to throw your life away, but it's mine to keep living, to weather the storm until we come out the other side," Aexie said.

"I'm sorry that we cannot see eye to eye on this, sister."

"As am I, brother," she said, then vanished.

Alexius could feel that she'd left this world. She was always so much better at teleporting than the rest of them, slipping so easily from world to world.

Alexius sank down on the couch and shivered at the loneliness. He should have sent a note for Thali, a message, something. He also regretted not parting on better terms with Aexie. Who knew if she would return or if that was her moment of judgment. Was she done with him now? Alexius wondered, too, whether he had truly saddened

Xerus with his choice to take a blood oath with Thali. Not that Xerus was one to talk since he had taken the blood oath with his mate early on, and that had turned out to be a bad decision. As a result, he paid the price everyday now that he always had an enemy in his head.

Alexius felt a pang in his chest. He did regret leaving Jax. Jaxon had always accepted Alexius, been kind enough if not also tough but fair. He knew Jax would miss him greatly. Jax was always the steady one, the one you could count on. And Alexius had always made it a priority to maintain his daily training with Jax because it made him happy, at least until Alexius had left on his mission. *Have I been making all the wrong choices?* he wondered miserably.

CHAPTER THIRTY-SIX
Thali

THALI WOKE ABRUPTLY. SHE glanced around, forgetting for a moment where she was. Then she remembered and took a deep breath, trying to calm her racing heart. She wasn't in her drab, cold room at school, and she wasn't in the plush bedroom of the manor by the school. She wasn't even in the luxury of her beautiful green palace bedroom. No, she was in the white-and-gray bedroom of a palace of dragons in a magical realm. She rubbed her head as she realized how valid her panic was. For sixteen years, there had only really been two places she'd ever slept: her family's ship and her own bedroom in Densria. A wave of homesickness hit her as she missed the comforts she always enjoyed at home: Marcus's strawberry tarts, her wall of gifts, each one a memory of something or someone. She looked down at the ring on her hand.

She wondered how Elric was, how Daylor and Tilton and Mia were. She wondered how all her friends were and then started to wonder how long she'd been away. Time moved differently here, and she wasn't sure exactly how many days she'd been here. Maybe a week? Maybe two?

A knock on her door pulled her attention back to the present. It cracked open. "Are you decent, Rou?" Rommy asked.

Thali nodded, then realized he wouldn't be able to see it. She wrapped a fluffy robe around herself. "Come in," she said. She tried to smooth her hair down, but there was a weird bump that seemed to defy gravity.

Rommy pushed through the door carrying a tray. He brought it to the bed and sat cross-legged on the end. "I've brought you something special this morning."

"Why?" Thali asked.

"Can't a brother be nice to his sister?" Rommy asked.

Thali rolled her eyes. Rommy was always full of surprises.

She looked at the tray and gasped. Two bowls of white congee with egg, scallions, and pork floss sat on the tray with a plate of ordinary dumplings. "It looks like home," Thali said with a sigh. Whenever they got home after a long trip at sea, they would sleep in their own rooms, but by the second night, it felt strange not to be as close together as they were on the ship. So, Rommy would scoop Thali up when he woke, and they would crawl into their parents' bed. The next morning, her father would bring in four bowls of congee and plates of dumplings. They'd stay in bed all morning as they ate. Those were some of Thali's favorite memories.

Rommy waited while Thali shifted, tucking the blankets around her to make a more stable surface. He handed her a bowl and proceeded to use his sticks like knives as he cut the dumplings in half so they would be bite-sized, just like he had done when they were younger and she was learning to master the sticks. Something in the back of her mind started to bother her then, but she shoved it away, slamming a door in its face as she enjoyed this moment. Rommy put some crunchy fried wonton scraps into her congee and then handed it to her. She closed her eyes as the heat seeped from the bowl into her hands. She held the bowl in her hand on top of the pillow table she'd made for herself, and Rommy did the same.

Thali took the first mouthful and fought the urge to lay back as she savored the delicious warmth sliding down her throat. "This is just as I remember it," she said.

"Good! I slaved over the recipe. I even had rice brought in from our world."

She devoured the whole bowl; it was gone too soon. But then, she picked up her sticks and took half a dumpling. She looked inside, expecting the meat to be purple or pink, but it was the normal gray color that dumplings were in the human world. "Are these from our world, too?" Thali asked.

"Only the best for you, Rou," Rommy said.

For a moment, she was reminded of someone else who always insisted she get the best of everything. A wave of sadness hit her as she thought of Tariq ... and Bree. Tari had been so angry at her for letting Bree get hurt. She was mad at herself for not protecting her sister. She had been so wholly unprepared to protect her friends, and while people kept saying there was nothing Thali could have done, nothing anyone could have done, she knew she was the only one who could have done something.

Rommy pressed his knee to hers, yanking her out of her thoughts.

"When do you think I'll be ready?" Thali asked.

"What do you mean?"

"Ready to go back, to help protect Adanek."

Rommy looked at her and cocked his head. It was a rare occasion when Rommy had to pause to think. He always had answers at the ready. "After breakfast, I want to show you something," he said instead.

Thali's brow furrowed. That hadn't been a real answer.

Rommy took a dumpling and put it in her bowl before taking a half for himself. They always shared dumplings like this.

"I can do it myself now, you know," Thali said, a grin on her face.

"I know. I'm just taking care of my little sister," Rommy said. He patted her knee through the blanket before grabbing another half of a dumpling, letting her grab her own half this time. They moved on to discussing the different creatures they'd seen in this world. There were still a couple that Thali wished she could see in person from Rommy's description of them.

Finally, they each took their halves of the last dumpling, then sadly stacked all the dishes back on the tray.

"Get dressed and meet me in the hallway?" Rommy asked.

Thali nodded. She didn't move until he'd gone. Then, as she dressed, her thoughts returned to how starkly different her life with Rommy was versus her life at the palace. Maybe it was waking up and not knowing where she was earlier, but she couldn't help comparing her life now to her life in the palace, her life at school, her life at home, and her life on a ship. Her life here reminded her of home. There was a simple routine to it: training, learning, basic comforts. Her life at the palace was so overwhelming, with so many people depending on her and on the decisions she made, her skills, and her abilities. Everyone always wanted or needed something from her. Then there was the overabundance of luxury.

She sighed. Then, she shook her head and put her hand on the door-knob. Only then did she realize she'd dressed in her usual trousers, shirt, and vest, not something princess-like.

Rommy was outside her door, speaking softly with Xerus. They glanced up, and Xerus nodded at her.

"Rou, come. I want to show you something," Rommy said.

Thali nodded at Xerus as she walked away with Rommy, down the hallway to another hallway. This was the more public part of the palace, filled with offices and bland rooms specifically for meetings or receiving guests.

Rommy stopped at a set of doors opposite Xerus's office. She won-dered if this was Jax's office or whether her brother had his own office now, too. Rommy pushed the wooden door open and revealed a simple table and a grand desk, with a chair, a couch, and a wall of books the only other furnishings. There was nothing particularly special about the space besides the shiny red hide of the chair. It reminded her of dragon skin, but surely that would not be acceptable in a place where dragons lived. She swallowed, too afraid to ask.

The gray slate of the furniture left the office feeling cold. It was not the office she would imagine Rommy to keep. "Is this yours?" she asked.

"It is, but it's not all of it. Come," he said as he strode to the bookcase next to the desk. He moved a couple of books and then pushed on the door. The books were like a key, each pulled out to a specific distance like tumblers in a lock. Rommy pushed on the shelf then, and it swung open to another room the same size as his office. This room was much more reminiscent of her brother. Here, a deep-blue carpet and tapestries in blue and yellow hung along the walls to soften the harsh slate gray. There were a couple of bookshelves here too, but before Thali had the chance to look at the titles, her attention was caught by what sat in the middle of the room: a large octagonal table, atop which rested a map of their world, her world.

On the kingdom of Adanek, a tiny sculpture of her sat with a tiny Elric. "Rommy, what is this?" she asked. Surrounding the sculptures were moving arrows leaving Adanek and entering other kingdoms. The map was clearly magic.

"I think you're ready to see what I've been preparing for the last three years," he said.

"What do you mean?" Thali didn't understand. For the last three years?

"I always knew there must be a reason you have the abilities you do. I know our parents forbade it, but I knew it was a beautiful and useful skill. Three years ago, when Mupto rejected me, I knew I had to prove my worth to Rania, get her to leave Bulstan for me. And what better incentive to leave Bulstan than to have something better to go to." He waved his hand over the map, and Adanek lit up in blue. Then, a tiny island in the shape of a star lit up, and gold dots started to stream out of it.

"Rommy, how did you ..." The blood rushed in her ears, sounding as if she were falling into a violent ocean during a storm. As she watched, the golden dots flooded the whole world.

"You marrying Elric just made this all the easier. It's like you were reading my mind," Rommy said. He waved his other hand over the map again, and little blue figures started to pour out of Adanek. They moved south, mixed with the golden creatures, and suddenly the kingdom to the south of Adanek turned blue. Then, the golden creatures and blue figures doubled and moved east and west, toward Cerisa.

"Rommy, what is all this?" Thali asked. Her throat was dry. She couldn't believe her eyes. Surely she was mistaking his intent.

"It's my plan to take over the world, for you and me and Rania," Rommy said. He didn't take his gaze away from the map as he spoke, so he didn't see the emotion Thali was trying to choke down. His eyes glistened as he watched his plan unfold on the table.

"*You* made me open the portal," Thali whispered disbelievingly.

"This is what we were meant to do, Rou. You and me. You raise the army of magical creatures, and we take over the world. We don't even need soldiers eventually. Look," Rommy said. He touched the northeastern islands, and her tiny figurine flew there and called the creatures already there. The magical creatures filled all the lands. "You can control them for us. We only need to take over a few key kingdoms, and the others will bend a knee."

Thali looked at him. How was this person her sweet brother? She swallowed. The rushing sounds came back, and she stumbled as she stepped backward. Her foot caught on the rug, and she started to fall backward. Rommy was there immediately, holding her arm so she wouldn't fall. His instinctive reactions were still the same. But what of his mind? "Rommy, what happened? What made you want to do all this?" Thali asked. It felt like her brother had been replaced with a dangerous, strange animal.

"Rania. I wanted to marry Rania. Mupto rejected me, said I didn't have enough to offer and Rania was not one for ocean travel. I knew then I needed an empire. Now I'll have one. Rania will join you and me, and together, we'll have an empire."

"And Elric," Thali said.

"Oh, of course, and Elric," he said. But he didn't meet her gaze. He just stared at the table. His thumb rubbed his fingers, almost tucking under and Thali knew there were things he wasn't saying.

She tried to swallow, but it wasn't easy. She backed up and sat in a chair.

"I know, it's a lot to take in, but you're going to be an empress."

"I thought Rania would be the empress," Thali said.

"We'll have the whole world. We'll split it so you can have half, and Rania and I will have half, just like with our dumplings."

"What about Bulstan?"

"I was going to leave that for Tariq. Rania will probably want to keep it as a summer home, anyway," Rommy said.

Thali's ears started ringing.

"What do you think?" Rommy asked.

"I think it's a lot to take in," Thali said carefully. She suddenly wanted to be away, far away from her brother. She didn't even know him anymore. But she knew she would have to watch her words. "I think ... I think I'm going to be sick," Thali said, and she rushed out of the room and down the hall. She knew she wasn't going to make it to her rooms, so she ran outside and spewed into a bush. She placed her hand on a tree trunk. The solidness of the tree calmed her and grounded her. The world slowly stopped spinning and then Rommy was there, holding a handkerchief out. She took it without thinking. He was always there for her. Whatever she needed, he gave her. She loved him. He had been her brother, her confidant, her protector for so long that she couldn't reconcile him with that person who wanted to take over the world. What was she going to do now?

Chapter Thirty-Seven
Tilton

TILTON BLINKED. HE STOOD in a hallway, but he wasn't sure why he was there. Lately he'd been finding himself in places he didn't remember going to and running on autopilot for far too long. He never found himself somewhere he shouldn't be when he became aware again, but that didn't really say much. Tilton shook his head and walked back to Thali's apartments. He, Mia, Daylor, and a few guards were the only ones repainting and redecorating as they didn't want it to be obvious that Thali was still missing, so he had to pull his weight.

It was early evening when Tilton walked into Thali's rooms this time. He wanted to check on the progress and make a list of the tasks they had left to do before tomorrow. He was hoping they would be done the project by the end of the next week. He pushed Thali's office door open and saw candles spread out everywhere.

Daylor rose from his chair. "Hello, my love."

Tilton looked around, confused and a little worried that someone would see. "What is all this?"

"You've been working so hard lately, I thought I'd do something special," Daylor said. He led Tilton to a chair and sat him down at the new table they'd chosen for Thali. It was round and solid cherrywood, but Daylor had put a cloth over it. "I didn't want to accidentally scuff it or get wax on it," he said.

Tilton thought it was an incredibly sweet gesture. As Daylor sat down, Tilton looked around. There was no food on the table. But just then, Mia swept into the room wearing a cute apron and placed a dish down between them. She smiled extra big, and Tilton wondered why.

"It's a great time of the month," Mia said as she winked at Tilton.

"You're ... relieved then?" Tilton asked.

Mia nodded. "You two make the cutest couple, by the way."

"How did you know?" Tilton asked.

"Oh honey, I've known since the second year of school," Mia said, and she sashayed back out of the room.

"Did you know she knew?" Tilton asked.

Daylor looked down. "Do you remember when we were in school, and I took Mia to the ball? And then afterward she and I weren't together suddenly?"

Tilton nodded.

Daylor continued. "She simply said she wasn't interested and then left me alone rather suddenly after the ball. It was odd, but to be honest, I was relieved. One day a few weeks later, she cornered me, told me that I should go after my heart's desire because I was lucky to have found someone I love."

"She knew? Even then?"

"Yes, she knew," Mia said as she swished back into the room. "You two were always together, and I saw the way he looked at you when you were dancing with Thali. You glanced back at him and in that moment, I knew." She presented a couple of dishes of roast meat with vegetables though they hadn't even touched the previous dish yet.

"And you're ... you're all right with it?" Tilton asked. He felt terrible for saying it out loud. He hated himself for it, and for his cowardice.

"I'll say the same thing as before. You two are lucky to have found your other half out of everyone in the whole wide world. If anything, I feel envious," Mia said.

"You don't think ... well, less of us ... because we're both men?" Tilton asked. He felt gross saying it, but he had to know.

Mia put her hand on his shoulder. "No. Love of all kinds is beautiful. In some cultures, it's preferred."

"Really?" Tilton asked.

"You should ask Thali about it. She knows better than I do. I just remember her telling me about it a long time ago," Mia said. She turned to leave.

"So ... you think Thali would be all right with it, with us?" Tilton asked.

"Honey, Thali would love it—if she doesn't already know," Mia said.

"Personally, I assumed that since she's so oblivious to her own romantic interests that she wouldn't pick up on other people's," Daylor added. His cheeks were red.

Tilton felt terrible for saying some of his thoughts out loud, but this, this had been important. And it made him feel better that Daylor had been unsure of Thali's stance, too.

"She's oblivious when it comes to herself, yes, but she's very perceptive when it comes to other people. Honestly, she probably assumes everyone knows," Mia replied on her way out. "Eat before it gets cold. Talk after."

Tilton and Daylor were alone again. Tilton cut into his meat and stuffed the food into his mouth. Food was definitely better when you lived in the palace. He'd never eaten as well at home as he had at school and here. So many vegetables and roasted meats. He was almost done eating when he noticed Daylor sneaking peeks at him. "Daylor, I'm sorry. I ... I had to know," Tilton said as he rested one hand over the other in his lap.

"It's all right," Daylor said. He opened his mouth and then closed it. Then he did it again.

"It can't be worse than the things I just said." Tilton stared at his hands, at Daylor's hand reaching across the table seeking his own.

"Are you in love with Elric?" Daylor asked suddenly.

"What?" Tilton looked up in surprise.

"I've ... I've seen you tailing him. A lot. And often. The heart wants what it wants. I know that Mia just said all those nice things, but I can't help but notice you've pulled away from me. I know, this is a weird conversation to have when I've set all this up, and I don't want to taint it. But I have to know. It's been killing me."

"No," Tilton said. He looked straight into Daylor's eyes. "I love you. No one else, and certainly not Elric. He's Thali's husband."

"I know, but again, the heart wants what it wants, whether it can have it or not. So if you're not in love with him, why have you been following him like a puppy dog?" Daylor asked.

"I ... I don't know..." Tilton said. He tried to think of how often he'd been in Elric's presence lately.

Mia came out then with dessert, cleared their plates, and left without a word.

"Daylor ... I've been having these strange—" Tilton started.

The door burst open, and Tilton and Daylor jumped up at the same time as Elric burst into the room. He stopped and looked around frantically. Then he looked confused. "I saw the flickering light under the door ... and I thought for a moment she'd come back." Elric's gaze swept the room. He looked frantic, and Tilton's heart leaped for him.

"Sorry, Elric, she's not here," Mia said as she came back.

Elric looked around again, taking in the scene anew. "Oh, I'm sorry to have burst in." He tilted his head a bit and smiled. "I love that you all spend time together. You're welcome to use lanterns, though. Surely it gives off more light than a dozen candles."

It dawned on Tilton that Elric didn't realize this was a romantic dinner.

"I'm sorry we're using Thali's rooms," Mia said, holding another plate of dessert.

"Oh no, don't worry about that," Elric said. "No one else is using them right now, and you've all worked so hard lately. Please use them at will."

"Thank you," Mia said.

"I'll leave you to it, though. Have a lovely night," Elric said as he turned and left.

When Tilton turned back around, Daylor's jaw was clenched.

"I'm sure it was an honest mistake," Mia said before melting back into the other room.

"There are no laws against us being together. I'm sure he just didn't think anything of it, especially with Mia here," Tilton said. He had to calm Daylor down.

"It's awfully insensitive of him to make assumptions," Daylor said.

Tilton thought Daylor was making his own assumptions and wondered if it was partly because he was still jealous. "Hey," he said, moving closer to Daylor. He looked down and saw the dessert Mia had put on the table. He took a piece of chocolate-dipped fruit and sat in Daylor's lap. Daylor lowered his head and loosened his jaw. Tilton put the strawberry to Daylor's lips, and Daylor opened his mouth and took a bite. Tilton tossed the end of the strawberry over his shoulder and touched his lips to Daylor's. Daylor's muscles released their tension as their lips and tongues explored each other. Tilton felt a rush of fire consume his body and he let himself burn.

Chapter Thirty-Eight
Mia

MIA WAS UPSET AS she refolded the freshly laundered bedsheets and put them away in a nice stack in Thali's closet. Elric's timing couldn't have been worse for poor Tilton and Daylor. She had tried not to listen in but couldn't help but hear the difficulties they were having. If Thali were here, she'd fix this. She'd go right up to Elric and tell him how insensitive that had all been, then probably pay for their wedding and start some kind of initiative to help others in the same situation.

"I'll add it to the list," Mia said. She had a running list of things to tell Thali that was just getting longer and longer. It made a distant memory float up.

"You've been away for so long. I missed you so much and I can't even remember all the things I have to tell you!" Eight-year-old Mia hugged eight-year-old Thali until she couldn't breathe.

"I missed you too!" Thali said when Mia finally let her go. "I'll help you remember, and then next time, you could write a list so we can talk about each one," Thali said.

Mia looked at the ground. "I don't have parchment and quills, or ink. There's some in the shop, but that's just for my mama's use."

"Come," Thali said. They strolled slowly home from the dock as Mia filled her in on all that had happened while Thali was away. When Mia was done, Thali asked about certain people that she'd not heard about. Mia always felt special because she felt like she was a spy for Thali sometimes, listening in at the shops for all the newest gossip.

When they finally reached Thali's house, Mia was out of breath from all her talking, so they sat by the koi pond and Thali fetched them some water. They drank it, then ate the fruit sitting at the bottom of the water glasses while Mia caught her breath. Then, Thali led Mia to her rooms and pointed to a stack of books with blank pages. "Pick one."

"Any of them?"

"Whichever one you like best," Thali said.

"Oh ..." Mia said. She moved a few around and looked at them. She picked one that was so brightly colored, it almost shimmered.

"And here," Thali said. She got a quill and ink from a drawer and gave them to Mia. "Now you have the supplies to make a list or write me or whatever." She looked around as if she was wondering if there was something she was forgetting.

"Thank you," Mia said.

Thali shrugged. "It's not getting any use just sitting here, so you might as well use it."

They spent the rest of the day at Thali's house, and Mia took the writing materials home after she dined with Thali's family. Forever after that, Thali always included new blank books, parchment, quills, and inks—sometimes in fun colors—as part of her birthday gift to Mia.

There was one book exceptionally special to Mia. It was covered in pink and yellow silk. She had never used it until recently when she had gained her new station at the palace with Thali. Now, it held all her learnings about her new job. She'd drawn a map of the palace and made lists of tasks that needed to be done and when. It was practically a guidebook for Thali's lady-in-waiting.

Mia closed the pink-and-yellow silk notebook and ran her fingertips over it. Sometimes, the softness of the silk calmed her nerves like a cool balm. She had needed to tell herself more and more often that Thali would be okay. Her best friend always came back from her trips. Mia wasn't doubtful of that. Plus, Rommy would ensure it. But she wasn't sure if Thali would come back the same person—or a person she could still love. Mia had never said anything out loud, but the last time Rommy had been here, he had seemed different, as if a darkness had settled in him that hadn't been there before. She hoped the same darkness wasn't in Thali when she returned. Thali might not emit the sunshine that Elric always seemed to exude, but she was always sunshine adjacent.

Mia shook her head and made some notes on the sheaf of parchment next to her book. She always made a list at the beginning of the week of the tasks and duties she had to accomplish. Then, she would pin it to the wall in Thali's closet, where she had set up her workspace. Every day, she checked them off as she went, moving the completed tasks to a pile on her desk. Since Thali had left, Mia's tasks were slightly different, so she'd made two piles of completed tasks. One was from when she and Thali had arrived at the palace and life had been normal, and the second pile was for when Thali had disappeared and Mia's duties had been modified. The stack representing the time when Thali was gone was slowly growing larger and larger, making Mia wonder if it would grow taller than the first pile.

Chapter Thirty-Nine
Tariq

"WHAT IS THE MEANING of all this, Father?" Tariq asked. He and Bree had just done the impossible and found the bear-man. The bear-man could help them find Thali and navigate this new world they faced. But now, as they left the cave, Tariq and Bree faced dozens of royal guards on the beach. Tariq looked around at his friends and colleagues. For the second time this week he was facing them, not standing with them.

His father's face softened for a moment, and Mupto approached them. Tariq had already placed himself in front of Ambrene. Tobias, who was trying to melt back into the cave he'd just come out of, was behind her.

"Father, what is all this?" Tariq asked.

His father looked wistfully at him. "Son, you're opening wounds that were never meant to be reopened," he said.

"And this, bringing the whole army to guard against me, that is your answer?"

"No, son, the army is here to protect you. The bear-man, he is more dangerous than you think," Mupto said.

"He's been living in a cave, hiding, for centuries. We didn't force him out. He came out of his own free will to help us, and I have promised to treat him fairly. Then, you greet us with all this?" Tariq motioned at the army.

"We will treat him fairly, but this *is* fair. These soldiers are here as much for his protection as yours. They will protect you from him and him from outside harm. I will welcome him no other way."

"And I suppose you'll put him in the stables to sleep?" Tariq asked.

"He will occupy the guest house on palace grounds."

"Oh great, even farther away than the stables." Tariq rolled his eyes.

"These are still my lands, Tariquin. My lands, my rules," Mupto said.

Tariq now knew he better shut his mouth soon. If his father was using his full name, it meant he was reaching his limit.

"But why, Father? What scares you so much?" Tariq asked.

"He is a bear. And he has magic. We don't know what he can do," Mupto explained.

Tariq tried one last time. "He's been living here in seclusion for so long. If he really wanted power, wouldn't he have just taken it? He's had the time to do so."

"Perhaps. But perhaps this is the game." Mupto looked over his shoulder. "We should return soon if we want to get back before it gets dark."

Tariq nodded and turned to the bear-man. But the guards all moved like an ocean wave and surrounded Tobias. However, Bree had anticipated them and already taken the bear-man's arm, whether to protect him or ensure he didn't run, Tariq couldn't say. He grinned.

"I am walking with this gentleman here. You may lead the way," she said to the guards.

"I'm sorry about this," Tariq said through a couple guards. There was a wall two guards thick between him and Bree and Tobias.

"It's all right. It's an honor to escort this lady home," Tobias said. He behaved like a generous gentleman.

Tariq was surprised that so much time in isolation had not affected the bear-man's manners and was glad that the bear-man hadn't run off deep into the cave when they'd emerged to see so many soldiers.

Tariq kept a close eye on Bree and Tobias all the way back, not completely trusting either Tobias or his father. When they arrived at the palace, Tariq nodded to Tobias and let Bree make sure he was comfortable and settled in. He went to his father's private office to have a discussion with him.

He knocked on the door, and when he heard his father say, "Come in, Tariq," he knew that his father would have tea and cakes beside the roaring fire. It had been chilly on the last stretch of the trek home, made much longer since they hadn't been on horseback this time.

"Father," Tariq said as he looked around the room and sat down.

"Son," Mupto replied, cracking a grin.

"Father, what is going on? Why would you treat someone who has come out of isolation—originally caused by our ancestors at that—so poorly? He is our guest."

"He has magic. He's not like us. You don't know what his true motivations are or what he really wants," Mupto said.

Tariq shook his head. He could not believe the words coming from his father's mouth. "I have magic, Bree has magic, and you've never felt like that about us. What about Routhalia? She has infinitely more magic and power than the rest of us combined." Tariq crossed his ankle over his knee as he took a cup of hot tea in his hands.

"It is not the same. He is different."

"Much like we are different from the rest of the world?" Tariq asked.

"Yes and no. We are the same as the humans of the rest of the world, even with our different skin color. He doesn't even resemble a person. He's a creature, and we haven't been able to trust creatures thus far."

"He is a creature, but that does not mean he does not act honorably."

"True, but it also does not mean that he *will* act honorably." Mupto crossed his ankle over his knee just as son had and sipped his tea.

"By ostracizing him and treating him poorly, you give him reason to dislike and to resent." Tariq placed a hand on his knee. He hoped he looked supplicating.

"We will treat him well and fairly but with caution," Mupto said. He imitated Tariq with his hand placement. Tariq realized this was the middle ground. His father would not see things as Tariq did, and he would not bend either, so this was the compromise.

Tariq put his cup down and brought his hands together. "We agree to disagree then." He bowed his head over his hands, and Mupto did the same.

"He will stay in the guest house then and be escorted by four—"

"Two," Tariq interjected.

Mupto swallowed. "Fine, two guards at all times when out of his room. You and Bree will be the only two visitors allowed, and the door must stay open during your visits for safety."

"I will take one guard with me or Ambrene into the room for safety, but the door will be closed if Tobias wishes it," Tariq said. He flipped one hand palm down on the knee closest to his father.

"That is settled then," Mupto said, flipping his own hand palm down.

Tariq wondered if he'd been too easy on his father, if there was something he was missing. "You break bread with him twice a week," he added.

"How often do you plan to dine with a bear?" Mupto asked.

"Once a day at least. You're welcome to join us."

"Can the bear-man use utensils?" Mupto asked.

"We rarely use utensils to dine, and we've accommodated other guests who do not understand our customs," Tariq replied.

Mupto's eyes narrowed, and he turned his other hand over so it was palm down on his knee before continuing. "I will promise two meals a week and attempt more."

Tariq nodded and turned his other hand, so both were now palm down. Both men were still for a minute, waiting for the ancient magic of a Bulstani deal reached and settled to fall over them. When it did, Tariq felt a weight descending upon his shoulders like a heavy blanket. It pressed down on him, and when he saw that his father's shoulders did not budge with the pressure, Tariq was determined to keep his straight, too. Tariq started to clench his teeth with the pressure, and then it finally lifted. He felt a patch of skin on his leg, just above his right knee, warm and change color. It was just a small square of slightly darkened skin. His father would have an identical square. Their skin would return to their original coloring once the deal had been completed, but now they were bound to each other by it.

His father stood before Tariq did, and Tariq lowered his head in a nod.

"Will I see you for supper this evening?" Mupto asked his son.

"If Tobias is invited, yes," he said.

Mupto nodded and left.

Tariq followed moments later. He was convinced that Tobias would do well here. Tariq himself would make sure of it. He strode down the hallway, out of the palace, and to the guest house, where four guards stood. He swallowed to contain his anger and then nodded at his personal guard to stay outside. His father had either not sent the order or it had yet to reach the guards. Waving for one guard to follow him, he opened the door and saw Bree rearranging some flowers on the table. There was no bear-man in sight. His heart did a flip as he wondered if Tobias had changed his mind and decided they weren't worth it.

"He's in the bathing room, says he hasn't had a proper bath in decades," Bree said.

"Reminds me of Thali," Tariq said.

"There's a reason I try to wait until *after* Thali's had her bath before I see her whenever she arrives for a visit." Bree grinned as she turned around to kiss Tariq on the lips.

"Thank you," Tariq whispered on her lips.

"Whatever for?" she asked.

"You handled the situation beautifully." Tariq combed her hair with his hands, getting them caught in the curls. He gently extracted his hands so as not to pull on her hair.

"You did, too." She kissed his nose.

"Maybe I should have stayed in the cave," Tobias said as he entered, a large cloth wrapped around his bottom half. Human feet peeked out the bottom as he approached them. "Yes, prince, my bottom half is human, though perhaps a bit hairier than most," he said.

"There are trousers in the bottom drawers in your bedchamber," Bree said without turning around.

"Thank you," he said, turning back to the bed chamber.

Bree smiled and Tariq kissed the corner of her mouth. He held onto her hand but guided her to the couch. His own guard was posted just inside the sitting room, looking out the window.

The guard opened the door when a knock sounded, and a kitchen helper came in. She set down three teapots and more cakes and pastries, along with slices of cured meats and fruits.

"Thank you," Bree said.

The girl left after a quick curtsy.

"You stay out of the food. These are for our guest," Bree said as she gently smacked Tariq's hand away. He pouted.

Tobias walked in. "Am I interrupting something again?"

"Not at all. Please join us, Tobias. Refreshments have arrived." Bree set about pouring tea for him and Tariq.

Tariq in turn poured Bree's tea and watched as casually as he could as the bear-man picked up the delicate cup with his furry paws and gently sipped his tea.

"We have more dexterity than the average bear. That's the human side." Tobias turned to Tariq and pointed his outermost digit out and up for effect like a human dandy would.

"I apologize for my rudeness," Tariq said.

"It's not a problem. I welcome the curiosity, and you humans are always so curious," he said. He gently picked up a sandwich and popped it into his mouth. But after watching Bree put one on a plate before taking a bite, he took a plate and stacked it with pastries and sandwiches, bringing the plate to his lap.

"What do you know of Etciel?" Tariq asked.

Tobias's eyes narrowed. He glanced outside in the direction of the portal. "Why do you ask of such a place?"

Tariq looked at Bree, who nodded as she looked at him and said, "You might as well."

"All right," Tariq began. "The short version is that my best friend was tricked into opening a portal—not ours but the one to Etciel. She inadvertently released magical creatures back into our world. Her brother is enslaved to dragon royalty, and she journeyed to Etciel to learn how to control her own magic. But we really need to get her back."

Tobias froze with a pastry inches from his mouth, blinked, then asked, "Does she want to come back?"

"I don't know, but I want to go there and ask her," Tariq said.

"You said her brother was enslaved by dragons?" Tobias put the plate back on the table and furrowed his brow.

"Yes," Tariq and Bree replied together.

"That is false. Dragons are not allowed to enslave anyone. It is dragon law."

"Then ... then there's something else going on, but her brother at least works for them. He says he's not allowed to—or can't—stay in this world for long," Tariq said, wondering why Rommy was lying.

"Interesting," Tobias said. Bree and Tariq waited for him to elaborate, but he kept quiet.

"What can we do for you in return, Tobias?" Bree asked.

Tariq was a little surprised by her boldness.

Tobias looked at her for a long moment, and to her credit, she held her head high and matched his stare. "I would like a seat at this court, some land, and a home, not hidden away, but recognized. I would like to join your community," he said.

Bree nodded. "Deal."

"I'm not sure we can—" Tariq said.

"You are the crown prince. This you can do, without your father's approval," Bree said.

Tariq nodded. He would do it then. "We'll have to take it slow, but we will bring you into the community."

"I don't expect to live here for free. I think I have a lot to offer," Tobias added. "Your weapons training, for example."

"Oh?" Tariq's interest was piqued.

"You are good warriors, yes, but I have to say you've gotten a little sloppy since I taught your people." Tobias crossed his arms.

Tariq was not at all surprised that Tobias had watched their training. When you had that much time and were that stealthy, he supposed you learned how to watch everything with no one knowing. *Though a bear-man might stick out a little*, Tariq thought, wondering if Tobias could become invisible.

As if reading Tariq's mind, he said, "And I'm very good at reading people. I do not have the power of invisibility, but I can stay still for a very long time." Tobias piled six fish sandwiches on his plate and brought it to his mouth. He ate each with a single bite, popping all six in his mouth like grapes before needing to chew and swallow.

CHAPTER FORTY
Garen

G AREN SAT LISTENING TO his captains at his usual table in his tavern as they discussed what to do with shadow creatures on the loose.

"We should go after them," Ilya said. He had a soft spot for Ella and the brothel.

Sesda disagreed. "We know what to look for, and they likely won't come back. So why spend our time chasing them about when there's real danger to concern ourselves with? What if something else gets through the barrier?"

Fletch and Garen remained silent as his captains debated.

"Time to vote," Garen finally said. He looked around. They'd been discussing this for an hour. "Who wants to go after them?" Two hands went up, including Fletch's. "Who wants to leave them be?" Two hands went up this time, too. He would be the tiebreaker.

"They'll be on everyone's minds until they're found and captured, boss. Might as well direct the energy that way and get them gone," Fletch said.

"Why waste our energy when they're obviously going to stay away? You said it yourself. We know what to expect from them and what to do about them," Ella argued.

Garen was surprised that Ella didn't want to go after them. He'd seen more women from the brothel in the tavern lately, taking time off. He'd guessed they were afraid of the shadow creatures. That settled it for him. "We go after them," he said. "Tomorrow night, we start our hunt."

Everyone nodded at that. Once he had made his mind up and broken the tie, everyone was on board. They left the tavern then without a word. Even if some disagreed, they knew what they had to do. Garen put his cloak on and left the tavern out the back. He would visit Foxall and find out what needed to be done to find the things or draw them in.

Strangely, he didn't mind the bell at the top of the door that announced his arrival. He walked into the apothecary's shop amid the bottles and vials and overflowing barrels. The walls—what little of the walls you could see—were a dark purple-blue that seemed to change and shift as your gaze traveled. Most, though, were covered in tall wooden cabinets, all with grids of tiny drawers. There must have been hundreds of drawers in each cabinet. Almost all the drawers were a dark gray, but one set looked like they were being repainted a light gray.

"Gives it a brighter look, don't you think?" Foxall said from the counter.

Garen nodded. "We plan to go after the shadow creatures. Can we set a trap to entice them to show themselves somehow?"

Foxall whistled. It was a little off key, but then Garen remembered he was a dragon in human form, so there was bound to be eccentricities. "You can take the one of its kind we have and flash it around, threaten its life. The others will probably come to you then," Foxall said. "They will be angry though, so move quickly and attack quietly. Your people best be ready—oh, and they could use this ..." he said as he disappeared into the back. When he emerged, he held a ladder. It looked freshly painted white. "I was priming it in the back, but no worries. It's almost dry." He placed it on the rail in front of the cabinets, then climbed up, leaving footprints where his feet lifted the paint off. Foxall slid the ladder to the middle cabinet. He started looking in the various drawers, humming and hawing before finally shouting, "Aha! Here it is!" He shimmied down the ladder and then turned his palm up. A round disk in his hand sprang open to reveal a net of the finest silver filigree. "This is enough net to cover the town square. Your people will need to work together to catch them under the net. Then I can bottle them or eat them."

Garen swallowed and nodded. He'd forgotten that Foxall wanted to eat them.

"You should keep the square dark but carry torches ready to light. They will be stunned by sudden light. If you all light torches at the same time, they will be stunned enough that you can throw the net over them," Foxall said.

"Will we need to uncork the vial the other one is in?" Garen asked.

"No. Definitely don't do that. And keep the vial in the double pouch I'll give you. Now that I think about it, I think I'll go retrieve it now. We don't want it hearing or seeing anything to warn the others." He turned and rummaged in another drawer before pulling out a leather pouch.

Garen nodded. He followed Foxall to the opposite wall in his shop. There, Foxall opened various drawers until he pulled a familiar pouch from one. He opened it, showing Garen the vial for a moment before stuffing it back into the pouch. Then he slid that pouch into the other one.

"There," Foxall said as he tucked the package into an inner pocket.

The prince of thieves, for his part, went to tell his captains of the plan. They spent the next day gathering torches and setting them up in the square as the sun started to set.

That done, Garen stood in the square and looked around. All his people were in place. They were just missing Foxall now, and he had the bait. It was getting dark quickly, and the apothecary was to have arrived before the sun set. Worried, Garen himself went to the apothecary's shop. Knowing Foxall, he had probably forgotten the time.

When the bell dinged over the door, Garen stepped in and froze to let his eyes adjust. Then, he marched in, went right into the back, and found his brother and Foxall leaning over a small, vined plant.

"What is this?" Garen asked.

Joren looked up. "Why hello, brother, it's good to see you too. Don't mind me. I'm just contacting the world your beloved is trapped in on your behalf."

Garen's heart leapt as he stared at the plant.

"I was able to open the smallest of portals. Even after draining himself for weeks keeping the barrier in place, Alexius sent me enough magic to help me open a tiny gate for Joren to snake a vine through," Foxall explained. He tapped the table where tiny black gems were spilled around the plant.

"She wants to come back," Joren said. He was focused on the plant, sweat dripping down the sides of his face and leaving streaks through his face paint.

"Hmm ... if she wants to come back, then that will make this considerably easier," Foxall said.

"Is she all right?" Garen asked. His throat was parched as he continued to stare at the plant. He recognized Thali's handwriting on its broad leaves as the vine scrawled across the table.

Brother not himself.

Need to come home.

Joren wrote on another leaf with the pointed nail of his index finger.

Garen here too.

The reply came on another leaf.

I'm all right. Safe.

The vise around Garen's heart loosened a little, but not a lot.

The bells on the door signaled that someone else had walked into the shop. Garen wanted to yell at them to go away, but he remembered why he had come.

Before he could remind Foxall of the trap, the apothecary forestalled him. "I have a way to get her out, but she will need a guide, someone she trusts."

"Send for Elric," Garen said.

Joren looked at him incredulously.

"Elric left the city today, boss," said Fletch from behind him.

Garen looked at Fletch, then at Joren. Could he trust his brother with this?

"I have to hold the connection," Joren said. He examined his nails as if he was bored.

"Boss. You need to go. She's our princess too. We'll handle the trap," Fletch said.

Garen managed a tight smile for Fletch. The kid was too noble for his own good.

"It's true," Ella added as she popped her head in the back of the shop.

Garen spun around to look at her, and at her nod, strode to the front door where he found all his captains.

"You go bring her back. We've got this handled," Ella said.

Ilya agreed. "Garen, she's our princess too. We want her back almost as badly as you do. And if you go, we know she'll make it back."

Garen's heart expanded with pride. He was so proud of his family. "Let's bring her back then."

Foxall appeared beside him. To Garen's amazement, the dragon stepped to the side, then stepped outside himself. There were now two Foxalls, one more translucent than the other. "What?" Foxall shrugged. "This way I can be in two places at once, though someone else will have to hold the pouch. I'm more of a mind than a body right now. My shadow self can help trap the creature and keep the little portal open, but I can't go to Etciel. Thali doesn't know me." Foxall pointed to the thick pouch on the counter and Fletch took it. "My other self will join you once Garen's journey is underway," Foxall told the captains as the transparent Foxall left with them.

"Good luck," Garen said, though he knew they wouldn't need it. He trusted his family.

"All right. Let's get started," the more solid Foxall said as he dashed around the shop collecting different ingredients.

That done, they headed back to the plant. There, Joren handed Garen a blank leaf on the vine and leaned away as if suddenly very interested in the wall.

Garen stared at the leaf for a long time before writing anything.

Coming for you. –G

That was all he wrote. He had to admit, it was tougher to write with his fingernail than it was with a quill.

There was no response for some time, and Garen stared at the plant, waiting for a leaf to start changing to show she'd replied.

The leaves crumpled then, and Garen's heart leaped into his throat.

"They were covered or suffocated or something. Someone must have walked into the room," Joren said. He shrank the leaves until they were just tiny, barely noticeable pieces.

"Have we lost the connection?" Garen asked.

"No. Just made it smaller, more discreet," Joren said.

Foxall was dumping things into a bucket. Then he stood with his hands on his hips. "Now, we just have to wait for Alexius."

The bell chimed then. Moments later Alexius appeared in the shop's rear.

"Good timing, my boy," Foxall said. Alexius nodded at Garen, glanced at the plant and Joren, then helped Foxall carry the bucket over to the plant.

"Can Alexius go?" Garen asked.

"No." Foxall and Alexius said at the same time.

Foxall explained. "He has to maintain the barrier here, or we'll have madness descend upon us." With that, he dumped the contents of the bucket on the plant.

"Why don't *you* want to go?" Joren asked.

"I don't know if she wants to see me," Garen said. "What if she won't come back with me because it's me?"

"Thali's not an idiot. She'll come back with you. She just said so," Joren said.

Garen glanced worriedly at Alexius, who was concentrating on the plant. Suddenly, a door started to emerge beside the plant.

"Ohh ... that tickles," Joren said as he shimmied his shoulders. Everyone ignored him.

"Hold onto the plant all the way there and all the way back," Alexius instructed. "It will guide you to her, then back here. Do no stray and do not let go. You have five minutes, our time," Alexius said.

Garen nodded.

"Good luck, my boy. See you when you return," Foxall said, turning and leaving, for his part here was done. He locked the front door on his way out, and at that, Garen took a deep breath and stepped through the shimmering doorway.

It was like walking through pudding. He tried to take a small breath and felt his lungs fill, so that was good. He put one foot in front of the other, always keeping two hands on the plant. It felt like he had to fight for each step, like he was walking through quicksand. Garen kept pushing though. He was starting to lose his sense of direction and orientation when finally he reached solid ground that didn't give like the pudding he'd been walking through for what felt like ages.

He opened his eyes and saw Thali standing there. His heart leaped. She had her back to him and was speaking to a tall man whose blue hair was neatly tied back at the nape of his neck. His gaze slid to Garen for a moment, but he did not react, just continued talking, though Garen could not hear anything.

He looked around him. The stillness of the air around him told him not to move. He must be concealed in some way. Then, he saw the figure in the chair next to the tall man who reminded him in some ways of Alexius, only much older. It was Thali's brother, Rommy. So that was why she had minimized the connection. Rommy sat there, talking and smiling. Garen was forced to read his lips to know what he was saying.

"Come on, Rou. Are you sure you don't want to play just one game?" Rommy asked.

When Thali turned to reply, Garen could see her lips. "No, that's all right, Rommy," she said. "I'm tired. Xerus has me training really hard, and I need to rest for tomorrow's training."

Rommy gave a fake pout before rising. "Well, all right then. If you must. I suppose it's a good thing, for all our benefits. The stronger you are, the easier it will be. I suppose I have paperwork anyway, eh, Xer?"

"Yes, there are plans to be made," the blue-haired man said.

Rommy left then as Xer held the door open for him. Alexius's brother left too, but before he closed the door, he glanced at Garen.

Prepare for war, said a voice in his head. Then the man was gone. Thali stared at the door, remaining frozen for a full five seconds. Garen was starting to worry that she didn't want to see him, but then she turned around and his heart expanded in his chest and burst. She looked healthy and well, glowing even.

"Garen," she breathed. She hurled herself into his arms and started to cry. He wrapped his arm around her. "We have to go," he said as gently as he could. He didn't know when she would be missed, but he was sure it would be soon. And they might be able to catch up to him.

Thali nodded.

Despite the soaked shirt, Garen kept his arm around her, supporting her. "Is there anything you need to bring?" he asked.

Thali reached around, hanging onto Garen with one arm, and grabbed a blue gem as big and round as an orange. She put the stone in her pocket, though it did not bulge. Surprisingly, she turned her face into his chest and nodded. He felt her curling up against him and wondered what had happened here. But for now, they had to get out of here, so he readjusted her in his arms as she tucked her head into the space between his chin and chest just like she used to.

With one hand on the vine, Garen walked back into the pudding. There, he swallowed. He had missed her so much. As he pushed through the pudding, he wondered what would happen if he stopped, if he let go of the vine. Would they be able to live in this in-between place forever?

"What if we let go? Could we stay here forever?" Thali asked, sensing his thoughts as always. Garen wanted to so badly. Living in pudding would be worth it if he was with her.

Chapter Forty-One
Thali

THALI COULDN'T TELL IF her heart was breaking or melting. What was Rommy thinking? Did he really think taking over the whole world was feasible or reasonable? Or necessary? How was it that he'd never mentioned it before? Part of her refused to believe it, and part of her was breaking because of it. Her whole world was broken. How could she love Elric but also love Garen enough to melt into this little puddle with him. He had picked her up and carried her, reading her mind. Without more than a look, he'd felt her crumbling and now held her together, squeezing her tight, and she knew she could be all right. So what if they left the world to fall apart and stayed here instead? Weren't they entitled to happiness and love, too?

As Garen carried her, she felt the weight of this world on them. The air, the ground, were thick and heavy, and Thali pushed her threads out around them to help clear the way as he pushed through with each step. It barely took a drop of her magical energy. She felt Garen's chest relax as the weight eased, and he placed his cheek on her head as he continued walking.

Thali used her magic to follow Garen's muscled shoulder down his arm to the hand that held on to the plant they followed.

"What if we let go? Could we stay here forever?" Thali asked. She felt Garen's throat bob. He'd been thinking it too then. She smiled as she felt a laugh rumble in his chest.

"Do you really want to live in pudding?" Garen asked her.

She smiled against his throat, and she felt him smile in response. "With you, yes."

Garen took a few more steps, though Thali noticed he had slowed. "But could you really live knowing the world was in trouble? Your family? Your friends?" he asked.

Thali buried her face in his neck. "I wish I could."

Garen wrapped more of himself around her. "Me too."

Thali didn't want to say anything else. She was already starting to feel the shame of her lack of loyalty to Elric, of wanting another man. Though strangely, she didn't feel as guilty as she thought she should.

Thali could feel warmth as they neared the end of the vine.

Garen stopped for a moment, right before the doorway. "Thali, I won't ever stop loving you. I promise to find you in every lifetime and make it up to you. I'm sorry this is your burden to bear." He pressed a kiss to her forehead and stepped through the doorway.

Thali squeezed her eyes and took in one more deep breath, savoring this last moment with Garen. Then, she felt something strange on the other side. Garen put her back down on her own feet, and Thali stepped beyond Joren, nodding her thanks to him. She followed the strange feeling—part vibration, part buzzing. Once in the front of the apothecary's shop, she caught sight of the magical creature hiding in one of her dearest friends.

CHAPTER FORTY-TWO
Tilton

Come to the town square tonight, before sunset.
–F

That was all the note had said. Tilton would be lying if he said that he wasn't a little apprehensive about going, and he was glad that it had been so easy to convince Daylor to go with him. Tilton had kept a line of communication open with a man he'd had a brief dalliance with in school. The note was his reply to the message Tilton had sent saying that Elric had left the city to follow a lead about a gate's location. According to Avery as she had rushed to prepare him, Elric had insisted he wanted to go himself.

Now Tilton was headed for the square with Daylor at Fletch's request. He froze for a moment and would have tripped if not for Daylor reaching out to grab his shoulder. Tilton had just realized this would be the first time Daylor would truly meet Fletch. And Daylor knew nothing of his previous dalliance with Tilton.

But now was definitely not the appropriate time to tell him.

"Are you all right?" Daylor asked.

"Yeah, sorry," Tilton said.

They kept walking. The sun was starting to touch the horizon, and as they got closer, they noticed lots of people were gathering in the square. It wasn't a market day, but you wouldn't know it looking at all the people streaming in.

Tilton and Daylor made their way to the center of the square, the big empty space where the first market vendors to arrive early in the morning would sell their wares. The square was empty now. Everyone was gathered along its perimeter.

"Hi." Fletch's voice made them spin around.

Tilton's heart pulled a little at the memory of how quietly Fletch always appeared. It pulled a little more when he saw Fletch. "Hi," he said. It came out raspier than he'd expected.

"Hello," Daylor said.

Tilton noticed his voice was a little lower and softer than usual.

"Thanks for coming," Fletch said. He always spoke quietly, but Tilton was a quiet person too, so it had been something they had bonded over. Fletch's eyes narrowed as he looked at Daylor, then Tilton, and he swallowed. He looked as if he had something to say but held it back. "We're trying to capture a shadow creature. Take a torch, and when they give the signal, light it, and hold it toward the center," Fletch said.

Tilton nodded. If he hadn't heard the stories, he would have been surprised by the request. There was much he wanted to ask but didn't. He swallowed it down. It wasn't the time.

Fletch placed a hand on Tilton's arm, pausing a moment. "It was good to see you." Then he took two steps, turned a corner, and was gone.

"But where do we get ...?" Daylor began to ask when they saw a man even larger than Daylor walking around with a wheelbarrow full of torches. When he neared them, he nodded as they each took one. Daylor always had his flint and steel with him, and the torches were already soaked in fat that would ignite quickly. They stood there along the square's edge, watching and waiting. Everyone else was waiting, too.

"So ... that guy ..." Daylor started.

Tilton felt his cheeks burn. "What about him?" he asked, not looking at Daylor but out at the square instead.

"You and he used to ..." Daylor started.

Tilton finally turned his head a little, waiting for Daylor to finish. His eyebrows were raised, and he looked like he was waiting for Tilton, who just stared at him.

"You're going to make me say it?" Daylor asked.

Tilton turned his attention back to the center of the square. "Say what?" Tilton asked.

Daylor put a hand on his shoulder. Tilton turned then. "Look, I know seeing me with those women before, it mustn't have been easy. And I know that you had a life before me. I just didn't expect it to be ..." He leaned in close to Tilton. "... with one of *them*." He murmured it so close to Tilton's ear that shivers ran like fire down his spine.

He swallowed. "We had a brief dalliance while I was in school. Nothing more," Tilton said. He didn't want to say more than he had to. He didn't want to tell him that it had been his first experience with another man and that it had solidified his identity in some ways.

"You two still talk?" Daylor asked.

"No, but we're friendly. And we send each other information, work related," Tilton said.

A noise caught their attention. A shrieking in the middle of the square sounded. It started like a hiss, and suddenly the apothecary stood in the middle of the square waving around a vial with a dark liquid in it. Or was it dark smoke? He was too far away for Tilton to see clearly. The shrieking continued, getting louder by the second.

"Now!"

Daylor stumbled a moment with his flint but lit his torch, touched it to Tilton's, then pointed it in the direction of the square. Tilton moved with him, as did everyone else. They formed a ring with their torches, and the shrieking worsened.

It hurt Tilton's ears so much that he slapped his free hand over one ear and tilted his head to dampen the sound with his shoulder. He watched as a huge shadow swirled like smoke in the square. Each time it poked at darkness and tried to disappear down an alleyway, its path was blocked by fire.

The torches closed in, and with the others, Tilton walked forward until the ring closed. He looked up as silver strands soared over them. The shimmery net sailed into the air and opened. The apothecary waved his arms. Now, he held an empty vial in his other hand, and Tilton could see his mouth moving as he threw a powder in the creature's direction. Then, the net landed on them both. Tilton's heart leaped to think the apothecary might be wounded or killed. Another shriek rent the air, and the net shrank so quickly, it was as if the smoke and shadow had been suddenly sucked out.

The square stilled. No one moved. Tilton shoved his torch into Daylor's hands and ran over. He grabbed the net, which felt oddly soft like silk, and pulled it away to see what was left underneath. The apothecary huddled there, both vials securely in his hands as he held them to his ear. He muttered something, shook the vials, then listened again. Then he nodded.

Tilton offered him a hand up, and the apothecary smiled as he took it. Suddenly, he stopped and looked into Tilton's eyes. The apothecary's eyes narrowed. "Come with me," he said, clamping onto Tilton's hand. The apothecary shoved the vials in his pocket, and without a word to anyone, pushed through the crowd with their torches, down an alleyway, then down another and another. He didn't let go of Tilton's hand as he unlocked the shop doors. Daylor and Fletch caught up to them just as they were heading inside.

"What's going on?" Daylor asked.

The apothecary didn't answer. He just hauled Tilton with him as he rifled through his drawers. "Eat this," he ordered, shoving a date into Tilton's mouth. Tilton blinked as the sweetness flooded his mouth.

"Now this." The apothecary grabbed a milky-white vial and popped it open with his thumb before putting it to Tilton's lips.

Tilton did as he was told.

"Wait, don't ..." Daylor said.

Fletch melted to the back of the room and watched quietly.

"Ah, there it is," the apothecary said. Then he turned around rather suddenly and hit Tilton on the head. Tilton reeled a moment and then sat down, conveniently, on a barrel. The apothecary took a swathe of cloth and wrapped it around Tilton's eyes then.

"What are you doing? Why did you—" Daylor asked.

"Foxall knows what he's doing. Trust him," Fletch said.

"Open," Foxall said.

Tilton felt fingers touch his jaw and squeeze. He opened his mouth, and a pair of wooden sticks touched his tongue. Then, it peeled something away from it, something he hadn't even known was there. Tilton wanted to close his mouth, was tempted to and tried, but the apothecary had his thumb and finger shoved between his teeth from the outside of his cheeks.

"What is that?!" Daylor shouted.

"Come help me hold him. It will not come out willingly," the apothecary said.

Tilton felt Fletch's warm hands on his head. He took the apothecary's spot, keeping Tilton from closing his mouth. Then, he felt Daylor's hands under his shoulders.

"We're going to put you on the table, boy. Lay still if you can," Foxall said.

Hands wrapped around his legs, and they lifted him onto the wooden surface. The wood felt cool against his skin, and he realized he must be warmer than he thought. Tilton felt the something pulling away from him, and he tried to follow it, to put it back in his mouth, but Daylor's hands held him down. Tilton tried to yell, but the only thing that came out was a moan. It felt as if a second skin was peeling off his tongue, out of his insides. He gripped the sides of the counter with his hands. Tilton thought he might throw up. He wanted to get off the table, but then it started to hurt less as the something peeled away from his middle.

"Alexius?" Daylor's voice asked as another pair of hands landed on his hips.

"Tilton, you have a creature acting as a spy inside you. I suspected but could not confirm. Foxall is removing it. You must try to stay as still as you can. It will want to stay because to leave would be to leave its connection to its children," Alexius said.

Tilton's insides turned to fire then, not the good kind but the bad kind. He burned from the inside and writhed on the counter.

"It is trying to convince you that it should stay. It will try every tactic. You must be stronger," Alexius said.

"Tricky little buggers they are. Let's hope it doesn't blow up my shop," the apothecary said. He sounded farther away now. Then, it was Tilton's loins that pulled uncomfortably.

"This next part will be the most painful. I'm sorry," Alexius said.

"Baby, it's okay. I'm here for you. You can do this," Daylor said.

Fletch said nothing.

Tilton felt the consistent pressure of six hands on his body and the table solidly beneath him. He gripped it again as hard as he could and nodded. His groin felt like it was being ripped in two. "Faster," Tilton managed to whisper before his mouth wanted to clamp shut again, but Fletch's fingers did not allow it. The ripping felt like a sword cleaving him in two, from the inside of his ribcage down to his knees.

"Out," a new voice commanded. It was familiar, but Tilton couldn't quite grasp it in his pain. But then like a breeze, the pain that had seared his body calmed like he had been sewn back together and now rested on a soft fluffy cloud. A balm soothed his body like a wave over the beach where flame and pain had once been.

"Thali," Fletch breathed.

Tilton pulled his blindfold off and saw a shimmering pearlescent serpent swimming around in an orb above him. He could only turn his head because he was still being held down, but there Thali stood like she'd just come from the back room.

"Ah, thank you, dear. Welcome back. If you could place it in here," Foxall said.

Thali nodded, and without moving, turned the ball into a thread and pushed it into the vial the apothecary held open.

Fletch was the closest, and he flung himself into Thali's arms. Then, he bowed at her feet, putting her hands to his forehead. "We've all missed you so much, my lady," Fletch said.

"Thank you, Fletch," Thali said. She gave a small smile as she pulled him up.

Garen was standing behind Thali, his hand on her shoulder. Tilton nodded at him. He nodded in return, then Fletch went to Garen. His hand trailed down Thali's arm, staying on her elbow as he leaned away to talk to Fletch.

"You're back!" Daylor rushed over to her next and swept her up in the bear hug he was known for. Garen kept a protective hand on her arm all the while.

"I missed you guys so much," Thali said. When Daylor put her down, she went to Tilton—after taking and squeezing Garen's hand before releasing it—and hugged him. She seemed healthy, warm, and more muscular, but sad.

"Did you just get back?" Daylor asked.

Thali nodded. She let go of Tilton and glanced at Alexius. Tilton knew they were talking mind to mind. She always had this tiny smirk on her face when she spoke with him like that.

Alexius took three steps then, and she wrapped him up in a hug, too. He patted her on the back awkwardly, looking uncomfortable. Fletch was gone, but Garen had stayed, drifting closer to Thali. She drifted closer to him in return, and Tilton wondered what had happened between them just now. He didn't doubt that Garen must have gone to get her, but he saw something between them that was similar to, but different from, when they'd once been together.

Thali stood back and looked at them all. She nodded at the apothecary.

"Foxall, at your service." The apothecary bowed.

"Foxall, what was that?" she nodded at the vial.

"A signat," Foxall said.

Thali's brows furrowed a moment and then she nodded.

"And for the rest of us who know nothing?" Daylor asked.

"A spy," Foxall said.

"Do you think—" Thali asked.

"No, it was disoriented. It will not have seen anything it could understand," Foxall said.

Tilton felt left out. He knew something major was happening, but he wasn't privy to the information. He knew, though, that Thali would tell him later if he asked.

"Did it do any permanent damage?" Daylor asked as he pointed to Tilton.

"Shouldn't have." Foxall turned to Tilton. "You'll feel ill for a day or two, but then you should be back to your usual self. You might notice a decrease in appetite. Hosting a signat takes a lot of energy." He started putting his things away.

Garen interrupted him. "And those shadow creatures. Are there more than we thought? Do we need a new trap?"

Foxall looked over his shoulder at Garen and said, "No, we were wrong. These two are mates. They came here together, but nothing else came with them."

"How can you be sure?"

Foxall chuckled. "Because they don't want me to eat them." He winked.

Garen nodded as Thali went to the back of the shop and returned a mere second later, her brow creased. She locked eyes with Garen, who raised an eyebrow. She shook her head. Tilton made note to ask what that was about.

"We should go," Alexius said. He walked out and stood holding the door meaningfully.

Daylor glanced at Thali and Garen. Tilton wanted to slap Daylor for how obvious he was being. Instead, he took Daylor's arm, and they walked outside together.

"Don't you want to see what happens?" Daylor leaned down to ask Tilton.

"It's none of our beeswax." Tilton crossed his arms.

"It is if we're going to be out of a job soon," Daylor said.

Tilton followed his gaze to a particularly shiny plate reflecting the light inside the shop. Beside it, Garen and Thali still stood, looking at each other and murmuring things rendered unreadable; for their heads were bowed together. It looked heartbreakingly sad.

"They cannot be together," Alexius said out loud.

Tilton jumped. He had all but forgotten that Alexius was there.

"I know," Daylor said. "The kingdom needs her, and she can't do what she needs to do if she's with him. But she just ... seems so .... at ease with him, happy," Daylor said.

Alexius nodded. "They are true mates."

Tilton watched as Garen's hand gently trailed along Thali's jawline to wrap around her neck as they stood with their foreheads together. It was a more intimate moment than he'd ever witnessed, so Tilton looked away.

A minute later, the door pushed open, and Thali cleared her throat as she came out. When the door closed, Tilton heard the door latch though he'd seen no one do it. Thali took a deep breath in and then exhaled. She pressed her lips together, swallowed, and turned her face to the shop. She looked at the place she'd been standing moments ago for a long while, then took a deep, shuddering breath. Tilton guessed she had tears in her eyes.

"Well, shall we?" She pulled up the hood of her cloak, swiping her eyes surreptitiously.

Tilton had been right—wait, did she have a cloak on a moment ago? He snaked his arm around her waist, and Daylor put his arm around her shoulders. They started walking toward the palace as Daylor filled her in on the recent news.

She stopped. "Wait, how long have I been gone?"

"Three months," Daylor said.

Thali's eyes went wide, and she hurried her pace.

CHAPTER FORTY-THREE
Alexius

T HE MOMENT THALI HAD stepped into this world again, he'd felt it. He'd felt like himself again. The anxiety, the lack of patience were all gone. Then, the next thing he felt was how powerful she was. Magic flowed from her like she was the moon pushing and pulling the ocean on a whim.

Alexius allowed himself a moment to revel in her return as he followed the three friends. Then he said in her mind, *There is much we need to discuss.*

I missed you too.

I mean it, your brother.

Yes. I know.

Alexius felt the confusion and the hurt in her.

When they reached the palace gates, all she had to do was remove her hood, and the guards nodded—looking surprised—as she walked into the palace and straight to Elric's office.

"He's not here," Tilton said.

"Where is he?" Thali asked.

"He's following a lead about another gate," Tilton said.

"He's on his way back," Alexius said then.

"How do you know?" Daylor asked.

"I may have sent a messenger when I knew she was on her way back," Alexius explained.

"How very ... undragonlike," Daylor said.

Alexius shrugged. *I knew he wouldn't forgive us if we didn't tell him.*

Thank you, Alexius.

We need to talk before you do any more magic.

Thali nodded, then turned and strode back down the hall to her rooms. "Tilton, I assume there's a mountain of work for me?" she asked as they walked.

Tilton nodded but was saved from explaining just how much as they reached her rooms. She pushed open the doors and headed straight for her private quarters. She froze, then looked around at the redecorated rooms. "It's ..." Thali began. She rushed up to the shelves as she took it all in.

"Alexius said you had something similar in your room at home, and I thought it would be a nice way to bring a piece of your home to the palace," Tilton said. He held his breath.

Alexius felt it before she expressed it. She was so happy.

"I love it, so much," Thali said. One wall was all shelves filled with the items Alexius had brought with him when he had returned from Densria. And he had returned just in time too, as Elric had been about to send out a search party when he hadn't reported for duty as scheduled.

"Alexius mapped out where everything was in your room at home, so we made an expanded version. I hope you don't mind that we added some of the gifts you've received recently," Tilton said. He pointed to a purple book amongst the other things they'd added.

"I'm so lucky to have you all as friends," Thali said. She hugged Tilton and wrapped an arm around Daylor.

"I hope you know you can always tell me if I'm wrong or if I'm being too much," Thali said. She'd said it so quietly, it was only because Alexius was a dragon that he could hear it.

"And you won't chop off our heads?" Daylor asked.

"Never. Please, always feel that you can tell me anything. I promise never to hurt you," Thali said.

"In that case, we're pretty hurt you left without us—or anyone else," Daylor said.

"I'm so sorry. I had to leave in a hurry. Besides, I couldn't separate you two," Thali said.

"What do you mean?" Tilton squeaked.

Alexius felt Tilton's heart race.

"You two lovebirds come as a pair, no?" Thali asked.

"So you know? About us?" Tilton's eyes widened, and Alexius forced a laugh back.

"Doesn't everyone?" Thali asked before slapping a hand over her mouth. "Oh sorry, am I supposed to keep it a secret?"

"No, it's fine," Tilton said. He blinked several times.

"And you're okay with it?" Daylor asked.

"Why wouldn't I be?" Thali asked.

"Because we're the same gender," Daylor said.

"You can love who you want, and you two ... well, it's undeniable. And you know, it's considered a more powerful bond in some cultures," Thali said.

"I don't know if I'll ever fully understand human customs," Alexius said.

Tilton and Daylor turned to him, worry etched on their faces.

OF SPOOLS AND BILLOWS

"That's not what I meant. What I meant was you humans are so judgmental. My brother's mate is also male. I think I have a cousin who's asexual, and my sister is bisexual. Male to male, female to male, female to female, genderfluid, you are who you are." Alexius shrugged.

"The dragon's not mad at us," Tilton whispered as he sagged. Then, he clapped his hand over his mouth as Thali had. "Sorry!"

Alexius chuckled. Tilton was an anxious individual who always seemed overly concerned with physical harm. So Alexius held in another laugh as he refrained from telling him that dragons preferred psychological harm as a consequence as it was much more challenging.

"Now that that's all settled ..." Daylor put his hands on Tilton's shoulders. "Let's leave Alexius and Thali to catch up and prepare for Elric's arrival."

The moment the door was closed, Thali went to her bedroom, and when Mia launched herself at her friend, Alexius noticed the only reason Thali stayed on her feet was her magic.

"You're back!" Mia said.

"Always, I always come back. I don't break promises," Thali said into Mia's hair.

"I was so worried. I mean, I knew Rommy would keep you safe, but still, another world, magical creatures, you never know," Mia said. She squeezed Thali and continued to hold her.

"I'm sorry, but Rommy is ... different. Don't trust him if he comes here, all right?" Thali said.

Mia nodded into her hair.

You know the truth? Alexius asked Thali in her mind.

I know that my brother has it in his head that he needs to take over the world. I don't understand it. But he wants to use the animals and my magic to take over each kingdom until it's just one empire for he and I to share.

Alexius nodded. *I guessed as much. You need to know that my siblings and I, we were forced to obey him. I broke out when I took the blood oath to you, but it also cut me off from them.*

That explains a lot.

I have so much to tell you. I didn't before because I thought we had time. That's been my mistake and I'm sorry.

"Thali?! My love?!" Elric burst through the door then, and Mia backed away, nodding to Alexius and mouthing, "Thank you."

Mia left then, and as Thali and Elric embraced, Alexius noted a strand of hesitation in Thali. It was small, but it was there. *I fear what may happen if we wait too long.*

I will come find you tonight, Thali said.

Alexius bowed and left the room, too. When he stepped outside, he saw Thali's animals waiting to get in and Nasir scrawling on a piece of parchment. He held the door open for the animals, then said, "Go send it. I will stand here until you return," Alexius said.

Nasir nodded. "Thank you, brother," he said before hurrying down the hallway.

CHAPTER FORTY-FOUR
Elric

I T HAD BEEN YEARS since Elric had ridden out as the sun was setting. He felt the exhilaration of almost being free despite the tension of the unit of guards surrounding him. They weren't exactly subtle as they plowed along the road. Eventually, they stopped at an inn so he and his myriad of guards could get a drink and some quick food before continuing onwards.

"Sir, a royal messenger," Stefan said.

Elric looked up to see a liveried royal messenger nearing. He hopped off his horse and recognized the messenger as a newer one, young and quick.

"Your Highness, Alexius from Her Highness's guard bade me get this to you as quickly as I could." A royal guard took the messenger's horse and led it to the stable.

Elric took the note, holding his breath.

> *She may be back tonight.*
> *-Alexius*

Elric's brow creased even as his heart raced. Now, he had to make a choice. He was chasing a promising lead, and Alexius hadn't said for sure that she would be back, only that she *may* be. He was so close to talking with this old acquaintance who might know something of Thali's disappearance, yet he needed to be there if and when she did return.

"Do we head back, sire, or do we go forward?" Stefan asked after Elric handed him the missive.

Elric ground his teeth for a moment. "We keep going. We're almost there, so let's go see what this person has to say and then return."

After a quick bowl of stew and mug of ale, Elric retrieved his horse and continued his journey, only Stefan and a handful of his guards following. Soon after leaving the inn, they passed a school and came to a small plot of land boasting a large garden and a small house. Elric stopped and dismounted outside the garden, leaving his guards and horses behind. Stefan came with him, however, hand on his saber as they walked up to the house. The door swung open as they neared, and Elric wondered if this man he was meeting might have magic. Maybe he should have brought Alexius with him. But no, Alexius should be at the palace to help Thali return if he could.

"Hello," Stefan said as he stepped through the darkened doorway first.

When they stepped into the small cottage, they saw a fire dancing in the hearth and a man in simple brown robes sitting at a table.

"Master Brown," Elric said. He thought it strange a man wouldn't stand to greet his prince.

"Your Highness, you'll forgive my lack of protocol and hospitality as I don't often have guests. Would you sit with me?" Master Brown said.

Elric nodded and sat. He saw then that Master Brown had one leg wrapped and raised on a makeshift barrel.

"I slipped on some wet cobblestone in the market. I've never really gotten used to cobblestone streets," Master Brown said as he followed Elric's glance. "My apologies for not greeting you as I should."

Elric nodded. This man had been appointed to Thali's school directly by Thali's father, so he should not be dangerous. He was, after all, a teacher, one that had taught Thali for three years. So why were Elric's instincts saying otherwise? "You wrote to us with news of your princess and future queen?" Elric asked. He wanted to impress upon this man Thali's importance to the kingdom.

"Yes. I know her well enough, better than she realizes, actually," he said. He avoided truly answering the question, and Elric raised an eyebrow. "You see, Your Highness, I was hoping to join the royal guard, specifically, the princess's guard."

"And why is that?"

"Because I am sworn to protect her, something a lot easier to do as her personal guard."

"What do you mean? Who did you swear to?"

"Her father is an excellent and fair merchant," Master Brown said.

Elric nodded, frustrated. They were still so far from discovering more about the magical lands, and this man wasn't answering any of his questions.

"Did you know that in my culture, when we're children, we're all told our destiny?"

"No." Elric swallowed his impatience.

"Mine is to die for the queen."

"I see," Elric said. "Thali is not yet queen."

"No, but she will be."

"Yes." Elric swallowed again. This man was starting to make him uncomfortable. He glanced at Stefan, whose eyes were narrowed, but his hand had moved away from his saber.

"To protect her, I need to be near her," Master Brown said.

"All right." Elric was starting to feel more and more wary of this man. "You want to be in her guard. I will speak to my captain to see if it's possible. But you wrote to tell me that you had information about Thali and magic."

"Yes, yes. I was getting to that. There will be a war, and you must choose her."

"Sorry?"

"There will be a war and you must choose her."

"That doesn't make any sense. I've already chosen her."

"In the moment when the real decision is before you, you will know what I mean. You will have a choice, and you must choose her."

"Of course," Elric said, barely keeping his temper from flaring. This was a waste of time; he should have turned around. "Thank you for your information. We will be in touch about the position in the royal guard."

"Thank you, Your Highness. May you live long," Master Brown said.

Stefan coughed. "Is there anything else you'd like to share with us?"

Master Brown pushed his lips together. "No, I don't think there is."

Elric rose, then nodded and went out the door.

Once outside and mounted, Stefan caught up to Elric as they trotted away. "I'm sorry that was a waste of time," Stefan said.

"It's not your fault. I should have known. What nonsense. I can't believe that man teaches."

"He hasn't taught since Thali left school."

"Has he applied to the royal guard?"

"Yes, multiple times from what I've been told. Lord Ranulf himself has requested his denial."

"Why?" Elric asked. "Never mind, I can guess." Elric thought then he should send a letter to Lord Ranulf asking about Master Brown's history.

Elric and Stefan picked up their pace, as did the rest of the guards as they made their way back to the palace. If they rode just a little faster, they could make it back in a couple of hours. Elric couldn't believe he'd chosen to follow the lead instead of going back to the palace. Thali could be home right now wondering where he was. Or she could be injured. He hoped she wasn't injured. Brother or not, he would have Rommy strung up if she'd been harmed in any way.

Elric was lost in his thoughts as they rode back. He blindly followed the guards as they stopped at a town to switch horses and continue onward. The moon was high in the sky by the time they could see the tallest towers of the palace.

Their horses were lathered in sweat by the time Elric slid off his horse in front of the palace and ran up the steps. Avery was there to meet him. She nodded and Elric raced through the hallways and into the private wings with Avery and Stefan on his tail. As he neared the rooms he shared with Thali, he could hear soft voices on the other side of the door and see the soft glow of light. He reached out and threw the door open before the guards could do it for him. She spun around, radiant as ever. Before he knew what he was doing, he was crashing into her and they were together, bodies pressed, his lips on hers. Elric beamed wider than he ever imagined he could. "It's you? It's really you? I've missed you so much," he said.

"I've missed you too," Thali said. She stepped back, though they still held each other's elbows as they took each other in. He was covered in mud and dirt and travel grime, but she was fresh and grinning in her usual trousers, shirt, and vest. She looked stronger, if that was possible, and perhaps more confident, more self-assured.

"Now, where are my lovely friends, my tiger, dog, and snake?" Thali asked as Alexius opened the door on his way out. The animals sprang free, barrelling into Thali and Elric. Thali was soon flat on the floor covered in orange, gray, and green as the exuberant animals greeted her. Elric realized he wasn't the only one who had been miserable without her.

CHAPTER FORTY-FIVE
Thali

A WEEK LATER, THE strangest mix of people gathered in the same room.

"Everyone ready?" Thali asked, standing just outside the door. Tilton nodded. She'd asked him to gather these specific people because no matter the turmoil that tore her heart and childhood memories apart, everyone had to be warned. Then, it was up to them. It would be out of her hands, and she was almost excited not to have to worry about it anymore.

Thali leaned in close to Tilton and whispered in his ear. "You let your informant know?"

Tilton nodded, then held open the door while Thali walked in. He opened the window closest to the woods and nodded ever so slightly. He remained there as the meeting got started.

Thali looked around the room as it quieted. Elric moved next to her, took her hand, and gave it a squeeze. Tilton, Daylor, Mia, Avery, various advisers and councillors, the captain of the guard, and the army general were already present. Another set of doors opened, and everyone curtsied or bowed as the king and queen walked in.

"We're so glad you're back safely," the queen said softly in her ear as she placed her hand on Thali's wrist.

Thali nodded. She waited for the king and queen to be seated and then looked for Alexius. He slipped out from the crowd to stand on her other side. She looked around once again to see if everyone was there and saw Nasir and Isaia come in and Stefan flank Elric. She was so glad to see them, all of them. Fighting back some unexpected tears, she took in all the people she loved. They were all here, except for her mother and father. She wished they were here, and though she suspected they were on their way, the earliest they'd make it was tomorrow morning.

"Thank you all for coming together," Thali said. "As most of you have probably guessed, or know already, I've been away a long time. What many of you don't know is that I journeyed to a world called Etciel. It is a land very different from ours. It is where the strange creatures of our stories reside. But there is also magic there, magic that I've learned to use to help our kingdom because we may be going to war." Thali stopped and swallowed. Alexius sent her a wave of calm, and Elric squeezed her hand, pressing his leg against hers.

She took a breath and continued. "My brother wishes to use the magical animals that have been attacking our countryside, attacking our neighbors, to take over the land and build himself an empire."

"But why?" Councillor Strawman asked. He was a valuable ally and had always smiled at her but had never said much to her besides complimenting her pretty dresses.

"Does it matter?" Elric asked.

"It does. Perhaps he will not come here. You are, after all, his sister. This is his home kingdom. Would he not go out and conquer others instead?" the councillor insisted.

"He wants to use me to conquer all the kingdoms," Thali said.

"How can he use you? You're here," another adviser, Councillor Liman asked. Thali took a deep breath. She hadn't wanted to show her magic, and a small part of her was still hesitant, still most comfortable hiding it, still wanted to keep it a secret.

Elric patted her hand. Thali swallowed. She reached out to the nearby birds living in the tallest turret. They were coming. She turned her attention to the window, and a moment later, a flock of twenty birds swooped into the room. The group gasped. The birds flew in a swirl over the table, then flew in a circle over Councillor Strawman before leaving. She sent them a thank you and directed them to the berry bush in the forest she often ate from.

"That was ..." Councillor Liman said.

"Just birds. How can you take over an entire kingdom by making birds do acrobatics?" Councillor Strawman asked.

Indi sat up then, popping her head above the table they were all gathered around. Thali pet Indi's head. She really did think this tiger could understand her better than most humans.

Thali could feel Alexius starting to get angry. *Don't, you'll terrify them,* Thali warned.

They don't seem to understand the importance of what you're saying.

It's because I'm a woman. Or maybe because I'm half Cerisan.

Alexius simmered but calmed.

"What can we do in preparation?" Elric asked.

"I'm not sure," Thali said.

"You're not seriously considering this? I mean, look at our kingdom. We have not seen any attacks on our city or even the palace. Sure, there have been attacks further out, but who's to say the creatures aren't just hungry and attacking the countryside for food?" Councillor Liman interjected.

Elric looked at Alexius, who clamped his lips shut.

"The risk to the kingdom is too great if we don't take this seriously," Elric said.

"He's not made a move in our direction. He's not—"

"I AM THE MOVE!" Thali shouted.

The councillors all looked at her in horror.

"Rather, I was *supposed* to be the move. But when I realized what he wanted to do, I left. I came home to warn you, my family, my kingdom," Thali said.

"If you're such a risk to us, then maybe we should lock you up," Councillor Liman said.

Indi growled and Alexius edged closer to Thali. She felt him right behind her to her right.

"You will do no such thing," Elric said.

Councillor Liman looked at the king.

The king looked between Thali and Elric. His eyes narrowed as he thought. He leaned over to his adviser and whispered a few words. Then the adviser ran over to Elric and whispered so quietly that Thali could not hear.

Elric coughed. "Father, I would like to introduce you to Princess Routhalia's adviser, Alexius."

Did I just get promoted? Alexius asked Thali.

I suppose so. Though the king cannot offer you any station unless you've been introduced to him first.

What would you like me to say?

I don't know what he's going to ask.

"Alexius, what do you know of what the princess has said?" the king asked.

Confused, Alexius looked at Thali before speaking.

Thali knew he was confused that no one was acting, and he was hoping to convey that.

Alexius took a deep breath and said, "I am not from here, so please forgive me if I err with your customs. The danger she speaks of is very real. There is currently a barrier that protects the city and the palace, but the rest of your kingdom is not under such protection. Hence the attacks there, not here."

"Who created this barrier and how?" the king asked.

Should I tell him it was me? Alexius asked Thali.

But then who held it when you weren't here? It might force you to reveal more than you want to if you say it's you.

I've sworn a blood oath to you. This is as much my home as it is yours now.

Thali swallowed in response.

"I did, Your Majesty," Alexius said. It was a risk.

"You took it upon yourself to create a barrier for the city? On whose authority?" Councillor Liman was practically purple with rage.

I think we should tell them. Scare the trousers off them, Thali said.

Is that wise?

What are they going to do? Lock us up?

I don't know. Maybe.

Thali looked at Elric. He looked flabbergasted, like he wasn't sure what to do and was soaking it in as much as everyone else.

"My duty is to protect the princess," Alexius began. "She, as she has told you, has much magical power, power that attracts other magical creatures and therefore invites a lot of unwanted attention. I used a barrier to deflect their attention, and while I'm sorry others outside the barrier have been harmed, there's much more damage to be done in a city," Alexius said.

"You should both be locked up," Councillor Strawman said.

Elric gasped. "Be very careful with your next words, councillor. You speak of the kingdom's future queen." He looked ready to murder someone as he stared the councillor down.

"If your princess is truly dangerous, if her brother and those creatures are after her, then perhaps we should send her away to protect the kingdom, protect the people," Councillor Liman suggested.

"No," Elric said. "She is my wife and partner."

"Perhaps you should go with her," the king said.

"Father?" Elric asked.

Thali couldn't believe her ears. They would send her and Elric away instead of preparing for war? They would be so incredibly unprepared. If they sent her and Alexius away, there wouldn't be anyone to protect the city.

"We have not seen the danger you speak of. I have not seen proof of such an attack on our kingdom, and I don't know that the beasts will attack unfairly. If they are drawn to the princess, and if her brother is also drawn to her, then perhaps it makes sense if you three go elsewhere, just for now. Consider it a honeymoon," the king said.

Elric's face was filled with hurt and shock. "Where will we go?"

"I know where," Thali said.

Elric looked at her.

"We will be twenty days away. I hope you do not regret your decision," Thali said, turning on her heel and leaving the room. She was so angry and hurt that they wouldn't even listen, let alone take her seriously. Her animals rubbed up against her, trying to comfort her.

Elric followed her, as did Alexius, Isaia, and Nasir.

"They'll come around. They'll change their minds," Elric said as they rushed down the hall. "Let me go talk to my father alone."

"He's made his feelings perfectly clear, Elric," Thali said. She had left her brother because he was crazy. But at least he listened to her. He took her seriously. She'd come back here, left a dream of a life with Garen in another world to come back here and protect a place that didn't see her as anything more than a decoration. She returned to her rooms and was surprised when a whole slew of people walked in behind her. All her guards, Elric and his guards, Daylor, Tilton, Mia, Alexius, and even Nasir and Isaia had followed her. When her gaze landed on Tilton, she had another thought. *Garen. Garen's people would ready for war.*

"We're leaving for Bulstan tomorrow morning," Thali announced.

"But ... but Thali, you just got back. Are you sure—" Elric asked.

"Are you coming with me or not? I'm not wanted here. Until I am, I will go to Bulstan. Tariq said he would always have a place for me there, and I trust him."

Elric nodded. "I'm coming with you."

"Good. Be ready to leave tomorrow morning," Thali said.

Elric took her face in his hands. "We'll have an adventure all our own," Elric said. "Promise not to leave without me?"

"Promise," Thali said, meaning it. "I'm going out tonight, and I need you to trust me."

Elric searched her face for three seconds and nodded. "I trust you completely." Thali nodded. He pressed his lips to hers and practically skipped into his closet to go pack his bags.

Thali thought it was cute that Elric thought of this as an adventure. "Stefan," she said before he left.

He turned around.

Thali said, "Make sure his weapons and armor are packed."

His eyes narrowed a touch; then he nodded.

Now only her family was left, her dearest friends. "You don't have to come, but you're all welcome to," Thali said.

"We want to come," Mia said.

"We don't want to be left behind this time," Tilton said.

"We might be leaving only to come back right away," Thali said.

"We do have some sailing experience," Daylor said.

They all grinned at each other. The mood had lightened.

"You'll be my crew then." Thali smiled. She finally felt like herself for the first time in a long time.

As her friends left to go pack, she thought of the conversation they'd had so long ago about packing and what to bring on a ship.

"All our weapons?" Mia asked now. At Thali's nod, she nodded too and scurried off.

Thali grinned. She was glad that Mia had taken her seriously when they trained as children. Mia didn't like fighting, but she could defend herself and others in a pinch.

Thali turned to her guards next. "I'm not sure what this means for you. I'm sure you can go back to the royal guard, but if you come with me, we might be on our own. We might permanently live in Bulstan, or we might sail the oceans, but there are no hard feelings. I know this is not what you all signed up for. You are free to choose your own path."

A couple of the new guards nodded and slinked off, but Thali was a little saddened to see that so many of them would follow her. "I can't promise you anything." Thali looked each of them in the eye.

"I owe a life debt to you," Isaia said. "I go where you go. Plus, I can sail."

"I am yours, on orders from my own prince. And I will be thrilled to visit home," Nasir said. "Also, if we live in Bulstan, all my brothers and sisters here are welcome at my invitation."

The other guards nodded their appreciation.

Thali smiled. She realized there was a community within the palace, her community after all. "Then, see to your things. We leave in the morning. We may have to stop in Densria on the way to pick up my ship and supplies, but we will continue on within the day," Thali said.

They all nodded and left, except Nasir and Isaia.

"We would like to come with you tonight," Nasir said.

"Tonight? I didn't say I was going anywhere tonight."

"We heard what you said to Elric and would like to meet your other citizens," Nasir said.

Thali nodded. Tonight, she would resurface as the Princess of Thieves.

Chapter Forty-Six
Garen

G AREN WAS ON A rampage for all the wrong reasons when he'd returned from listening in on Thali's meeting and he knew it. He tried his hardest not to take it out on his people, but his heart had broken anew. They'd had a chance to live together, to live in peace together forever, but they hadn't taken it. There were too many people that depended on them. And then, Thali had felt the evil in this world, and their decision had been made. They'd said goodbye again.

At least this time, they'd broken their own hearts. But it hadn't even been worth it.

Everyone kept well away from him except to make the necessary reports, nothing more. He noticed Foxall was with them now and was treated well by his people. He was glad. It would be good to have an apothecary join their family.

"Boss." Fletch appeared.

Garen nodded. Fletch had stepped up and used all his contacts to get everyone to the town square to help capture the shadow creature. His captains had done him proud. All his people had. Even Tilton and Daylor had helped.

Fletch handed Garen a piece of parchment. It wasn't much bigger than his palm. But the moment Garen glanced at it, his heart did a flip-flop. He would know that writing anywhere. His eyes narrowed as he looked at Fletch, who blushed and shrugged.

Tonight. We must prepare. -T

"That's all I got," Fletch said.

"But—" Garen began, then his heart leaped like it knew before he did. The tavern door opened and there she stood. She wore a simple purple dress, but her body was crisscrossed with leather straps holding various weapons. A plain dagger sat next to another with a red gem in its pommel on her belt. Her skirts had long slits for her legs, and Garen caught the glint of metal on them. He gulped. His heart was about to explode with pride at seeing her standing so confidently. And then, he saw a flicker of doubt cross her face. It was only there for a moment. He didn't know what she had to be unsure of and it cracked his heart a little. She stood there with her tiger on one side, dog on the other, and snake draped around her neck like a goddess. Two warriors even stood behind her. Everyone in the tavern stopped and turned. She lifted her chin a little, and bless Fletch because he approached her and bowed, his head almost touching his knees.

"My lady, welcome home," he said.

"Cheers to our lady!" the whole of the tavern said, and their mugs of ale *thunked* as they touched them together.

The severe look on Thali's face melted and she smiled. She'd clearly been worried they would turn her away. Garen's chest swelled with even more pride as his people showed her she had a place here.

Fletch offered his arm and walked Thali over to Garen.

Ana raced ahead and jumped up to lick Garen's face as Indi hopped up on his bench and positioned herself on its back so no one would miss her presence.

Thali smiled tightly at him and slid onto the bench but on the other side of the table. "You got my note?"

Garen nodded. She looked concerned. He turned his full attention to her.

She swallowed. This was clearly difficult for her. He wanted so badly to reach out and touch her hand, but as his gaze fell on it, he was reminded of the giant ring on her finger and kept his hands where they were. She was married to someone else.

The air stilled around him. He knew it was her magic. She had created a bubble so no one would overhear them.

"My brother is coming. He wishes to take over our world. He wanted to use me to do it, but I think he still has a way to do so without using me to control the magical animals. He wants to take over our neighbors first to the south, then to the west. You have to warn the others."

Garen nodded. "I know. You must know I was listening." After her brief hesitation and slow nod, he asked, "What is going to be done here?"

"They're sending me away, me and Elric. We will go to Bulstan. They didn't believe me, Garen," she said. "They think *I'm* the danger."

Such a pained look crossed her face, he twitched, wanting to hurt whoever had hurt her this way.

"They're in denial. And they're sending Alexius away with me. The barrier will fall in two days."

"You will be safe in Bulstan?" Garen asked.

Thali nodded. "You must get everyone to stay indoors once the barrier falls. The creatures will come, and they will attack. Is there anywhere underground you can go?" she asked.

Garen nodded. He reached out to cover her hand with his, not caring about Elric right now. "I'm sorry they didn't listen to you. We will. What else can we do?"

Thali's face relaxed a little. He did not like seeing creases in her forehead, and it made his heart lighter to see that he could ease some of them.

"Thank you. I ... I never expected to be ignored, let alone sent away."

"They are fools. Scared old fools," Garen said.

Thali swallowed. She was upset but trying not to show it. He knew that look. She took a breath and said, "Remember, get everyone to stay inside in two days. Leaving would be even better."

"Anything else?"

She thought, then nodded. "Teach them to meditate, to close their minds so they can't be infiltrated." Thali choked on a sob, and he wanted so badly to wrap his arms around her, but that would be too much.

He squeezed her hand.

"Come with me," she breathed.

Garen's heart squeezed again.

"You know I can't. I can't leave my people, and you have Elric," Garen said.

A tear rolled down her cheek, and Ana turned to lick it off her face. Then, Ana shoved her nose into Thali's eye and Thali laughed as she redirected Ana's long snout. Garen smiled to see her laugh. They stayed quiet for a few moments.

"Will you promise me you'll stay as safe as you can?" she asked.

Garen nodded.

"Alexius says he found an old, abandoned building that's sunk into the ground. It's made of stone and should keep some folks safe. Will you get as many people as you can in there and stay inside? Foxall will help. Maybe there are some hidden caves even?"

"We know of many places. I promise, I'll do everything I can."

"Foxall's presence alone will make many creatures think twice, but still." Thali's shoulders slumped and she sighed. "Thank you."

Garen patted her hand, wanting to do so much more. "Do what you must," he said. "We'll help any way we can."

"Keep them safe," Thali said, looking around at the people in the tavern. She took another deep breath and squared her shoulders. The air moved around him again.

He knew they were no longer being obscured. "We'll hide you if you want to stay," Garen said.

"No. I want to go to Bulstan. Perhaps I can find some answers, something that could help," Thali said.

Garen wondered if she wanted to get the sparkly prince involved. His people were great warriors after all, and they would not react the way Adanek had.

"Two days, sun up to sun down," Thali said. Garen nodded. She stood and slowly weaved through the room before leaving with her snake, tiger, dog, and two guards. Garen had noted the two guards with her didn't have a lick of royal colors on them, so they'd come to show him they were on her side. No matter what happened, they would stay with Thali, not Thali the princess but Thali their friend.

CHAPTER FORTY-SEVEN
Thali

T HALI SWALLOWED AND LOOKED around her perfect bedroom, wondering if any of it would be here when she returned, if she returned. Her eyes slid to a beaten up armoire that made her smile. She'd not realized how much she would miss until she'd been forced to leave. Councillors Liman and Strawman and the king and queen had already gathered at the palace entrance. Elric's parents hadn't spoken a single word to her since his father's decree.

Thali said goodbye to her new home and went down to the official receiving room to join Elric. He had taken it all well, though he looked angry at his parents for going through with it.

"You'll be back in no time, son," the king said.

The queen only hugged him close. Then, it was Thali's turn. "I tried so hard to tell them not to do it, but they prefer ignorance," the queen said.

"Please, the day after tomorrow, the underground mushroom gardens are a lovely place to spend the day," Thali said.

The queen nodded her understanding.

Thali put a smile on for the king then and curtsied. But she did not approach him for a hug, nor did he offer one. The councillors had the gall to wave as Elric took Thali's hand and they walked down the steps to the carriage. They would take a carriage to the edge of the city and then their horses to shore. They numbered twenty people as they traveled the short day's ride to shore, and Thali would be glad to be away from the politics.

Their departure and transfer to horseback was smooth and efficient, and they traveled in peace, stopping only once at the top of a hill just before the school and the harbor. As they crested it, they could see the ships, and Thali recognized a few of the flags in the harbor as those of her family.

"I sent a messenger ahead last night to tell them to wait at the harbor for us to join them," Elric said as he caught up to her. His horse was fast, but Arabelle hadn't been on a journey in some time and was exhilarated by the freedom.

"Papa," Thali whispered, and she took off with Arabelle. The dozen guards and her friends all chased after her as she rode as fast as she could. It was perhaps not the wisest decision, but she didn't care. She couldn't wait to see her parents.

Arabelle slowed when she got to the dock, and Thali leaped off and threw herself into her parents' waiting arms. She held them tight. "Rommy ... he's... he wants to use the animals and the creatures to take over the kingdom, to take over all the kingdoms," Thali blurted out. It got easier each time she said it, though she braced herself for her parents' disbelief. Rommy was, after all, the golden child.

"I knew something wasn't quite right when he came back to us. I wondered if we would find out before it was too late. So tell me, what is the king doing about it?" her father asked.

"He does not believe me," Thali said. She let the tears flow then, and Lord Ranulf folded his daughter into his arms as they made their way to the ship and their quarters. Elric joined them as she told her parents all that had happened.

"So now you are going to Bulstan?" her mother asked.

Thali nodded.

"Then we will go with you," she said.

"But ... but it's summer. You always go north," Thali said.

"It sounds like the world is about to suffer through some big changes, and you shall be at the center of it. You matter more than our business," her mother said.

"Thank you," Thali said, choking back another sob. She hugged her mother then, burying her head in her chest. Thali hadn't known what her parents would say. But she was overjoyed that they believed her.

"We will stop by Densria to help them batten down the hatches before we leave." Her mother took command.

"Densria will be safe." Alexius had slipped into the tight family quarters amongst some of the guards.

"Why's that?" Thali asked.

"The caladrii. They're not creatures you want to cross, so everything gives them a wide berth. They're powerful. And they've made a home in Densria, so they'll keep it safe. In fact, you may have many people come seeking refuge and recovery once the war starts," Alexius said.

Thali silently asked, *Did you bring the caladrii to my home?*

I wish I could say I did. But I did not. They go where they wish, and they wished to establish a home in Densria. It's the first time I've ever seen caladrii make a home. I think it's the first time in centuries, if I'm being honest.

Is there something they want?

They are the purest of the pure. Their motivations are true and theirs alone.

"So, Densria this afternoon and then off to Bulstan," Lord Ranulf said. He stood to survey the group. "How many did you bring with you, daughter?"

"I believe we are twenty, Papa," Thali said.

"Isn't that what you need to staff your ship?" her father said as he raised his eyebrows.

Thali's eyes lit up. She hadn't seen her own ship in years.

"We'll be a bit snug this afternoon, but we'll take two ships to Bulstan then," her mother said.

"Guess those sailing classes will come in handy after all," Daylor said.

"Your Highness, daughter, you may sleep in here with two guards each on the floor. The rest of you, to the crew's quarters," Lady Jinhua said.

Thali knew her mother's expressions well. She knew Lady Jinhua would be thinking about what Thali had said and what both Thali and Elric being here meant. She wondered when her mother would corner her to dig deeper about what was going on. All she could do was wait.

It took them some time to get organized, but with her family's experienced crew, they were out on the ocean in no time, heading home briefly before heading to Bulstan. Thali tried to connect with Tariq, sending him a message down the thread that was his in her mind, to tell him they were coming, but she could not reach him. She thought maybe she was just too far away, but she wasn't sure. She had done it before from here. Perhaps with the tumult in her life and the stormy season at sea, it was too much to get through. All she could do was hope he saw her message.

CHAPTER FORTY-EIGHT
Thali

"**H**OW DOES IT FEEL?" Thali asked Daylor.

"Like I could spend my life doing this." Daylor cracked a grin and they laughed.

Thali ran a few steps to the rope ladder and leaped on it, climbing up. She'd never felt more like she'd been living out a dream than these last few days. They'd arrived in Densria and left shortly thereafter. She'd sent word to Garen by bat to send people to Densria and to Mia's family to stay in town, close to the fluffy chickens that were the caladrii. Thali and her family had stayed only long enough for a bonfire, a send off, and to resupply for the trip to Bulstan and beyond should it take them longer in the stormy season.

They'd had some beautiful weather though, and her ship sailed along-side her parents'. Daylor, Tilton, Isaia, and Alexius were all putting what they had learned in school to good use. They even taught the other guards. It turned out one had been a sailor years ago, so he had slipped into the rhythm of their assignments easily. Thali had done a little bit of everything, correcting this or that, while being the captain she'd always dreamed of being. The icing on her cake was that Mouse, part of her family's crew, had been kind enough to join her crew as an extra hand.

Have you gotten through to the prince? Alexius asked.

No. I wonder if the connection was broken when I went to Etciel.

Perhaps.

Thali was getting impatient. She just wanted to get there. She wanted to see Tariq, to see what he'd discovered because she knew him well enough to know that he would not have sat idle all this time.

She tugged on a thread in her mind, bringing a bat to her from the hull. This was something else she'd missed, communicating with the animals as a team and sending bat messengers. Thali was going to try something to speed up the process, so she sent the bat with a message to her parents. Once the message was received, her parents watched her crew as she instructed Daylor and Tilton to make a loop of rope. Mouse went to tie the end to the bow. They found a small barrel to place the loop around and tossed it over the side. Her parents did the same after watching them from afar.

Thali reached into her mind and found some large whales nearby. She requested their assistance in return for the location of a krill swarm. The whales swam over, and she instructed them to take hold of the small barrel and to swim gently before picking up speed.

"Drop the sails!" Thali said. Her crew worked quickly, though some were clearly confused. Her parents' crew followed her lead.

"Is it okay if I go to the bow and watch?" Elric asked.

Thali nodded. She took his hand, and they went together. The whales hadn't surfaced yet, so she and Elric watched as the masses finally breached the surface and slowly opened their mouths a crack as they took hold of the barrel. A couple more latched onto the barrel her parents had tossed over. Their crew finished dropping their sails just then. Suddenly, the ship lurched under her feet. Thali reminded the whales to start slowly, and she smiled as she felt them slow. All the crew members from both ships were on deck watching the enormous whales towing them.

A bat arrived with a message from her parents.

You gave them the correct direction? What will they require in payment? Did you ask them nicely? How does that work anyway?

Thali wrote them back right away.

Yes, yes, and yes, and I'll explain it later.

Alexius appeared at her other side then. *It was kind of you to ask.*

I refuse to demand it. They are living, breathing creatures with families and lives.

We haven't had a chance to discuss what I need to tell you. Alexius glanced at Thali.

How about now?

Sure. You might want to sit down.

Thali gripped the rail a little tighter and shook her head slightly, ready for whatever Alexius threw at her. Elric put a hand over hers and she smiled at him.

Alexius began. *Magic has a price. In Etciel, when you used it freely, something else paid the price. When you took over the hornsnoads' minds, what you didn't see is that they killed themselves afterward. They consider invasion of the mind the worst offense, and since they have a hive mind, the invaded one kills themselves so the others in their community are not tainted.*

Thali covered her mouth. She'd had no idea that all the toady-type creatures were so ... so sophisticated.

I know the truth was hidden from you, but I also knew it would pain you to find this out. I also knew you'd want to know so you could use caution going forward.

What of the magic that was in the air there? How I could feel it surround me?

Alexius said, *In Etciel, magic is like air. There is enough air for everyone, but while it is free, when you take too much, you take from someone else who might need it.*

Then how do you know when and how much to take? Thali was confused.

You don't. You proceed with caution. The only place with limitless magic is the lake of birth.

I was there. I refused to go back.

What did you create?

Thali brought up an image of the bird she'd drawn as a child, of it coming to life.

Well, at least it's interesting and probably not dangerous.

A cough interrupted them, and Thali turned around.

"Captain, what do we do now?" Daylor asked.

"Prepare for arrival," Thali said. With the whales towing them, she suspected they would gain days of travel time.

We're reaching my limits, Alexius said then.

Thali swallowed and almost asked the whales to stop. After this, her beloved kingdom could fall. She looked around. At least her family was here. Or part of them. They would be reunited with the rest soon. "Alexius has reached the limit of his magic. Adanek is now unprotected," Thali said quietly to Elric.

He squeezed her hand. "At least we have a way to return quickly should we need to," Elric said as he put an arm around her waist.

"What do you mean, 'should'?" Thali asked.

"Well, I'm hoping that maybe they won't attack. We're way out here. Why would they attack there if you're here?"

"Because my brother wants to take over the world. Were you not listening before?"

"Thali, it's not that I don't believe you. It's that I'm hoping you're wrong. I'm hoping that what you described is the worst-case scenario. You can't fault me for that, for wishing the best for my kingdom. I might not have a kingdom to return to, but I can hope."

Thali was angrier than she should be at his words. She felt it rising in her even as she recognized it as something more than what it was. Of course a small part of her hoped she was wrong, but it felt like even Elric didn't believe her.

Indi bumped her head into her thigh, and Thali stooped to pet her. The tiger looked up at Thali as if to make sure she was okay. Thali took a moment to reassure her tiger that she was indeed all right.

She held her breath, then slowly exhaled. She felt the barrier whimper in her magical eye. It was difficult to describe. It was like having a third eye that saw things no one else could. "Best of luck to all our friends," Thali said, taking Elric's hand.

"How long will it take us to get there now that we have help?" Elric asked.

"We might be there tomorrow morning," Thali said.

Elric nodded. "That's a lot faster than the usual two weeks."

"Sure is." Thali smiled. She would see Tariq soon.

Elric was asleep before Thali even climbed into bed. But she just lay there, unable to sleep. So, she eventually got up, wrapped her cloak around her, and went to the galley. She knew they'd be gambling there, and she felt like being around people.

Sure enough, Mouse had started a game of cards. A few guards looked up in surprise when they saw her, but she waved them down. She didn't mind if they gambled, or rather, she didn't mind that Mouse would take all their money. There was no way her royal guards and friends could handle the game like Mouse could.

Thali hovered and watched a few games, happy to just take in the atmosphere for now. Everyone had noticed her, but Mouse continued and she didn't say anything, so they kept playing. Watching was exciting enough. Eventually, Mouse glanced up and asked if she wanted in. She shook her head.

Mia sidled up to her. "How are you holding up?"

"What do you mean?"

"Well, you were basically exiled from your home, no one believed your warnings—well, almost no one—and now we're sailing away like we did something wrong, leaving some of your dearest friends to be attacked by magical creatures while we take a little vacation on the sunny island of Bulstan."

"Wow. When you put it that way, it's a lot, isn't it?" Thali said.

"It is. It's a lot. And we're here for you." Mia wrapped her arm under and around Thali's.

"I think I'm still stunned that they didn't believe me. I can't even fathom what's about to happen in Adanek. I hope my brother calls his plans off now that he doesn't have me, but I'm not sure what he'll do."

Mia glanced at Thali, then went back to watching the game. "I think he'll either come after you, or he'll take over the world and offer you a chance to join him."

"You really think so? I made it pretty clear that I wouldn't be part of it."

"He'd be a lot more powerful with you than without," Mia said. "That might be enough for him to try and entice you again somehow. Or threaten you."

"I still can't believe Rommy is so ..."

"Wrong?"

"Delusional. I don't get it. He's never wanted—"

"To take over an entire merchant empire?"

"I guess, but—"

"I don't think it's a huge stretch from merchant empire to world empire."

"Really?" Thali asked.

Mia shook her head. "Think of all his connections. He knows so many nobles, kings, queens, and leaders. He's been dealing with them since he was a child."

"That's exactly what bothers me," Thali said. "How could he take over their homes, their lives, their people? That's ruining millions of lives, so many of whom he knows personally. He's never been so ruthless and heartless. What happened to him?"

"That's where you and he differ. You think of the people, Thali. He just thinks of the power, the ability to say that he's achieved this or that and commands this many people, these armies. He was so destroyed by Mupto's rejection that he's thinking *only* of achieving, succeeding, being stronger and more powerful than anyone else so he can have Rania. He's not thinking of the people involved or what it takes to actually run an empire."

Thali was impressed at Mia's insight. "All that may be true, but he knows how to run an empire."

"He knows how to run your family's empire, yes, which is lots of trustworthy people all working toward the same goal. I don't think he'll have as easy a time with his plans as he thinks." Mia patted her arm.

"When did you become so wise and perceptive?" Thali asked.

"When I started working at the palace with you," Mia said. She threw her hair over her shoulder.

Suddenly, raucous laughter roared, and when it calmed, Mia yawned. "Well, I'm off to bed. I like sleeping in those hammocks more than I thought I would."

Thali felt terrible that Mia had to sleep in a hammock, but her best friend hadn't complained and had gotten dirty working like the rest of them. "Sleep well," Thali said, hugging Mia.

Eventually, Thali sat down to watch the games closer. Later, she rested her head on her hands to watch as she got tired. Before she knew it, she was waking up in the morning with a few heavy cloaks draped over her, Isaia and Nasir asleep nearby. She wondered if they'd fallen asleep here or had chosen to stay near her. She guessed it was the latter. Thali wasn't sure what she'd done to deserve such loyalty. She tried to rise slowly and quietly, but one of the cloaks around her had something heavy in the pocket and it *thunked* on the ground as she stood, waking Nasir and Isaia. "Good morning. I'm sorry I kept you from your beds," she said.

"I'm impressed you slept through last night's shenanigans," Isaia said.

"I suppose it's an odd place to fall asleep, but I've been doing it since I was a child."

"You didn't have a bed?" Nasir asked.

"Why would I go to bed when there was so much fun to be had?" Thali asked. "My parents stopped trying to keep me away after the first three times I snuck in here to watch the games. It got to a point where there was always a blanket laid out on the bench for me."

Isaia laughed.

Thali's favorite cook appeared from the back with a pot of coffee and some pastries filled with ham and cheese. She took one and bit into it, closing her eyes as she enjoyed it. "These are amazing. We're so lucky to have you," she said.

"Thanks for trusting me to feed ya," he said. He left the coffee and pile of pastries on the table. Nasir and Isaia came to join her.

"No wonder you want to live on a ship," Isaia said as he popped an entire pastry into his mouth.

"We've gotten pretty lucky, that's for sure," Thali said. Between the three of them, they polished off three pastries each and the coffee. As the first people started trickling into the galley for breakfast, Thali went up to the main deck to start her exercises. Her mother was probably already wondering where she was.

Her parents' ship had pulled in close to her ship, and the whales were still swimming swiftly. Her mother had put a plank across their ships so they could cross over to train. Thali stepped over easily.

"Good morning, daughter. I see you slept in the galley," her mother said as she raised an eyebrow.

Thali nodded. Then, after Crab came over and ruffled her hair and she hugged him, she took a staff and started her warm-ups. Much of the crew came over and took turns sparring lightly with her. She knew they were warming her up to face Crab and then her mother.

All at once, Thali realized she could use magic, and she grinned as she turned to with her mother.

"Ready?" Lady Jinhua asked.

Thali nodded. She attached her threads to her body parts and was excited to move them in her mind as she sparred with her mother. At first, she didn't move very quickly, but then as her mother sped up, Thali moved faster and faster. She flew through the motions, deflecting her mother's strikes and landing her own until she finally landed a hit on her mother. They stopped then, and Thali worried her mother would be angry. Instead, her mother shimmered with sweat and grinned.

"Finally," Lady Jinhua said.

"Finally?" Thali asked.

"I've waited a long time for you to land a hit on me," her mother said, stretching to keep from getting too cold too fast in the wind.

Applause went up around them, and Thali looked around to see that everyone had gathered to watch their match. She felt a little guilty for using magic.

"You used magic, didn't you?" her mother asked. "You moved a little too fast from some defensive positions to offense."

Thali nodded, wondering again if her mother would be angry.

"You need to use every tool you have to overcome your enemies. And I would say your new technique is sharper, more cohesive."

"I trained with someone who really knows their stuff," Thali said. She thought of Jax and was saddened that she hadn't said goodbye to him. She wondered if she would ever see him again.

"I hope to meet him one day," Lady Jinhua said, wiping her brow.

Thali used her own sleeve to do the same. She was mentally as tired as she was physically now.

I see Jax taught you well, Alexius said.

He's remarkable, Thali replied.

He's the best warrior I've ever seen. And I would love to see your mother spar with him. That would be a match for the centuries, he said.

"That would certainly be a fight worth seeing," Thali said out loud.

"You should change. We'll be there soon," Lady Jinhua said.

Thali nodded. She crossed back to her own ship and went to her rooms.

Elric was awake. "You woke up early?" he asked as he finished dressing.

"Oh no. I couldn't sleep last night, so I went to the galley and ended up falling asleep there," Thali said, grabbing a towel to wipe the sweat away.

Elric nodded. "You're a very different person on a ship."

Thali felt her defenses rise. "Oh?"

"It's interesting. You're much more confident, more comfortable," Elric said.

"Is that a good or bad thing?"

"It makes me sad that I've torn you away from it," Elric said.

"I chose to leave it. I do miss it sometimes, like now. But it'll be worth it."

"I hope I can make sure it is," Elric said. He put his hand over hers, and they slid toward each other to embrace. Even though she was sweaty, and he was still mussed from sleep, they stood together quietly, just holding each other.

When Thali emerged from belowdecks, she looked immediately to the right. The whales' threads pulled at her. The were confused, even a bit frightened. She squinted and looked around the ship in all directions.

She mentally followed the threads to try and see what they were seeing. They recognized land masses more as directional changes in ocean currents. And these currents had changed. They weren't behaving as the whales had come to expect in this location.

Have we not made good time like we were supposed to? Thali wondered. She looked around again. She looked to the right again, to where she expected to see land the moment she'd come above. Grabbing the spyglass from Mouse, she searched for the natural rock formations that prevented the island from suffering any real storm damage. They weren't there. There were no trees, there was no shore, there were no turrets or flags piercing the top of the landscape. It was eerily quiet. The whales left then and swam away.

Thali looked around, not quite believing her eyes. "Bulstan is missing," she whispered.

THE ADVENTURE CONTINUES IN...OF GATES AND TYPHOONS

Out December 2024.

Visit https://geni.us/OfGatesandTyphoons to buy now or scan this QR code:

A Note from the Author

This book is a little different from the others in that we're following multiple perspectives. After Soxkendi, which is written in first person and with multiple perspectives, this started as a nanowrimo (National Novel Writing Month) personal challenge. It was a good fit to follow multiple people because many of the characters are in a different place physically or mentally. I wanted to see if I could develop the story through many characters while also giving them their own arcs. The only downside to this experiment was instead of a five book series, this book pushed it to a six book series. I didn't get through nearly as much story as I was hoping to! Thank you for allowing me to explore my storytelling.

I've been asked whether Alexius and Thali were ever romantic. They are not. If you haven't already, I encourage you to read Soxkendi to give you more background on Alexius. He is strictly Thali's mentor, but he also finds a lot of healing within these adventures too.

Tilton and Daylor have always been together – in my mind, they were attracted to each other right from the first book, and if you look back, there are hints (Tilton being very upset as Daylor gets female attention right before Daylor falls into the river, and Tilton being super concerned and knowing that Daylor doesn't know how to swim). They get together in the second year of school and have been inseparable since.

If you're curious about the poem that's quoted in chapter nine, it's Shakespeare's Sonnet 116 – one of my favorites.

ACKNOWLEDGEMENTS

Wow, book four in Thali's story and my fifth published book. It's difficult to fathom that a year ago, I was toiling on my own, almost secretly.

Always first and foremost, I'm so grateful to you, dear reader, for choosing this story to read and I hope you're entertained.

Thank you to my communities that have rallied around me. For buying my book, for telling your friends and family about it, for taking the time to read it. I hope you get to see a piece of me in my work and that you are also entertained!

Thank you to my editor – Bobbi Beatty of Silver Scroll Services. I couldn't do this without you and your attention and care with my story are things I cherish with much gratitude.

Thank you to Lorna Stuber, proofreader extraordinaire! I think I learn something new about the English language every book...

Thank you also to Tanya, who has used her magical skills to help this author with all the things she hates doing, I'm so grateful for your time, your skills, your knowledge, and your friendship.

I'm grateful to the very talented artists at MiblArt. Your group puts the most beautiful covers together for me and I appreciate working with you!

These books are possible because of the amazing support I have from my family. Thank you to my husband for everything, but especially in making sure that this author is fed on time. Special thanks to my mom for telling everyone she knows and selling my book to all her friends and acquaintances.

To my steadfast furry friends, Truffle & Udon, thanks for reminding me to get up every few hours and keeping my toes warm and keeping me company as I tip-tap away. To Kali, thank you for making sure I get outside for some fresh air and get dirt under my nails once in awhile.

About the Author

Camilla is a lover of many mediums of storytelling. She loves to write strong heroines with animal sidekicks, who can kick butt and find the love of their life. She always has projects on the go and loves to consume stories of all kinds—books, shows, movies, plays, amongst many others.

When she is not writing, Camilla is often found exploring animal behavior, crafting, drinking a hot beverage, and clicker training her animals.

Come visit her at CamillaTracy.com or on instagram @camilla_tracy. Sign up for her newsletter by visiting: https://geni.us/CamillaTracynewsletteror scanning the QR code below:

Manufactured by Amazon.ca
Bolton, ON

39098653R00176